SORGINA

The Wicked

"There has to be evil so that good can prove its purity above it."

– Buddha

Contents

Chapter One: Delayed Roadwork

It was October 1972. Workers were busy with the relocation of a widely-used road in the Pittsburgh area, Interstate 279. I-279 consisted of the freeway stretching from downtown Pittsburgh to Interstate 79; the road was designed to easily connect travelers to and from Pittsburgh and all points north.

Construction came to a screeching halt on August 30, 1972, when some of the workers stumbled upon an old cemetery which was not listed on their maps. The workers thought that could only mean one thing; the workers had stumbled upon a Native American burial ground.

Because the city and all the major committees involved were terribly afraid of the bad press they would receive if the gravesite held the remains of any Native Americans, the officials called an important meeting of the newly-formed freeway construction committee immediately upon the discovery of the cemetery. The committee consisted of members of the city planners and union bosses. An unheard-of, unanimous decision was quickly reached, without any need for dissented party's discussion. That type of thing was unheard of before, and it remains to be unheard of ever since.

###

The following morning, before word could get out about the unusual burial grounds, city officials had contacted the Smithsonian Institute, per the party's unanimous decision.

The Smithsonian Institute, having people on call for that type of emergency, immediately sent a small team of scientists to handle the issue.

###

It took nearly a month for the Smithsonian employees to unearth forty-six separate gravesites before they determined the cemetery had been used by a nearby deserted church, and the only bodies buried in it were Germanic in origin. They were relieved they had not stumbled upon a Native American burial ground as they feared.

Although it seemed an interminable amount of time to the construction committee for the Smithsonian scientists to identify the two-hundred-year-old bodies and move the remains to a nearby "active" cemetery, the scientists were rushed at every turn. The construction had to be resumed as soon as possible, and that wasn't going to be accomplished by the scientists taking their time with their tasks.

That created a heavy burden for the scientists. The union bosses followed their every move. They were constantly checking their workbooks to see if and how the actions of the scientists adversely affected their members. On top of that, the city fathers were wining and dining the scientists every night, trying to find a fault in the Smithsonian process. Because of all that, the scientists found very little time to report on and discuss their findings.

Adding insult to injury, as quickly as the scientists completed moving the cemetery, they found they were required to turn their reports in to the cities' fathers for their final approval.

As a result, the Smithsonian scientists returned to Washington, feeling their investigation of the cemetery was woefully incomplete. Had they been given the proper amount of time to carry on their experiments, they felt certain they would have obtained conclusive evidence.

In particular, the scientists would have liked to have spent more time investigating the old Bible they had found. That was the most interesting part of their research thus far.

They were aware Bibles had historically been the repository of all the settlers of a given area. The holy books included their birthdates, occupations, and deaths. Unfortunately, the union boss had snatched the Bible from the very eager hands of a scientist. The union boss claimed the book contained personal items, which was just his excuse to prevent anyone else from looking at the Bible's contents.

However, as was the Smithsonian employees' habit, they discussed their findings during the plane ride back to Washington, DC. They spent a great deal of time talking about what, if anything, the scientist who had held the book was able to find during the few seconds she possessed the Bible. The union boss had snatched the book away from the scientist so quickly she barely had time to open a random page of the document and skim its contents.

Though the scientist didn't have much time to look, she swore the page she saw referenced the burial of a woman listed as the personal assistant to one of the founders of the village, a Prussian colonel named Beck. That information later placed the scientists in a bit of a tizzy because no such young woman was found in the cemetery, despite them expending their greatest efforts to find her. Frustrated upon their non-discovery, many insisted the scientist in question had made the whole thing up.

Construction on the freeway resumed the day following the Smithsonian scientist's departure.

The crews were just settling into their constructional groove when a heavy equipment operator accidentally unearthed an unmarked crypt. The worker who had operated that piece of machinery was working in an area close to the original cemetery, but on unconsecrated grounds.

Hoping to avoid any more delays because they were behind enough as it was, the operator's supervisor quickly looked inside the burial chamber. Because there was no evidence of a Native American being buried there, the supervisor told the operator to quickly rebury the crypt.

Making certain the reburial was done in such a way as to preclude any further delays, the supervisor rode alongside the operator on the side of the machine, with the fire-resistant door open to enhance communication.

Distracted and rushed because of all that was happening, the operator struck an unmarked gas line, which exploded and engulfed everything surrounding it in flames, which promptly caught the attention of other workers.

The ensuing fire was extinguished as quickly as possible, and both men were medevacked to the nearest burn clinic.

Both men died at the clinic after undergoing very painful procedures which were meant to save their lives. The doctors were puzzled as to why those treatments didn't work because they had seldom failed before.

Upon the discovery of an additional body near the site of the gas line explosion, the newly-formed construction committee recalled the Smithsonian scientists and they had to begin the entire process all over again. They were told to make certain they had gotten all the bodies out of the old cemetery, including any that were still in the unconsecrated areas.

The Smithsonian scientists encountered the same roadblocks as they had before, with the union and the civilian bosses watching and dictating their every move. However, mostly because of their return engagement, some of the descendants of the original residents asked to meet with them, clandestinely.

The locals all agreed something unusual happened when the word *sorgina*, an old gypsy name for an evil witch, was spoken. Most of them later reported their hairs stood up on the backs of their necks. Though those people normally didn't give much into other types of superstitions, many of the locals had Romani ancestors who believed all those stories about their people were true. Some of those residents had distant ancestors who died lingering, unexplainable deaths, and that made them even more afraid of the *sorgina*.

The very day after they met with townspeople, the Smithsonian workers were asked to suspend all operations in the Pittsburgh area. The construction committee agreed to not press charges against the Smithsonian for defamation. In turn, the Smithsonian agreed to never permit the same group of employees to be assigned to the Pittsburgh area again. All parties agreed that was the best course of action.

For their part, the scientists were compelled to sign documentation stating they had never heard of, nor discussed, any totally unfounded *sorgina* superstitions, and they—the Smithsinian employees—had not encountered any local resident who spoke of the sorgina as real. It wasn't like the scientists believed in such "nonsense," as they had put it.

In their hurry to leave Pittsburgh, the scientists had not managed to find the crypt the committee members spoke of during their earlier meeting. They just wanted to resume their normal lives and workflow. However, the city fathers were more interested in stopping the rumor mill than finding a forgotten old crypt.

As the Smithsonian workers were preparing to depart the Pittsburgh area, with many thanks to the carelessness of the same union executive who had snatched the Bible from the very grasp of a Smithsonian scientist, they learned more than they would have had they stayed another month. They left the Pittsburgh area with more information than they could thoroughly discuss during the short plane ride back to Washington, DC.

The executive in question left the secured area where the Bible was stored just as one of the scientists emerged from the restroom. The executive never saw the scientist as she exited the ladies' room. The old timer had been taught women did not really matter in a man's world, so he didn't give it much thought.

Minutes later, realizing he had been taught wrong, the executive returned, accompanied by several of his female subordinates, but they were too late.

Chapter Two: Nekane

The union boss had been away from the document for but a few moments, which proved to be plenty of time for the scientist to learn where Colonel Beck's servant had come from, as well as the date she arrived in the village.

Most importantly, the scientist learned the servant's name was Nekane. That was a discovery none of them would have made during their first trip because they were pressured to rush through their research.

She eagerly shared her discovery with the other scientists, who once again became interested in the local Pittsburgh lore. Using that information as a basis, the Smithsonian scientists found they were able to reconstruct what they could of Nekane's life. However, because the gypsies were secretive about their lifestyle concerning their children, the scientists did not gather as much information as they would have liked to.

One of the important things they did learn was the direct translation of Nekane meant sorrow. Her parents must not have thought of that when they named her, but sorrow seemed to follow the young woman throughout her life. The earliest mention of Nekane, the scientists had found, was on the cusp of one such catastrophe.

###

She had lived during the sixteenth century. Nekane belonged to a troupe of gypsies who had wandered throughout Western Europe. From a very young age, Nekane would join the older women at the campsites. That group had danced for tips from the men who gathered around their wagons.

At the tender age of thirteen, Nekane had already blossomed. She was young and beautiful. It did not take her long to build up a reputation; word had quickly spread about the gorgeous youngster singing and dancing with the gypsy women.

As part of their northern route, Nekane's troupe crossed into France, setting up their encampment close to a military compound.

The gypsies were very much aware of the dangers, as well as the benefits, of setting up camp so close to a military base. Almost before they had completely settled in for the night, their encampment had attracted the company's bored soldiers, who were happy to join in the merriment offered by the gypsies.

The addition of the soldiers' money to the gypsies' encampmet ended all discussion about the choice before them, whether to move on or to stay, almost before it began. The chance of gaining more money was just too great.

Following a quick, but heated, discussion, the troupe's elders announced the decision to stay, much to the chagrin of Nekane's parents.

Many of the soldiers found Nekane captivating and were willing to part with their entire life savings for a single night with her. Her parents maintained she was too young, but that did not stop their daughter, or the soldiers who were willing to pay for the pleasure of her company.

Soldiers who lost all of their money gambling, or for an evening with Nekane, were questioned by superior officers concerning their losses. Because the soldiers were afraid they would face severe reprecussiions because of their wanton desires, they lied and accused Nekane of stealing their money as they lay sleeping.

As a result, an angry mob of military officials formed, demanding her execution.

Colonel Beck, who was stationed at the nearby compound, heard about the mob. Because he knew in his heart the girl was innocent, he smuggled Nekane from the camp during the dead of night.

Beck was a judicious man and waited for over a year to consummate his relationship with Nekane. They fell deeply in love and eventually migrated to the United States, where Beck founded a group of like-minded religious zealots. He became a founding member of a small community near the burgeoning city of Pittsburgh.

Because of their differing religious beliefs, they could not marry, but Nekane remained happy to be with the man she loved.

She spent much of her free time gathering herbs to prepare medicines for the minor injuries settlers always seemed to have. She also made other potions for the settlers unfortunate enough to be struck with illness.

Nekane fell in love with the small group of settlers and believed they had grown to love and trust her, as well.

During Nekane's twentieth year, the tragic meaning of her name once again identified what she had embodied, Sorrow.

An unknown illness devastated the population of the little village and began spreading to the surrounding areas.

Beck helped and cared for many of his friends during their final moments until he, too, died a horrific death associated with the disease.

That very night, a dozen men burst into Nekane's small room.

Blaming the young woman for the sickness that had spread around, they beat her unconscious, gagged her with an old rag, and bound her hands and feet.

They sealed her, alive and still unconscious, in an unmarked underground crypt separate from the consecrated cemetery. Then, they secured the crypt with thick padlocks so there was no chance she would be able to escape.

The deacon of the small village church, newly inflicted with the strange disease himself, oversaw the entire process. He, like the others, was quick to blame the young girl. None of them would even listen to her side of the story even if given the chance.

The deacon died the following day, but not before he transmitted the sickness to his closest associates. Soon, they, too, would suffer the horrible effects of the disease.

Nekane had regained consciousness to the sound of men chanting prayers as her burial plot was filled in. Too confused to wonder about the circumstances of her entombment, panic filled her mind as she sought to find a way out.

She screamed and fought, tearing her fingernails off as she attempted to claw her way out of the tomb. Nekane was unsure if any of them had heard her cries for help. Even if they had, the very hands which condemned and buried her would offer no assistance.

As Nekane slowly died, battered and bloody, the pain in her body seemed like nothing compared to the pain of her broken heart. Nekane had not only lost the only man whom she ever loved, but she also felt betrayed by the very people whom she had saved. How could they have been so quick to accuse and then abandon her? How could they have been so ungrateful for all she had done for them? Many thoughts such as that ran through her mind as she was encapsulated in her soon-to-be tomb.

Because of all the agony she experienced during her last hours, she uttered curses. Nekane condemned her tormentors, as well as their descendants, to die horrible, lingering deaths, just as she had.

###

It has been said it takes the cruelty and insanity inherent in mortal man to turn a good person to evil.

That notion had been attributed to various authors ranging in style from Socrates to C.S. Lewis to Shakespeare, those who were very familiar with the cruelty of which mankind was capable.

Regardless of when or where the saying came from, on that fateful day when Nekane was betrayed, a *sorgina* was born.

###

Ever since people have known about the existence of such an evil breed, the question they have asked is: How can one go about stopping a *sorgina* set on destruction?

A *sorgina* has only one viable enemy, another witch who had sometimes been an agent of goodness, a kind *mankukulam*.

A *mankukulam* is a Filipina witch who is inherently evil. However, some *mangkukulams* can take on the gentler role as a protector of good. People who encountered those mythical witches always knew if they were staring into the eyes of good or into the eyes of evil.

Mankukulams are a big part of the national heritage of the Philippines. However, because *mankukulams* are inherently evil, they are seldom spoken of. It is not unusual for a young Filipina to know little of her family's background because her family was afraid of bad luck associated with the mere mention of the word *mankukulam*, let alone being related to one. As a result, Many Filipinas went to their entire lives without talking about the *mankukulam* in the room.

Chapter Three: Tina Tupaz

A little over fifty years had passed since the completion of the relocation of I-279. However, it was under heavy construction yet again for standard maintenance. Throughout the decades, it was also deemed an extremely hazardous route by most of America's premier automobile clubs. Therefore, the workers had posted detours, as well as alternative "safe" routes.

It was on one fateful evening when an experienced young emergency room nurse named Tina Tupaz, in a hurry to get home, chose to travel on I-279, the fastest route to Pittsburgh's East End.

Because she knew the area well, she decided to ignore the numerous detour signs and greatly exceeded the posted speed limits. As a result of that, she found herself breezing through the construction zones.

There was an unusually dense fog bank that loomed heavily, covering the patch of road on which she was currently driving; that caused her to miss her exit.

A few seconds after she realized she had missed her exit, she sped up a little more, hoping to make up for lost time. That was completely out of character for her because others had known Tina for her safe driving; some even accused her of being overcautious at times.

Because of the recent course of events, Tina became uncharacteristically angry. She almost never became angry while driving, but she felt the orange safety cones and detours of highway construction were bad enough to justify her anger; no one was even working on the road at that time. Throwing an impenetrable fog into the mix just added insult to injury.

At the same time, Tina did not concern herself with encountering other vehicles travelling on the interstate. She had noticed only two other cars during her drive, a newer model Mercedes Benz being followed extremely closely by an older orange car; she could barely tell where one vehicle ended and the other began. Both vehicles were traveling so fast the nurse did not expect to see them again.

An experienced traveler, Tina had listened to several weather forecasts before beginning her journey. None of them had mentioned any fog, let alone some as thick and visually impenetrable as the patch she had just encountered. She hoped the fog bank would disappear just as quickly as it had materialized.

Meanwhile, the two vehicles Tina had seen, both traveling at least *twice* the posted speed limit, made their way quickly along the interstate. The older orange car relentlessly tailgated the Mercedes. As the vehicles approached the end of the construction zone, they became engulfed by an unusual fog bank, the very same one Tina had just encountered.

Both vehicles came out of the construction zone as if they were shot out of a cannon. The operator of the Mercedes chose that moment to attempt to gain an advantage over the trailing vehicle, only to find the older vehicle keeping pace, mere inches behind the Mercedes's rear bumper.

After a few more seconds of relentless tailgating, the driver of the orange car decided to maximize their vehicle's power and pass the Mercedes. However, the orange vehicle performed a classic pit maneuver, colliding with the Mercedes' rear quarter panel and sending it into an uncontrollable spin.

The Mercedes became airborne when it hit the highway's protective shoulder. It added a roll when the second set of tires went airborne. Then, it all ended abruptly when the Mercedes collided with the East Ohio Street on-ramp.

The driver of the orange car slowed considerably after colliding with the Mercedes, no doubt viewing the aftermath of the deadly race.

The driver then proceeded down the road and drove much slower than they had been, pausing only to honk their custom car horn at some old woman attempting to cross the freeway.

She stopped and gave him a look that frightened him so much he honked once more before taking off, leaving the accident scene behind.

Just as the surviving car drove away, the nurse's vehicle approached the scene. It was then when she decided to come to a sudden stop.

Because she had still been traveling too fast for the weather conditions, empty fast-food containers and other detritus of life flew about the inside of her car as she swerved and came to a stop near the off-ramp.

The nurse didn't know why she had stopped her car so suddenly; a thought had entered her mind and convinced her she needed to witness something, something very unusual. She wasn't sure where the thought had come from. It was as if another being had taken over her mind.

For a moment, she thought she heard a custom car horn in the distance. It sounded like it had played "La Cucaracha." Twice. She wondered if the horn had belonged to the orange car.

Unable to ascertain a problem at the spot she had been compelled to stop because the heavy fog was still hanging in the air, Tina decided to drive away.

However, at that precise moment, a light breeze came along, blowing enough of the fog away for her to see a dark-colored sedan wedged between the concrete of the East Ohio Street off-ramp and the ground below.

At first, Tina believed the fog and the dark sky were playing tricks on her. Where had that vehicle come from? She lowered her passenger side window for a better view.

Along with the view of the car, she could smell burning rubber and hear the ticking of cooling metal.

The breeze gusted, blowing the overwhelming metallic smell of fresh blood and the fetid odor of recent death in her direction. As a nurse, she was all too familiar with those odors.

Realizing someone might need her help, she sprang into action.

She popped open her trunk to retrieve the first aid kit, some protective clothing, and the flashlight; those were the items she always had in her car.

Standing only five feet tall and weighing fewer than one hundred and ten pounds, moving heavy objects did not fit within her skill set, but her mind had fully prepared her to offer emergency medical aid to those in need as she hurried toward the wreckage. Tina had an uncanny sense of when someone really needed her help, and she could feel an overwhelming sense of urgency at that very moment.

Tina kept moving toward the wreck until she came up against a high retaining wall, made from river rock, designed to keep the existing hillside from impeding on the highway. At the present moment, however, it was also keeping her from reaching the injured victims.

She decided to take a closer look at the barrier, hoping to find an easier route to the overpass. The wall, momentarily exposed by an errant breeze, gave her a golden opportunity to examine it for the spot where the car had passed over. Unable to locate one, her mind came up with a strange possibility. Tina envisioned a giant looking down on the car as it sped along the freeway, before picking it up in anger and jamming it under the on-ramp.

"It could have happened that way," she said to herself, shaking her head to clear the cobwebs. She wondered why her mind was picking up such strange thoughts.

Clearing her head also made her realize climbing over the retaining wall was the only way to get to the damaged vehicle. The sense of urgency she felt became stronger.

Tina then scaled the retaining wall, which wasn't easy, but she was able to make it.

Upon reaching the damaged vehicle, she peered through a narrow gap where a full rear window had until very recently had been. The putrid smell of death had now become more pungent.

When Tina saw the remains of a deceased person inside the damaged vehicle, she had to fend off the urge to vomit. After that, she felt a strange chill, which was followed almost immediately by overwhelming fear.

A bolt of lightning struck close enough for her to feel its powerful electrical charge. It seemed to be contained within a peal of thunder that roared furiously, shaking the ground beneath her feet.

Her tenuous hold on her newfound courage quickly evaporated. Tina covered her ears and screamed.

At that exact moment, the lights illuminating the off-ramp flickered and died, turning the Tina's world completely black. Her fear then turned into uncontrollable terror.

Without thinking, she ran toward her car, wondering why she couldn't see the emergency flashers and why she had bought a vehicle so white it disappeared in the fog.

Sobbing in fear as a strange whining sound came from deep in her chest, the young nurse jumped down from the wall. She then raced toward her vehicle's last known position.

When Tina could finally see the flashing lights of her own car, she turned in its direction, but tripped over an unseen object lying at the base of the stone barrier.

She tumbled forward, her flashlight and phone flying from her hands, making her invisible to passersby and eliminating any chance she had of calling for help. What was she going to do now?

Tina's momentum carried her forward for several feet as she slid across the wet grass. Shivering, soaked to the skin, and still in the grip of terror, she scrambled to her feet.

Prepared to continue running, she took a moment to turn and see what had caused her to fall.

Tina located a bundle of discarded clothing lying near the base of the wall. That reinforced her urge to run. However, she stayed put. The bundle of clothes was illuminated by the next series of lightning bolts; it turned out to be a man dressed in a bloodied and torn suit.

He sat up, looked at the young nurse with wide-open, terrified eyes, took a rattling breath before mumbling something, and collapsed.

Thinking she could not do anything to save the poor man, the sense of urgency passed yet again. All Tina wanted to do now was go home.

Another bolt of lightning flashed and illuminated the sticker on the rear window of her car. She remembered when her supervisor presented the sticker to her, when she had saved a man's life.

The sticker showed a sexy cartoon nurse holding two lightning bolts, accompanied by a legend. The sticker read, *Cute Enough to Stop Your Heart, Skilled Enough to Restart It.*

Tina took a deep breath, shook herself like a wet dog, and turned to the man lying on the ground. She was determined to perform the best physical inspection possible under the circumstances. The nurse then began CPR, thinking it would be hours before competent help would arrive.

Chapter Four: Questioned

Tina was never so happy to be wrong. The first EMS team arrived at the accident site in fewer than five more minutes.

The ambulance barreled through the fog, screeching to halt a mere ten feet from the nurse.

Then, the EMS team rushed to the rear of their vehicle, threw open the ambulance doors, and began pulling out equipment from inside.

The team rushed through the fog and darkness, directly into the nurse's field of view.

The remainder of Tina's fear evaporated with that team's prompt appearance on the scene. She thought of them as the best EMTs in the entire area.

Of course, her opinion of the team was probably slightly biased because the team leader, Jordan Best, had been her closest friend since high school.

His partner, Francis "Franky" Sinatra, was tall, skinny, and goth. He had ridden with Jordan since Franky had graduated from college. She adored Jordan and included Franky in the list of her top ten favorite people.

Jordan reached the victim, surprised to see it was his best friend who helped stabilize the man before help came. Then, he held his breath until he confirmed she was okay.

"Holy cow!" gasped Jordan, nudging Tina aside as he took over the chest compressions, "You really know how to scare a guy. What are you doing out here?"

"On my way home from my brother's house, I had a gut feeling something was wrong. I pulled over, saw the wreck, and tried to help. I think everyone inside the car is DOA." Tina attempted to sound normal, despite the maelstrom of emotions she was feeling inside.

"The storm came out of nowhere, and lightning struck right next to me," she continued, her fear returning as she spoke. "I panicked when the lights went out. I was hurrying back over to my car when I stumbled over this guy."

"I wondered why there weren't any streetlights," Jordan replied. "We didn't see any storm, but the sky is dark."

"The sky is black, and a dense patch of fog was visually blocking everything, Jordy. A typical Pittsburgh evening. I lost my phone and flashlight when I fell, so I couldn't call anyone. How did you find me?"

"Quit clowning around, yinz two," Franky said in his thick Pittsburgh accent, aggressively pushing his way over to the victim. "I got to get his jacket-n-at off to properly treat him."

Franky quickly cut away the victim's jacket before prepping him for movement.

"Thanks, Franky," said Jordan before turning to Tina and saying in a mater-of-fact voice, "The fog bank is very unusual. It is less than one fourth mile wide and is thicker than any fog I have ever seen before. On top of that, the horrendous storm you encountered only happened right here. Very strange."

"As far as finding you is concerned, don't tell anyone," Jordan whispered. "But I thought I saw a woman standing on the freeway. When I swerved to miss her, my headlights caught you in the distance. I was still going to drive on, but something in my head told me to stop. I decided to pull over to see if the call came from here."

"A woman on the road in a thin line of fog? This is a really strange night, Jordy."

"They are all strange when you're involved; a normal person would still be running," Jordan said, grinning. "But you need to get out of the way now. Me and Franky got it from here."

The EMS team loaded the victim onto a gurney, rolled him into their ambulance, and sped toward the nearest hospital.

While the EMS team worked, state police officers arrived.

They quickly determined there were no survivors in the wreckage, so they moved aside to allow technicians to employ the "jaws of life" to noisily open the vehicle, giving the coroner access to the bodies.

The streetlights lit up seconds later.

Following a brief search, Tina found her cell phone and dead flashlight lying in the grass behind her vehicle. Wanting nothing more than to go home, drink a glass of wine, and crawl into bed, she turned toward her car.

That was when she walked into a member of the Pennsylvania State Patrol, his "Smokey the Bear" hat worn low on his head.

Nervously clearing his throat, the patrolman said, "Excuse me, ma'am, I'm Trooper Young with the Pennsylvania State Police. May I have a moment of your time?"

"Of course. What can I do for you, Trooper Young?"

"I just need to ask you a few questions about the accident, ma'am. It shouldn't take long."

"I'll help in any way I can, but you know I didn't see the accident. It was over by the time I got here."

"What exactly *did* you see, ma'am?" asked Young, clearly disappointed.

"I was driving on Interstate 279 toward Pittsburgh. Then, I felt something was wrong, and I pulled over. The fog was so thick I couldn't see anything at first. When a stiff breeze blew some of the fog away, I could see a car jammed under the overpass." She paused. "By the way, aren't you supposed to ask me my name?"

"I'm sorry, ma'am," Young replied, sheepishly. "Please don't tell anyone, but this is the first accident I've had to write up on my own, and it's a doozy. May I see some identification, ma'am?"

"I have my license right here, Officer Young," Tina replied, handing him her ID.

Trooper Young copied the nurse's personal information into his notebook. "Your license says your address is on Kentucky Avenue in Shadyside. Is that correct?"

"Yes."

"Why didn't you follow any of the construction detours?" continued Young.

"I enjoy this section of the interstate when traffic is light. There is a sight that can only be seen if you travel on I-279. It is located just over the hill from the Bellevue exit. It makes the skyscrapers of the city below look like castles. It never fails to make me feel better."

Tina then glanced in the direction of the bypass and the vehicle wedged beneath it. She shuddered. "Usually."

"Is there any other reason for you being out here tonight, ma'am?"

Huh? Why would he ask such a question? Tina thought, hesitating briefly before answering. "My brother lives in Bellevue. I come out here often to visit. I was at his house tonight for a birthday party." She sighed. How much longer was the questioning going to take?

"Did you get right on the freeway after leaving your brother's house?"

"Yes."

"Can you tell me his address and what time you left?"

"Yes. Is that important?"

"It might help us narrow down the time of the incident."

"Okay, he lives at 213 Lincoln Avenue. I guess I left at about 7:30."

"What happened then?"

Describing recent events in detail might prove embarrassing, so Tina recounted the high points of her discovery of the wreck, leaving out the feelings of panic and wanting to run away. "I heard the cry for help and responded," she concluded.

"I'm sorry, I don't understand," Officer Young said, scratching his head.

"The man who was just taken away in the ambulance, he called for help, or something. Anyway, I heard a noise, went to investigate, and found him lying in the grass."

"Was he conscious when you found him?"

"No, but because he had just passed out, I began CPR. When the EMS team arrived, they continued treatment and took the victim to the local hospital, as you probably saw."

Young looked even more confused.

"You know, they did what EMS teams do," explained Tina, nearing the end of her patience. "He was alive, but very weak when they left. I hope he makes it."

"Me, too. Did he say anything before he passed out?"

"He mumbled something, but it didn't make any sense."

"Do you recall what he said, ma'am?"

Tina was exhausted, but she still tried to help the young policeman. She concentrated as hard as she could before finally turning to the officer. "I really don't know, officer. He might have been in shock."

Trooper Young gave Tina an appraising look, shrugged in disappointment, handed her his business card, and returned her driver's license.

Young was clearly disappointed she could not provide more information about the accident. "I understand. Thank you, ma'am; that will be all for now. If you think of anything else, please give me a call."

"Do you know his name?" Tina asked.

"Who? Whose name?"

"The man we were just talking about, the man from the wreck."

"I'm not authorized to share that information, ma'am."

"Am I free to go?" she asked, her patience at an end.

"Yes, ma'am. Thank you for your cooperation."

Fighting an impulse to gesture obscenely at Officer Young, Tina got into her car and sped off into the night.

Chapter Five: The Best Laid Plans of Mice and Men

The fog was now completely gone, which allowed Tina to drive home in fewer than twenty minutes.

As planned, she poured herself a glass of red wine and peeled off her cold, wet clothes. She left them there on the floor as she leisurely strolled into her bathroom.

Next, she stepped into the shower, allowing the hot water to run over her body, washing away the terrors of the evening.

When she finished showering, she drained her glass of wine and pulled on her choice of nightclothes, a very unsexy pair of jockey shorts and an old football jersey.

However, as soon as Tina's head hit the pillow, her eyes popped wide open, and thoughts about the harrowing events of the evening filled her mind.

###

After tossing and turning for the next few hours, she finally surrendered to the inevitable fact she wasn't going to get any sleep. Throwing on a tattered, old robe, she staggered to the kitchen and brewed a fresh pot of coffee.

Sleepy, bleary-eyed, and confused, Tina filled her favorite mug and plopped down at her kitchen table to think. The moment she stopped to think, the nagging urgency she felt at the site of the accident returned. She also couldn't stop thinking about the critically wounded man; she wanted mostly to know his name. She knew she wouldn't stop thinking about it until she had her answer.

Tina then began forming a plan for finding "her" patient. Once she thought the whole thing through, her conscience told her she had devised a stupid plan that could only lead to trouble. However, the voice that screamed urgency was stronger than the faint sounds of her conscience.

Tina finished her coffee, pulled her scrubs over her night clothes, and without even running a brush through her hair, she headed to the hospital more than two hours early for her shift.

Located in the southern portion of Pittsburgh's South Oakland neighborhoods, the hospital where Tina worked remained unscathed by city life. Different than other inner-city hospitals, theirs eschewed armed guards at every entry point. Thinking she had set a great plan, Tina continued to follow the process she had dreamed up at her kitchen table earlier that morning.

She parked her car in front on an unlit side street in front of a house with boarded-up windows. It was several blocks from the hospital. Under different circumstances, she would never leave her car unattended in such a shady part of town.

Because hospital security measures forced her to enter the building through the main lobby, she came in directly in front of the ER department. Tina sighed. That had derailed her plans before they even had a chance to begin.

Taking a deep breath, she boldly walked past the ER entrance directly over to the empty administration offices. Her ID badge was partially visible outside the oversized hoodie she had found in the back of her car.

A maintenance worker noticed Tina's ID badge. Captivated by her beauty, he watched her as she strolled toward the restricted administration area as if she belonged.

Tina brushed seductively against the maintenance worker, explaining to him she had lost her keys and would appreciate it if he let her in to the admin office.

The worker, being only human, almost allowed the beautiful young nurse to have access to the area. However, he liked his job well enough to take a deep breath and instead provide her with the phone number to the help desk, where she would be able to pick up a spare key.

The maintenance worker's surprising honesty caused yet another interruption in Tina's plans to locate "her" patient, which meant she desperately had to think of another avenue for her investigation.

Then, she remembered she had memorized Jordan's ID number for use in case of an emergency.

Tina tightly closed her eyes. She pictured a bright, beautiful angel perched on one of her shoulders, telling her to stop while she still had the chance. Perched on her other shoulder, a dark, evil witch told her not to worry; she would never be caught.

"I've got to stop watching cartoons," the nurse muttered to herself, shaking her head to clear away the imagined figures before making the decision that appealed to her the most.

However, fate stepped in and gave her another chance to redeem herself.

As she opened her eyes and began to walk across the hospital, one of her coworkers stepped into the hall from the emergency room.

"I heard you were here early," the coworker said. "We have a ton of patients today. One of our regular staff is on vacation, and we're understaffed to begin with. Would you be willing to start your shift early to help? We will repay the favor next time you need help from us.

Chapter Six: Business Antics

Though she was busy during the beginning of her shift, Tina noticed the emergency room business had slowed dramatically after sunrise. With a workload consisting only of an emergency birth, a couple of minor car accidents, and a gunshot wound, Tina's experience and talent allowed her to work on autopilot.

###

Shortly before lunchtime, Jordan strutted into the ER. He walked directly over to the nurse's station.

The remainder of the emergency room staff looked on with barely concealed envy. They knew they would never be Jordan, no matter how hard they tried.

Standing slightly over six feet tall with a face and a body that resembled a chiseled god in a museum, Jordan used his natural, shimmering beauty to sweep his way through life. He never quite understood how any nurse could resist him because he knew he could have virtually any woman he wanted.

Jordan smiled and headed over in Tina's direction. "I was in the neighborhood and decided you should take me to lunch," Jordan said as he smiled. Then, he looked closely at the nurse and frowned. "You look weird. Is everything all right?" The concern was evident in his voice.

"I need your help," she whispered. "Can you meet me outside in five minutes?"

Surprised by her response, Jordan turned around and marched out of the hospital without saying another word to anyone.

Waiting for Tina when she stepped outside, he confronted her before the automatic doors leading to the emergency room slid shut.

"What is going on?" growled Jordan. Clearly, he was both upset and concerned.

"Can you take me to get my car, Jordy? I didn't park in the garage this morning. I'm not even sure which street it's on, but I can get you there." Tina looked at the ground, carefully avoiding Jordan's eyes. "I'll buy you lunch and tell you the whole story."

"C'mon, I'm parked around the corner," Jordan replied with a shake of his head.

A brief time later, Tina found her car was safely parked on the employees' floor of the hospital's parking garage.

Tina sat across from Jordan in an old, worn-out booth of a local sandwich shop, telling him all about her morning.

Jordan frowned. "That's got to be one of the stupidest things you've ever done!" he exclaimed, staring at her in disbelief.

That got the attention of a few other customers, who stared curiously over in their direction.

Tina lowered her voice. "Why are you being so mean, Jordy? I know it wasn't smart, but I felt like I had to learn everything I could about 'my' patient." She wanted to tell him about the sense of urgency that kept finding its way back inside her head, but the better part of discretion told her she shouldn't mention that.

"First, he is *not* your patient; he never was. Second, all you had to do was ask me. I could have checked on him for you legally. You didn't have to go all *Mission Impossible*." Jordan paused, looking at the small puddle of condensation his soft drink left on the table. "Besides, I already looked at the file for anomalies."

"What do you mean you already looked at the file?" Tina hissed.

"I don't know why I did it. It was like someone was in my head, telling me to follow up on a patient I had already turned over to the hospital. Weird, you know?"

Jordon's reply shocked Tina. Could the same urgent voice have been communicating with Jordan, as well?

Tina leaned in closer, whispering, "What did you learn?"

Jordan shrugged. "I'm not sure I should tell you."

"Tell me, Jordy," she said, sweetly. "You know you want to."

Jordan sighed. "Okay, but I didn't learn much. I found detailed reports on the accident, the victim's injuries, and the emergency procedures performed, and nothing more. There was also the fact he was fitted for a halo device, the follow-up stuff I usually get after an accident."

"That poor man!" Tina replied, close to tears.

"Tragic," muttered Jordan, pointedly looking at his watch as he stood. "We're going to be late if we don't get back right now. I'll print out the reports and bring them to you at the end of your shift."

Tina coasted through the afternoon, her mind a million miles away. All she could think about was what Jordon had told her and the additional information he promised to get her at the end of the day.

Rushing out of the hospital as soon as her shift had ended, Tina was shocked to see no sign of Jordan.

He stood me up, she thought, angrily.

Exhausted and furious, Tina decided to just head home.

Being her mind was otherwise occupied, she failed to notice the large manila envelope lying on the front seat of her car until she almost sat on it. *What the...* she thought.

Seeing the words, *John Doe: You Need to Let Him Be!* written in bold letters on its cover, she snatched up the envelope and dropped it onto the passenger seat.

Holding the contents tightly to her chest, Tina looked furtively around the parking garage before getting back into her car and pouring the envelope's contents onto the passenger seat.

Her mind had completely let go of concerning thoughts about how Jordan was able to enter her car.

Tina stared at the information Jordan had given her. The reports covered every inch of the damaged vehicle, as well as the accident site. She had already been there and seen that.

Feeling disappointed because she had not learned anything new, she returned the documents to the envelope, more determined than ever to complete her quest. If Jordan wasn't going to help her, she was going to have to find out more herself.

Clutching the folder tightly under her arm, Tina exited her car once again.

She then locked the doors and then hurried back inside the hospital to find "her" patient.

Tina decided to try the surgical intensive care unit first.

Finding an empty nurse's station, Tina thought that was a great opportunity to see if "her" patient had even ended up in the SICU, but she quickly determined checking records would be unnecessary.

Tina had found "her" patient. He had been assigned a private corridor-facing room. In hospital speak, a private room contained only one bed. In the SICU, corridor-facing walls were glass, providing medical staff with a clear view of the patient within.

Privacy, as a layperson understood the word, did not exist in hospitals. Today, that had helped her out.

Tina strolled into "her" patient's room like she belonged to his medical team.

Standing inside the door to the patient's room, she immediately noticed a profound silence and felt an overwhelming urgency to check on the machines designed to keep a patient alive.

To her surprise, she found every machine was unplugged.

Tina quickly reattached the man's life support systems and inhaled deeply as soon as everything seemed like it was going to be okay. The sense of urgency was gone, and the nurse had lost any more desire to learn more about "her" patient.

Chapter Seven: Captain Decker

Tina sighed deeply, prepared to forget about the entire incident. However, when she turned to the exit, she encountered a giant man dressed in the uniform of the Allegheny County Sheriff's Department.

My life must be taking a wrong turn, Tina thought. *I keep running into police officers.*

Feeling at a distinct disadvantage under the glaring eyes of the six-foot-eight police officer, Tina took a few steps backward, making it possible to look directly into his face.

The patrolman's lips moved into what some people might call a slight smile. "I apologize for frightening you, ma'am," he said with a voice that seemed to rise from deep in the bowels of the Earth. "I am Captain Aloysius Decker with the Allegheny County Sheriff's Department. I'm investigating the incident involving this patient. I checked the nurse's station when I entered the ward, but no one was there. Then, I saw you with the patient. Again, I apologize for frightening you."

Having just saved a man's life for the second time in two days, Tina Tupaz should have been feeling ecstatic, but the giant facing her seemed to have let the air out of her balloons.

Tina's ID, hanging from a lanyard around her neck caught Decker's attention. "Ma'am, your ID card says your name is Cristina Tupaz. Is that correct?"

"Y-yes, sir, but my friends call me Tina."

"Are you the same Christina Tupaz who was at the scene of the accident involving this patient?"

"Yes, sir."

"I had been informed you work in the ER. Do you work this ward, also?"

"No, sir."

Decker scratched his head, moving his lips in a way no one would mistake for a smile. "Would you call this a coincidence, Ms. Tupaz? I don't think it is." He finished the sentence in his deep baritone voice.

"I don't believe in coincidences, Ms. Tupaz, I deal in facts. The fact you, the only witness to the accident involving this patient, have been found in his hospital room leads to serious questions. Would you be kind enough to accompany me, Miss Tupaz?"

Not waiting for an answer, he lightly placed a massive hand on Tina's elbow, guiding her toward the small office located behind the nurse's station.

Tina considered the chances of ducking between his legs and escaping, but she knew that would only lead to more problems.

Two nurses, who had just returned from rounds, watched as they approached.

"I need to borrow your office space," Decker announced, never breaking his stride.

"I'm sorry, officer; you are not authorized to enter this area," the larger of the two nurses said, attempting to block Decker's progress. The nurse glared defiantly at Decker.

He ignored her.

She backed off, looking seriously at her sensible shoes.

Decker strode into the office, dragging Tina in his wake.

The office, clearly meant only as a work area and not a meeting space, had barely enough room to hold the two generic metal desks and office chairs crammed in the narrow space. A metal folding chair stuffed into a corner acted as the only allowance made for the occasional guest.

Decker pointed at Tina and then the folding chair, watching from the doorway as she sat.

He then stormed out of the room, barking into his radio as he walked away. "Deputy Carlisle, report to the SICU nurse's station, ASAP!"

Decker moved down the hallway toward the patient's room, dropping out of sight.

Tina knew she needed to get rid of the John Doe file before Decker returned.

Finding no immediate hiding places in the tiny room, she slid the envelope onto the farthest desk, face down, amidst several others of the same size and color. Hopefully, no one would think to look there.

Seconds later, Decker returned to the office, accompanied by a female officer.

"Ms. Tupaz, this is Deputy Caroline Carlisle," Decker said, indicating the officer behind him.

Carlisle, only slightly taller than Tina, strode into the small office.

Dressed in a highly starched uniform, her light blonde hair and angular features were razor-sharp. Her leather shoes, holster, and belt, polished to a high sheen. Her sidearm gleamed. She squeaked slightly when she walked.

"Ms. Tupaz, regulations require a female officer to accompany a male officer when interviewing a female suspect," informed Decker.

"What do you mean suspect? I haven't done anything wrong!" cried Tina, her stomach twisting into a knot. She began to wonder if she should mention what she found when she entered the patient's room but decided to keep it to herself.

"Ms. Tupaz," replied Decker in a patronizing air, "a female officer is also required when the suspect has done nothing wrong. I have a few questions. If you answer them truthfully, we can all go home."

Decker quickly followed his explanation with his first question. "What were you doing in John Doe's hospital room, Miss Tupaz?"

"I was checking on him," answered Tina, quietly.

"Since we have already established you are not assigned to this unit, why were you checking on him?" persisted Decker.

"I found him when I stopped at an MVA last night. I had to perform CPR. I just wanted to make sure he was okay."

"Is that part of the standard operating procedure, Ms. Tupaz?"

With eyes downcast in fear, Tina shook her head.

"Ms. Tupaz, I believe this is a violation of hospital regulations. Are you acquainted with the victim?" Decker asked.

"The first time I saw him was last night."

"Did he speak with you?"

"He was unconscious; he had been in a horrible car accident!"

"Why were you traveling on I-279, Ms. Tupaz?"

"I enjoy the view. Why is that important?" Tina replied, sounding slightly defensive.

"This may sound like a cliché, Ms. Tupaz, but please try to remember *I* am the one asking the questions and determining the importance of information," Decker said with a snarl, his eyebrows rising in anger. "Where did you enter I-279, Ms. Tupaz?"

"I-I'm not certain. I think it was before the Bellevue on-ramp."

"Were there any other vehicles on the freeway?"

"Not when I got on; that's why I took I-279. Traffic was very light, especially early on a Friday evening. When I looked down onto the freeway from an overpass, there were only two cars on the road, one right behind the other."

There was a brief pause. Tina wondered if she should have mentioned the fact she had bypassed all the posted detours, but she thought the better of it.

"Did you recognize either vehicle?" Decker asked.

"No, but the second car was orange with a confederate flag painted on its roof."

Decker glared at Tina for what seemed like a lifetime. "Ms. Tupaz, don't try to make a fool of me!"

After another pause, he added, "I don't have any more questions for you at this time, but you will see me again; I guarantee it!"

Decker stormed out of the office without another word, with Carlisle following close behind.

Tina felt like her head was going to explode. No one in her family had ever done anything even slightly outside the law, yet Decker had just treated her like a common criminal.

She looked around the little office for something to smash but found her emotional rollercoaster ride interrupted by some movement.

Standing outside the office door, two nurses looked at Tina with concern.

Not trusting herself to speak, Tina nodded, acknowledging their presence and providing them with a reason to step inside.

"My name is Sue Cruller," a thin, middle-aged nurse said, firmly hugging Tina. "My partner's name is Barb Wilson."

The second, younger, and larger nurse, the one who had *almost* stood up to Decker, rewarded Tina with a beautiful smile and a firm handshake.

Within moments, the three nurses were seated around the small desk, bashing Decker and the mysterious Carlisle, saying, "Can you believe the nerve?" and "What is their problem?"

Buzzing from the nurse's station called the nurses back to work, leaving Tina alone in the small office. She retrieved the John Doe folder, clutching it tightly to her chest.

Departing the hospital through a back door, she rushed to her vehicle and carefully drove home.

Once inside her house, Tina sat at her kitchen table, carefully placing the John Doe envelope in front of her. She had retrieved it from the desk once the other two nurses left the room.

She stared at it for several minutes, watching as if it were a snake about to strike.

Sighing in resignation, she snatched the envelope from the table, poured its contents into a large old BBQ pot, and lit a match. She vowed to not let the sense of urgency get to her again as she watched the flames consume the papers.

Tina knew there were many regulations involved in keeping patients' information private. Her attempt at learning more about the victim was in violation of several of those regulations, which she intended to break no more.

Nauseous from excess trauma, as well as a lack of sleep, Tina felt she deserved a bit of fresh air. The small front deck she and Jordan had installed shortly after she became a homeowner supplied the best option.

She pushed herself away from the table and stumbled outside to be immediately encompassed by a fog that smelled like a primordial soup, Pittsburgh's answer to fresh air. Still, it was not as thick as the fog she had encountered on the highway.

She flopped into her favorite lounge chair, covered herself with a thick blanket, and fell into a dreamless sleep.

Chapter Eight: Suspension

Tina woke early the next morning to normal weather conditions in Pittsburgh, an overcast day with a chance of rain.

She took a little longer than usual as she prepared for her workday. Tina was still a little tired, sore, and very smelly after spending the night outdoors.

Rushing into the nurse's dressing room, almost but not quite late, she was met at the locker room entryway by her immediate supervisor, accompanied by the head of human resources. They were going through the contents of her locker, whispering loudly to each other.

They stopped talking when Tina entered the room.

"Good morning, Tina," Melissa Jones, the ER nursing supervisor, said nervously. Tall and thin, she was the opposite of the short heavyset woman conversing with her.

"I believe you know Belinda McBride, the head of HR," said Jones, indicating the woman beside her.

"There are several matters we would like to discuss with you, Ms. Tupaz. Please, accompany us to HR," McBride said in a snooty tone of voice.

"I'm sorry," replied Tina, valiantly attempting to shoulder her way to the lockers. "I can't go with you right now. It's time for my rounds."

"I called in one of the other nurses to cover your shift, Tina," Jones said, quietly.

"What's going on? Who gave you permission to search my locker?"

McBride harrumphed. "If you had read your contract, *Ms. Tupaz*, you would know management reserves the right to inspect personal storage areas as necessary. Your contract is quite clear on this topic. It is also clear you are required to appear at meetings scheduled by human resources to investigate policy infractions. Failure to do so can lead to immediate termination. You have two choices; accompany us, or I call security."

Tina watched silently as McBride turned and waddled out of the room, followed closely by Melissa Jones.

Momentarily toying with the idea of running in the other direction, Tina dropped her head in resignation. She knew she had no other choice.

She followed McBride to the elevators, like a lamb to slaughter.

Tina heard a familiar deep voice when the elevator doors whooshed open on the HR supervisors' floor, turning her shame and confusion into gut-wrenching hatred.

"Nice to see you again, Tupaz," said Decker, obviously pleased with the young nurse's situation.

"Mrs. McBride has reserved a conference room for us," Decker snarled as he turned and marched away.

McBride and Jones followed close behind.

Eyes downcast, Tina followed.

McBride seated herself at the head of an oval-shaped mahogany table surrounded by ten chairs. She silently directed Tina to take a seat on the right side of the table, immediately across from Decker.

A man whom Tina didn't recognize entered the room and walked to the end of the table, taking the vacant seat to McBride's left and placing his leather briefcase in front of him.

An elegantly dressed middle-aged woman entered the room next.

She stopped beside Tina's chair and scanned the faces around the table. She paused briefly when her gaze landed on Decker.

Turning to face Tina, she extended a perfectly manicured hand in greeting. "Good morning, Nurse Tupaz; my name is Lisa Williams. I'm the head of your nursing union. I heard they were bringing out their big guns over this pettiness, so I felt I had better make certain one of our best was properly taken care of. Mind if I join you?"

Not waiting for an answer, Williams sat in the chair next to Tina, leaning over to whisper into the young woman's ear. "I'm here to make certain they don't railroad you. As soon as we hear what they have to say, we can get out of here, and you can get back to work."

McBride tapped a pen on the table. "Good morning. I believe everyone is present. Before we continue, I would like to introduce Mister Gordon Russell, one of the hospital's corporate attorneys, and Captain Decker of the Allegheny County Sheriff's Department." Williams indicated the men to her left. "Due to the extreme nature of this incident, we have found it necessary to escalate this phase of the process to include the legal department."

"If you had contacted us before you let this 'incident,' as you call it, get out of control, we would never have gotten to this phase, Belinda," Williams said, sweetly. "Now, we have the police and corporate attorneys involved in what should be a simple reprimand."

"I have no intention of turning this into a legal hearing, Lisa, and I certainly don't want to incur the wrath of the union, but it is *because* the police are involved Mister Russel is present," snarled McBride.

"Which brings us to the reason we are here," continued McBride, reining in her temper. "I have provided copies of the reports relating to this case for review if any of you feel the need."

Lisa Williams practically jumped out of her chair, retrieved two copies of the report, and motioned for Tina to follow her. "Come along, Tina. I've reserved the conference room next door so we can speak in private."

Williams turned to McBride. "This may take a while," she said, smiling sweetly.

McBride didn't reply; her lips were squeezed together tightly in anger.

In the adjoining conference room, Williams grasped Tina lightly by her upper arms, looking directly into her eyes.

"Wait here, Tina," she said. "You look horrible. I'm going to find you some ice water to fortify your spirits and some caffeine to get you moving. We need you to get yourself together, or those jerks in the other room are going to eat you alive!"

Williams returned within a few minutes, carrying a tray laden with bottles of water, a pot of coffee, and some fresh pastries.

"Start with the water to flush your system," Williams said as soon as the door closed behind her. "Then, hit the coffee. The pastries are for a sugar rush."

"While you eat, I'm going to read the report out loud," intoned Williams in her public speaking voice. "If you have any questions or comments, just blurt them right out, okay? You got that?"

Afraid to speak, Tina nodded.

In the clear and concise voice of a radio announcer, Williams read the list of Tina's infractions from the previous day.

The file included screen captures from security footage, showing Tina's movements throughout the hospital the previous day, including entering the patient's room. Each photo was accompanied by written explanations of the depicted violations, including time, date, location, and the type of broken regulation. The report ended with a scathing statement from Captain Decker, stating his opinion Tina was determined to harm the victim of the accident.

"I'm screwed!" bellowed Tina.

"Tina, I know this sounds bad, but you can't give up before you start to fight. Finish your pastries. Then, we go back in there, see what they want, and we can work a deal. Okay?" Williams said, enthusiastically.

"Mrs. Williams, I have always been a very good nurse," whined Tina. "I don't know what happened to me yesterday. I never broke rules before!"

"Do you know why I'm here with you today, Tina?" asked Williams.

Tina shrugged, lethargically.

"I received an email telling me a lynch mob was after you, that you needed my help. Before I agreed, I checked your records. You've been an excellent nurse." Williams tapped the report. "Is this story true?"

"Yes, I was obsessed with finding a patient I had given CPR to at the accident site."

"You didn't stomp on regulations, as they claim. There is one thing I need to know; why did you spend so much of your time looking for the patient?"

Uncertain of the reason for her actions of the day before, Tina shrugged.

Astonished, Williams remarked, "Why would you…Never mind, I doubt you can explain anything you did yesterday."

Tina felt like the floor dropped out from beneath her. "Am I going to lose my job, Mrs. Williams?"

"I guarantee you won't lose your job, Tina, if you remember to let me do the talking when we go back in there. I am exactly like your attorney. If you are asked a question, don't answer it before consulting with me." Williams took a cleansing breath and completed her pep talk, practically yelling, "Let's go kick some butt, Tina!"

They returned to McBride's kangaroo court.

Tina took an empty chair *not* facing Decker.

Williams got right to the point. "Your report made for interesting reading, McBride, but I have things to do, so I suggest we get to the point. What do you want?"

McBride glanced in Decker's direction before answering. "After reviewing hospital policies, HIPAA regulations, and discussing the findings with hospital leadership teams, it has been decided Ms. Tupaz be terminated immediately, and her license suspended."

"Tut, tut, tut, McBride," Williams responded. "You know you can't make that kind of a decision without consulting the employee, and the employee's representative. That was clearly indicated in the collective bargaining agreement of…"

"Excuse me, Ms. Williams," Attorney Russell interrupted, "We are not concerned with bargaining agreements. Ms. Tupaz trampled over a dozen regulations, jeopardizing the lives of patients."

"Mister Russell," Williams snarled, "I'm not certain what your place is in this meeting, but I can assure you, your view of the report is questionable."

McBride peered over her horned rim reading glasses. "Let's not quibble over peripheral details, Mrs. Williams. As the employee's representative, what do you suggest?"

Williams smiled sweetly at the HR leader, "Tina Tupaz is one of the best nurses any hospital has ever had. She was recognized as the ER employee of the year. Twice. She has never been late for work and has always received exemplary reviews from her supervisors. You would never get away with terminating her on a first offense."

Glancing at the attorney, Williams continued, "Of course, if Mister Russell wants to bring in the union lawyers, I can make a call."

McBride responded like a wolf pouncing on a rabbit. "Before involving anyone else, Lisa, perhaps we can come to a compromise?"

As soon as McBride said the word compromise, Williams knew she had saved Tina's future.

It took another hour of negotiations, but Lisa didn't quit until she was completely satisfied she had wrangled the best possible deal for Tina.

Tina received a three-month suspension from her current occupation, with no guarantee of placement upon return. More importantly, however, she did not lose her license.

Decker watched the negotiations quietly, waiting until the parties had reached the final agreement before rising. He looked directly at Tina, growling in disgust, "I know you're dirty, Tupaz! You may have won this round, but I'm watching you!"

Williams jumped to her feet, "You're nothing but a bully, Decker! I have dealt with the likes of you many a time. Now, you either charge her with a crime, or get out. She will not talk to you again without her legal representative present! Do you understand?"

Decker, his face red with anger, stormed out of the room.

Williams motioned for Tina to accompany her to the hallway, not bothering with the common courtesy of addressing the remaining occupants of the conference room.

"Corporate policy dictates suspended employees be escorted by security. It's embarrassing, but necessary," added Williams, watching as two hospital security officers approached. "This will all be over soon."

After warmly hugging the diminutive nurse, Williams turned and quietly walked away.

Chapter Nine: New Job

Accompanied by security, Tina returned to her locker, packed her meager belongings into a small box supplied by HR, and left the building. Her movements were monitored while she loaded her car and departed the hospital property.

Automobiles were not a priority when Tina's Street was built. That meant, on some days, there was no parking to be found for several blocks. On that day, of all days, she was able to park her car on the street just a few doors down from her house.

Tina sighed as she went around to the back of her car to retrieve the small box of her belongings.

Glancing toward the house, she saw Jordan sitting on the front deck, comfortably leaning back in his chair, his feet propped up on the railing.

Storming toward the house in anger, Tina screamed, "Jordy! Where have you been? I've been calling and texting you for two days!"

"I had a lot to take care of, Tupaz," Jordan calmly replied.

"Like what? Covering your butt? I lost my job, Jordy!"

"No, you didn't. You got a three-month suspension."

Tina stomped up the wooden steps leading to the deck and dropped heavily into an empty chair. "It might as well be a year! I'm broke! How can I pay my bills?"

She paused as a thought struck her. "Hey, how did you know I got suspended?"

"Do you remember the day we met, Tupaz?" Jordan asked, pointedly not answering the question.

"I will never forget that day, Jordy, but you never want to talk about it, and you didn't answer my question," Tina sighed, her anger slowly dissipating.

Jordan casually leaned down, pulling a bottle of beer from a cooler at his feet.

"It's not even noon, Jordy; how can you drink this early?" asked Tina.

"Humor me, Tupaz. Tell me the story of the day we met," Jordan twisted the cap off his beer and took a long swallow, clearly ignoring his friend's questions.

Tina sighed in resignation. "I was attacked by three boys when I cut through a parking lot after my English as a second language class. I was only a freshman in high school. I probably looked like I was only three, but they didn't care. They hit me and started to rip at my clothes. They were dragging me to a van when they suddenly let me go and ran away. The next thing I knew, you were there, holding my hand and telling me everything would be okay."

"What about after that day, Tupaz? Do you remember?"

"Of course, Jordy," said Tina, sitting up straighter in her chair. "How could I forget? You knew I was terrified to walk to the bus stop alone, so for the rest of that year, you gave me a ride home."

"The point is, Tupaz, I knew you were in trouble when we were in high school. I didn't have any idea who you were, but I knew I had to help."

Jordan finished his beer, automatically reaching for another.

"Yesterday afternoon, I heard rumors about a crazy nurse breaking regulations to find a patient," he continued after a healthy swig of beer. "You also managed to anger some cop, so HR was sending the big dogs after you. You were in way over your head and needed my help."

"If Lisa Williams hadn't shown up, I would have been sunk," Tina remarked.

Jordan smiled. "Did you know I played football with Lisa's son, Marcus?"

"I should have guessed. You are very popular, Jordy."

"It worked out," Jordan said. "You ended up with three months suspension instead of being fired and losing your license."

"Do you know why they wanted to destroy me?" asked Tina, her calm demeanor returning.

"I'm not certain, but it probably has something to do with that cop," replied Jordan. "I'm not sure why he's even involved. Did you do something to him?"

Tina pondered Jordan's question and shook her head. "I appreciate the fact you saved my career, but to be honest with you, Jordy, I have zero dollars in the bank. I can't survive three months without a job."

"Do you remember meeting my aunt Joan? She is just a couple of years older than me."

"I think we met a few times," Tina answered. "I remember because she was the most beautiful woman I had ever seen." She stopped herself from saying his aunt had raised him after his parents died, knowing it was still a sensitive topic for him.

"Yeah, well, she owns a visiting nurse company," Jordan said, sliding his aunt's business card into Tina's hand. "I took the liberty of providing her with your resume. She was very impressed. Drop by her office tomorrow, fill out some paperwork, and you can start right away. You see, I'm still taking care of you, Tupaz!"

Jordan rose then nonchalantly strolled off the deck and off her property without another word. Jordan Best honked his horn and waved as he passed Tina's house, leaving behind a cooler full of beer and a very confused nurse.

Tina clutched the business card in her hand. She had to admit that things might work out after all.

Chapter Ten: Questioning the Survivor

Shortly after the accident, the lone survivor of the hit-and-run accident went through several lifesaving surgeries.

The surgeons who had performed the emergency action were pleasantly surprised at the patient's recovery, especially because his prognosis looked so dim upon his admittance. They happily signed off on his transfer after only one week, from the SICU to a private room in a different area of the hospital.

Although his transfer had been pushed by Captain Decker, the policeman learned of the transfer secondhand. He did learn, firsthand, how even the most innocuous change in hospital precedent can cause a nightmare of confusion.

In this case, it was a simple computer glitch which caused administration personnel to misplace the patient. It took over an hour for them to find him again.

By the time Decker gained access to the patient's room, he found him fast asleep.

Unwilling to relocate, Decker found an extremely uncomfortable chair, settling in to wait until the patient stirred.

Hours later, when the victim's eyes fluttered open, Decker was still waiting.

He jumped out of his chair, considerately positioning himself directly in front of the patient, cleared his throat for attention, and smiled.

"My name is Aloysius Decker. I'm with the Allegheny Sheriff's Incident Investigation Department. I'd like to ask you a few questions about your recent motor vehicle accident."

"I'm sorry for your loss, sir," Decker continued seconds after he had received no response. "I'll be as succinct as possible. If it gets too much for you, close your eyes, and I'll go away. However, the sooner we get some answers, the sooner we'll find the person responsible."

The patient mumbled in agreement.

Decker followed up with a quick question, "May I ask, sir, why was your daughter driving your car on the night of the accident?"

"Ashley; my daughter's name is Ashley," the accident victim said, choking back a sob. "She was driving the new car for the first time. It was a reward for being such a wonderful daughter!"

"Had you been drinking, sir?"

"What? No! Even if I had been, you know I wasn't driving!"

Decker pressed on. "You and your wife were dressed for an evening out. Did your daughter have to drive because you were intoxicated?"

"Absolutely not! We attended Ashley's volleyball game. I would never drink before seeing her play!"

Decker checked his notes. "You were wearing an Armani suit, and your wife was decked out in a black Versace evening gown. Hardly volleyball game attire."

"We planned on attending our twenty-fifth anniversary party after the tournament." The patient was becoming agitated. "And I don't like your tone."

He paused, looking at the police officer, appraisingly. "I remember you now, Decker! You led the investigation into my parents' deaths, but never found the person responsible for killing them. Your storied incompetence precedes you, officer! I believe this interview is over!"

Decker took a deep, calming breath. "I apologize, sir. My job is to find out what caused your accident. Sometimes, I need to ask tough questions to learn the truth. May I continue?"

The survivor glared up at the police officer for a moment before answering. "I want to get to the bottom of this, captain, but I reserve the right to end this conversation if I feel your questions are out of line." His tone was firm.

Decker nodded, "Because your daughter was driving, sir, where were you seated?"

"I was in the rear passenger seat. My son, Brad, was in the front passenger seat, and my wife was in the back seat with me."

"Did you always occupy the same seats?"

"No. I usually drove with my wife, Veronica, next to me and the kids in the back. We reversed the seating because Ashley drove."

"Our investigators determined your vehicle was traveling at over 130 miles per hour when it crashed." said Decker, checking his notes. "What caused your daughter to travel at such a high rate of speed?"

"She was pushed!"

"Did someone threaten your daughter?"

"No, I don't know," the patient answered, obviously confused, "I don't think she ever saw the Charger before."

"What Charger?" Decker replied, puzzled. "Please, start at the beginning, sir. What happened?"

The patient paused to gather his thoughts.

"I gave Ashley the keys and told her how proud I was of her," he said, sadly. "She was a winner! She was going to Harrisburg next week for the state volleyball tournament, and she was enrolled at Pitt for the fall. She had it all! Letting her drive the new car was a reward."

"She wanted to drive in the rain?" asked Decker, incredulously. "Our investigation said we were experiencing typical April weather for Pittsburgh: slashing, bitterly cold rain, with heavy gusts of wind."

"She complained about it, but when my wife asked her if she wanted someone else to drive, Ashley refused. It didn't matter; the rain stopped just as we were getting on the freeway. Ashley pointed out a detour sign located about fifty feet past the final exit, advising drivers to take alternate routes to avoid construction delays.

"The next sign said there were two lanes, one going directly to Pittsburgh with no exits, the other providing access to regular exits." Closing his eyes, he stifled a sob. "I told Ashley to take the Pittsburgh-only lane. I killed my entire family!"

"It was the only lane open, sir; the signs were wrong. Something else must have happened to cause her to drive so recklessly."

The patient took a deep, shuddering breath. *If the signs were wrong, why didn't anybody do anything about it?* the man thought. Then, he said to Decker, "We were only on the freeway for a few minutes before Ashley said we were being tailgated. I turned my head to look, but the car was so close the only thing I could see were headlights. My wife asked Ashley to slow down and find a place to pull over so the tailgater could pass, but he laid on his horn. It was one of those custom horns. It played the first few bars of 'La Cucaracha.'

"That caused Ashley to panic, and she stomped on the gas pedal. We must have been doing ninety when he hit us the first time."

"The following vehicle hit you?" asked Decker, furiously taking notes.

"The car had a heavy bull sweep grill protector, like the ones on tractor-trailers. Hitting us didn't even scratch his paint!"

"Is that when you crashed?"

Tears streaming down his face, the victim shook his head. "We hit the Jersey barrier, but Ashley regained control of the car and stepped on the gas again. She kept going faster. I leaned over the seat so I could see the speedometer. Ashley kept increasing her speed, trying to outdistance the tailgater, but the Charger kept pace, remaining inches from our back-bumper right to the end of the construction zone, even after we encountered the fog.

"Ashley stayed in the center lane, barreling straight ahead. I looked at the Charger as it started to pass us in the left lane. It suddenly swerved, clipping our left-rear fender, sending us into a spin. We went airborne when we hit the shoulder."

The man couldn't continue speaking. He turned away to hide the tears running down his face.

"There are several things I don't understand, sir," said Decker, unaffected by his interviewee's obvious discomfort. "You claim you were riding in the rear passenger seat. How do you explain landing over 100 feet from the vehicle when it crashed?"

The man took a deep, shuddering breath before answering. "I'm not sure. I must have been thrown from the car when it tumbled."

"I suppose that's possible, sir." Decker scratched his head, thinking. "Why have you repeatedly described the other vehicle as a Charger?"

"I saw the car earlier, on my way to the tournament. It was an orange, 1969 Dodge Charger with a *Dukes of Hazzard* custom paint job that came flying out of a side street, cut across three lanes of traffic, ran the red light, and turned left." The victim closed his eyes, trying to remember. "The driver pulled into a restaurant parking lot, jumped out of the car, and urinated in full view of everyone. Veronica wanted to call the police, but I talked her out of it. I didn't want any trouble."

"How can you be certain it was the same vehicle, sir?" Decker asked.

"I saw it as we passed under the exit lights. It was like *The Dukes of Hazard* car."

Decker looked puzzled.

"Don't you know that old TV show? They called the car The General Lee. It was orange with a confederate flag painted on its roof and the number 01 on the door."

"I never watched the show," Decker said, writing information in his notebook. "You mentioned fog, but no fog was reported that night."

"I know what I saw, Decker," the patient replied, defensively.

"How well do you know Christina Tupaz, sir?" Decker asked after a brief pause.

"I've never heard of her. Was she driving the Charger?" the patient asked, his blood pressure skyrocketing.

"We don't think she was driving the Charger, sir, she—"

The duty nurse stormed into the room, interrupting Decker. "Captain Decker, you agreed to inform the nursing staff when the patient woke so we could check his vitals *before* your interrogation! I will speak with the attending concerning this arrangement. In the meantime, I will have to ask you to leave."

Decker weighed the advisability of a confrontation with the staff, asking one final question, "Do you remember anything else about the Charger?"

"Yes. When he ran the red light, I caught a glimpse of a Pennsylvania license plate. The first three letters were JBB."

Decker carefully wrote down that information in his notebook, quietly closed it, and walked briskly out of the room.

He called the Pennsylvania vehicle registration office as he crossed the hospital lobby. "I'm looking for an owner and address connected to PA partial license JBB belonging to a 1969 Dodge Charger," he told the clerk over the phone. "Let me know the minute you learn anything."

After he disconnected the call, Decker exited the building and headed for his vehicle.

Crossing the highway in front of the hospital took him to the public parking garage where he thought he had parked his car. However, the police vehicle was not where he thought he had left it.

"Typical," Decker muttered to himself. *Every time I park where there are two or more adjacent parking garages, I always pick the wrong one,* he thought as he grumpily headed toward the next garage.

Chapter Eleven: Joseph Burns

His cell phone rang at the same time he pressed the panic button on his key fob. That emitted a repetitive horn honking so loud Decker couldn't hear the DMV report. After several attempts to turn the panic button off, he threw the key fob down on the ground and smashed it with his boot.

Unfazed, the DMV Clerk informed him the database showed only one 1969 Dodge Charger in Pennsylvania with the personalized PA license plate beginning with the letters JBB. It was registered to Attorney Joseph Brian Burns, who resided in a nineteenth-century mansion located in Pittsburgh's millionaire's row.

Decker arranged for a search warrant and then notified his team.

###

Early the next morning, three police vehicles invaded the well-manicured grounds of the Burns residence.

Like Genghis Kahn invading Rome, Decker sat ramrod straight in the passenger seat of the lead vehicle with Carlisle at the wheel, lights flashing through the pre-dawn darkness, casting eerie shadows on the lawn.

The cruiser, which was being followed closely by two black vans full of equipment and technicians, rolled along the serpentine driveway, coming to a stop at the front doors of the mansion.

The mansion's entryway, anchored to the drive by a set of three hand-carved marble stairs, seemed to dwarf Captain Decker as he exited the police vehicle.

Carlisle hurriedly donned her "Smokey the Bear" hat and rushed to join Decker as he climbed the marble stairs.

They reached the massive entry doors at the same time.

Decker reached out for a bright brass lion's head door knocker located in the exact center of each of the eight-foot-high oak doors.

Joseph Burns, with a self-satisfied grin, opened the doors just as Decker reached the knocker, proving Burns had been aware of the convoy almost as soon as it arrived. He had been watching the progress of the police officers approaching his property via security cameras.

"What do you want?" bellowed Burns.

"I'm Captain Aloysius Decker with the Sheriff's Department's Incident Investigation Unit. I have a warrant to search your garages," Decker answered in his most officious voice. He signaled Carlisle to step forward. She had the warrant in her hand.

Burns snatched the warrant from Carlisle's extended hand and scanned the document. "This warrant grants you access to the Charger, and only the Charger," Burns snarled. He waved the warrant under Decker's nose. "You will not touch anything outside of the parameters described in the warrant. To ensure you comply, I will be there, along with two of my assistants, watching you like a hawk!"

Burns turned to reenter his house, the warrant crumpled in his hand. He glanced at Decker before closing the massive oak doors. "I shall return in a few minutes. Until then, I suggest you do not move."

Carlisle looked at her boss, shrugged, and moved to join him in the center of the landing, where they waited patiently for Burns to return.

Ten minutes later, dressed in blue jeans and a faded T-shirt that read, *Trust Me...I'm a lawyer*, Burns stepped onto the massive marble landing.

Accompanied by two young men carrying video equipment, he strode past the officers without a word.

An Irish wolfhound bound out of the open doors, galloping for the garden, plowing over everything in its wake.

Carlisle latched onto Decker's shirt sleeve to keep from falling.

Decker, aghast at the contact, stared at Carlisle's hand.

She quickly apologized and let go.

Meanwhile, Joseph Burns continued walking toward the carriage house, waving the warrant over his head.

"This joke of a warrant grants permission for these storm troopers to inspect my property," Burns said to his assistants, speaking in the same tone he used to address a jury. "I am referring to the 1969 Dodge Charger collector's edition and its storage area. Nothing else! To ensure their integrity, you are to record every movement they make."

The small parade came to a halt in front of the carriage house.

"The Dodge Charger listed in this unconstitutional warrant is housed inside unit number two. Appropriately, access to the unit is limited to two people at a time," said Burns, officiously.

"My assistants have been instructed to take videos of the vehicle and the storage unit. I will hold you personally responsible for any damages caused by your goons." Burns directed his last comment at Decker.

Burns then opened a small plastic box attached to the door frame and discreetly entered numbers into a keypad. The door rolled open with barely a rattle, revealing an immaculate 1969 Dodge Charger.

The wolfhound rounded the building, tail wagging, tongue lolling to the side.

It pranced in front of Burns, seeking attention.

"I'm going to take Princess for a short walk," Burns said, lovingly scratching the wolfhound behind her ears. "When my assistants have completed gathering a video record of the Charger and its storage unit, your people may have access."

Burns made a kissing sound to attract Princess's attention and then strolled toward the rear of the house, Princess walking proudly by his side.

The four technicians facilitating the forensic investigation were divided into two teams. The first team was to enter the storage unit after Burns' people were through. They were tasked with taking scrapings of any foreign objects, such as skin, blood, hair, fresh paint, dirt, or plant matter found on the vehicle.

The second team employed laser-assisted measuring devices to search for any recent alterations.

The results of both the investigations were sent directly to Carlisle's laptop to compare the findings with vehicle information on file in the police database.

As soon as he determined the final pieces of information were processed, Decker moved from his position in front of the Charger's storage unit to review the results on Carlisle's computer.

Decker almost had to physically move Burns from his position in front of the computer before he could carefully read the final report. Burns had recently returned from his walk with Princess.

Decker took his time reading the reports, consciously ignoring Burns' childlike squirming.

When he finished a second review of the facts, he turned toward the attorney, and in his deepest baritone addressed him. "Mister Burns, the measurements we took were compared to the manufacturer's specifications for the vehicle. They were within the allowable parameters for a vehicle as old as your Charger."

The look on Burns' face turned from slightly angry to smug. "Fine," he sneered. "Now, you can get your idiots off my property!"

"However," Decker continued as if Burns had not spoken, "our cameras have discovered an anomaly on the right front fender that appears to be recent bodywork and touch-up paint."

Burn's face fell. "That's not right, Decker, and you know it."

"What I know, Mister Burns, is my technicians are going to enter the garage and take additional scrapings to determine if what the camera recorded is correct. If it is, we will impound the vehicle and take it to the lab for complete processing."

Furious, the attorney turned toward Decker, coming dangerously close to bumping his chest. "If those jerks mess up my car, Decker, you will pay for it!" Burns screamed into the officer's face. "I am a close, personal, friend of the governor. I have allowed this charade because of the respect I have for your boss, but my patience has reached its end."

Burns paused. "Why are you even looking at my Charger, Decker? I want to know before I call the governor. Why this sudden interest?"

"The reason for the search is in the warrant, Mister Burns."

"It's a generic warrant, Decker. You owe me more than that."

"Okay, Burns, an orange Dodge Charger of approximately the same year and model as yours was involved in a recent hit and run accident," replied Decker, calmly.

"Do you bother to check facts before you make a move, Decker, or is the art of investigation lost on you?" asked Burns, incredulously. "I've been in Paris for the past three months. I returned yesterday morning, so unless this accident happened during the past twenty-four hours, you are totally in the wrong! Don't touch a thing, Decker! I swear, if you allow your idiot technicians to touch my car, I will destroy you!"

Burns turned and jogged in the direction of his house, Princess prancing playfully behind.

Decker waited until Burns closed the massive oak doors behind him before signaling for the technicians to move on the Charger.

They proceeded to take paint and residue scrapings, placing them into clearly marked evidence bags.

Decker ignored his work phone when it rang and then shook his head when a call came over the cruiser's radio.

Out of curiosity, he looked at the caller ID when his cell vibrated again.

"He really does know the boss," Decker said, incredulously to no one in particular before answering the phone.

Fifteen minutes later, Carlisle, Decker, and the technicians were packed up and pulling away from the carriage house, leaving the Charger behind.

Watching from a second-floor window as the police convoy left the mansion's property, Burns made a conference call with his sons, Christopher and Charles, at Christopher's apartment.

"Who was driving my car?" Burns began yelling the moment Christopher said hello. "I never gave anyone permission to even *look* at the Charger!"

"I was driving," mumbled Christopher.

"Were you drunk?" screamed Burns. "You were involved in a hit-and-run in *my* car. You weren't supposed to be driving my car."

"Rachel was with us," Charley chimed in, speaking of Burns' present wife.

Burns squeezed the bridge of his nose, squinting out the window. "I'll deal with her later. Tell me what happened."

"Nothing," mumbled Christopher.

"We were following a Mercedes on our way to Pittsburgh," offered Charley. "It was going too slow, so Chris kind of helped it to move along. We may have been a little too close, but I know that Mercedes can move faster than it was."

"Where was Rachel?" demanded Burns.

"Your *wife* was passed out in the backseat," answered Christopher. "It wasn't her fault, or my driving. Just as we were passing the Mercedes, some woman dressed like an old hippie stepped in front of the Charger. When I swerved to miss her, I bumped into the Mercedes. It spun out of control and crashed. The stupid hippie woman jumped in front of me again, but when I honked my horn, she disappeared."

"Why didn't you stop?" asked Burns, quietly. He ended the call without waiting for an answer. He pressed his hands against his temples. What had those boys gotten him into?

Chapter Twelve: Bill Hughes

Tina Tupaz was a very fast study. She learned all the ins and outs of home nursing during her first week and quickly became the most efficient nurse Best Home Health had ever known. Because of her hard work, her higher learning curve, and her dedication, in less than a month, Tina was given the opportunity to run her very own patient.

The boss knew Tina would perform the job better than anyone else on her staff. Tina proved herself the moment she accepted the position. She had become the perfect manager.

She jealously protected the patient's anonymity and thoroughly researched the background of every member of her proposed staff before scheduling them to work with patients.

On the day the patient officially fell under the umbrella of Best Home Health's care, Tina discreetly parked her Toyota across the street from the patient's exclusive south Pittsburgh address. Her boss waited at the front door to greet patient 10142 when he arrived.

Tina stayed in her car until the large access van pulled into the semi-circle driveway and came to a complete stop in front of the house. Nervously rounding the back of the van at the same time the patient's wheelchair noisily inched its way to the sidewalk, Tina stood at her boss's side as patient 10142 turned to greet them.

Tina's was shocked when she realized she knew the patient; she needed to lean against the van to keep from falling.

"Good morning, sir," Tina's boss said, oblivious to the discomfort Tina was feeling.

Firmly shaking the patient's hand, she introduced herself, "I'm Joan Best, owner of Best Home Health. My staff will be providing your medical care while you progress through the next stage of your recovery."

"This is Tina Tupaz," Joan said, indicating Tina with a sweep of her arm. "She is my finest nurse and will be overseeing your care. I brought her portfolio for you to read at your leisure. I'm certain everything will meet with your approval.

"As Doctor Johnson, the hospital administrator, informed you, you are scheduled for our twenty-four-hour home care. Best Home Health can be trusted to address all your rehabilitation needs."

As the van driver propelled the new patient's wheelchair slowly into the house and through the two-story foyer, Tina stood up straight and moved to Joan's side.

They stopped in front of a ten-foot-wide stone fireplace located in the center of the spacious living room.

Joan removed a large pile of paperwork from her briefcase, laying it neatly on a nearby coffee table.

"Licensed contractors, under my direction, have made changes throughout your home, making it a comfortable and efficient headquarters. I have taken the liberty of providing receipts, formal project summaries, and P.O.s, along with Tina's portfolio."

"Is everything in order, sir?" asked Joan. "You haven't said a word since we arrived."

"I apologize, Ms. Best; I appreciate everything you've done," said the patient, rewarding Joan with a sad smile. "Doctor Johnson spoke very highly of you. Based on his assessment, I feel confident your choice of professionals has been carefully considered. Our first order of business should be getting rid of the HIPAA violation for using my real name. I am Bill Hughes, and I would appreciate it if you would refer to me that way from now on."

"Very well, sir, my staff and I will be happy to call you by your proper name. I will be on my way now, but Tina will be here to help you settle in and make certain your medical needs are taken care of."

"Come see me to the door, dear," she said, addressing Tina.

Taking Tina by the hand, Joan walked to her company car, which was parked a short way past the circular drive.

She presented Tina with the keys to the house and a friendly hug. "During the short time since Jordan brought you to me, Tina, I have grown very fond of you, but you haven't said a word since we got here. Hughes isn't speaking, either. Tell me the truth, Tina, are you sure this is what you want? Are you certain you're comfortable with this assignment?"

"Ms. Best," Tina said with a smile, helping Joan into her car, "I'm a little nervous about taking on this big of a responsibility, but I'll be fine once I start working; I promise."

"Thank you, Tina. I know you'll handle this assignment with your usual professionalism."

Tina smiled and waved as Joan drove away. Joan was followed closely by the access van.

Reentering the house, Tina sighed, thinking of the many changes she needed to make, beginning with opening blinds and windows to let some life in.

Pausing just inside the door, she waited for her eyes to adjust to the gloom, barely noticing William Hughes materializing out of the darkened living room.

"I apologize if I seemed a bit unprofessional earlier, Mister Hughes," Tina said as she approached her new patient, her hand extended in greeting. "I allowed Ms. Best to control the entire conversation without properly introducing myself. My name is Christina Tupaz—"

"Do you know a Captain Decker from the Sheriff's Department?" Hughes interrupted in a direct, no-nonsense tone.

Tina stared wide-eyed at Hughes, unable to find an answer she felt acceptable.

"I apologize for startling you," Hughes said, his tone of voice suggesting an insincere apology. "It's important you answer my question. Do you know Decker?"

Tina, finally able to find her voice, mumbled, "Yes, I've met the man."

"Please, explain yourself, Ms. Tupaz," Hughes said with a theatrical sigh.

"I would feel more comfortable if you called me Tina," the nurse replied, meekly.

"First, we need to clear up a few questions. If we are going to live under the same roof, so to speak, I need to be able to trust you." Hughes wheeled over to the coffee table, picking up Tina's personnel file, and holding it aloft. "This information packet says you are employed as an ER nurse. How is it possible for you to be here and in the ER at the same time?"

"I'm on a leave of absence," whispered Tina.

"I will need a little more detail, Ms. Tupaz."

"Decker found me inside your room at the SICU. You were unconscious. Decker thought I had something to do with your accident, so he railroaded me out of the hospital."

Hughes stared, his eyes speaking volumes. "Why were you inside my hospital room, Ms. Tupaz?"

"I am so sorry, Mister Hughes. I felt like I needed to check on you. Decker appeared out of nowhere. The next thing I knew, I was in front of a review board, and my union rep was bargaining for my job."

Tina took a deep shuddering breath. "On the night of your accident, I felt something in the pit of my stomach, like I was going to be sick. When I pulled over, I saw your car wedged under the bridge. I felt helpless. I shrugged the feeling off and walked slowly back to my car, but there was nothing I could do!"

Sitting heavily on the nearest chair, she dropped her head into her hands. She didn't feel the need to tell him about seeing the remains of his deceased family inside the car. He had already been through enough.

"Lightning caused all the lights to go off; the whole world turned black. I was so scared, I tried to run away," Tina continued, looking blankly at the floor, taking deep, shuddering breaths. "I didn't get very far. Before I could reach my car and escape, I tripped over a bundle of tattered, bloody clothing."

Tina was beginning to take control. "The bundle sat up and growled at me. It turned out to be you. You were a mess. Your heart stopped beating right after I found you. I began CPR and continued compressions until the EMS team arrived."

"That doesn't explain why you were dismissed from the hospital," Hughes replied.

"I was not authorized to check up on you. There are regulations in place that forbid casual contact across patient care lines," whispered Tina, almost ashamed to admit her actions.

"And now you're in my home. I believe you're stalking me, Ms. Tupaz. I am not at all comfortable with that."

"Wait. Mister Hughes, it isn't like that at all! Please, let me explain!"

"Against my better judgment, Ms. Tupaz, I will allow you five minutes to convince me of your innocence," Hughes said, glancing at his watch. "Then, I'm calling the police."

"Thank you, Mister Hughes," Tina replied, enthusiastically. She stood, took a deep breath, and continued, "Decker suspected something was up when he found me in your hospital room, but he has it all wrong!"

Hughes rolled his eyes before glancing once again at his watch.

"Okay, I know that doesn't make *me* look any better," admitted Tina, quietly. She began pacing back and forth across the room.

"Don't ask me why, but I was convinced I needed to protect you. I didn't cause your accident. It was over by the time I got there. I didn't even know anything was wrong until I felt compelled to stop. I saw your wrecked car, but you were the only person I could help."

Tina sighed. "When I finally found you in the hospital, you were very ill, but all your life support machines were turned off. Decker came in to your room just as I was satisfied you were okay.

"Decker pushed for a review with hospital HR. I still have my license, but I lost my job. Security escorted me out of the hospital. I have a mortgage and car payments. All I could think about as I was driving away from the hospital was how I was going to survive."

Pausing for a shuddering breath, Tina continued, "A friend told me about this nursing opportunity. I felt like I was getting a second chance. After that, my obsession with you disappeared.

"When I rounded the back of the access van and saw you, I was shocked. Up until Ms. Best used your name, I only knew you as a number. I didn't know what to say! If I'd have told Ms. Best what happened, I would disappoint her after she put so much confidence in me, so I didn't say anything. I hoped it would all go away.

"I know there is no one better at this job than me. I swear to you, Mister Hughes, I am the best nurse you have ever met, and as the head of your team, I promise you the most professional care possible." Tina wrapped up her story. She hoped she had done an accurate job professing her innocence.

"There are a couple of things we need to get straight," Hughes said after a long moment of silence. Tina knew he was intently listening to every word she was saying.

"Yes, sir," replied Tina as her stomach tied in knots.

"First, my name is Bill. Mister Hughes was my father. Second, I've lost too much weight since the accident, and I can't do much with this Halo device on. Would it be possible to hire a cook? I don't want some stranger cooking me meals. I already have enough strangers in my house." Hughes smiled. "You're from Pittsburgh, perhaps you know someone?"

Tina allowed herself a slight chuckle. "Thank you, Mister Hugh-I mean, Bill. I know a couple of people who may be available. In the meantime, my mother taught me all her special Filipino recipes. It will be fun to cook for you, but you may get fat."

Bill smiled before another awkward moment of silence. It appeared the two of them were finally becoming comfortable in each other's presence, much to the relief of both parties.

Tina, her social filters shut off, said, "Bill, I don't really like Captain Decker." She didn't even want to think about the man who tried to accuse her, and it was even hard saying his name.

"Neither do I, Tina," chuckled Hughes.

Then, he changed the subject, "My recovery plan has me walking in two weeks. Can you have me running in three?"

"I'm not your physical therapist, Bill, but I'll beef up your schedule, and we can adjust for your progress as each of your casts is removed, if it's safe to do so."

"I guess that will do," Bill took a deep breath. "For right now, because you are going to stay and take care of me, you should get to know the house. Let's take a tour. I'll navigate; you push."

They explored the house, getting to know each other as they investigated the new construction and discovered old, unused features. Tina pushed Bill's wheelchair slowly to the elevator to inspect the second floor, back down to the massive master bedroom which doubled as a safe room, exiting through its French doors onto the sun-lit patio.

They strolled like old companions along the stone-lined paths that wound through the garden, past the Olympic-sized swimming pool and clay tennis courts.

When the walk was over, Tina and Bill had learned enough about each other to form a cautious and rocky friendship which would hopefully improve over time.

Tina even prepared a light meal, ending the tour with a late lunch on the veranda, where the two of them enjoyed the rare Pittsburgh sunshine.

Chapter Thirteen: Murder Most Foul

Not in the same league with legendary drunks such as Hemingway, Picasso, or Ulysses S. Grant, Burns usually ended his revelries long before the lines between night and day became blurred.

However, there were exceptions to every rule.

"I deserve a night off," Burns slurred as his most recent lady friend, Julia, helped him into the back seat of his limo. He instructed his driver, known to Burns as Guillermo Escobar, to take the longest route home. Burns hoped he could sober up enough to think through his actions of the past few days. He wished to make certain he touched all the necessary bases before putting the hit-and-run issue to rest.

He had called in favors, threatened, and begged, all to save his boys from arrest and prosecution for the incident which had destroyed another man's life.

Guillermo grunted as he turned onto the mansion's winding driveway, the pistol in his shoulder holster digging into his armpit. It was uncomfortable, so he was relieved he would soon be out of the car.

Motion sensor lights ignited as he passed, illuminating the grounds with artificial light.

Pulling the limo as close as possible to the front entrance, he carefully surveyed the area for possible threats before opening Burns' door. Confident no hidden danger existed under the mansion's lights, Guillermo placed his pistol on the passenger seat as he drove away, leaving Burns to slowly mount the marble stairs of the main entrance.

The property's exterior lights blinked out just as Burns reached the landing, leaving him in total darkness.

Too drunk to let a little darkness concern him, Burns listened as Guillermo stopped the car in front of its storage unit.

The vehicle's dome light came on when the driver flung open his door.

Feeling secure in the knowledge of Guillermo being on the job, Burns turned his attention to finding the right house key.

The task took several minutes.

Burns unlocked the front doors, cursing in annoyance at the darkness which was now beginning to annoy him. He wondered why the burglar alarm didn't beep out its usual warning.

Suddenly becoming very frightened, he called out to Guillermo. "Guillermo! Call our electrician or the light company. Something's wrong!"

Guillermo didn't reply.

Burns stepped onto the landing, leaving the double doors ajar.

Princess, seeing the opening as an invitation to play, charged out of the darkness.

Phone in hand, looking in the direction of the carriage house, Burns never saw or heard the enormous canine rushing out the door.

She slammed into him on her way to the front garden, knocking him off his feet.

He tumbled down the marble steps into the grass, twisting his back and bruising his knee. Burns let out a stream of curse words.

Using the steps as a prop, he managed to climb to his feet. His cell phone had miraculously landed nearby, turned on and illuminating its presence.

Feeling something was wrong, he called his security team for backup.

Injured by his fall down the marble steps of his portico, Burns hobbled toward the limo, noticing as he grew closer to the building the storage unit's man-door stood open.

Burns pushed his way through the door into the eerie blackness of the garage, carefully making his way to the rear of the unit.

Using his cell phone flashlight, he located a small gun safe hidden against the rear wall. Using his thumbprint to unlock the safe, he snatched out of the lockbox a 9mm Ruger and a large watchman's flashlight.

Feeling certain Decker had returned to impound the Charger, Burns limped off to intercede, gun in hand.

Burns had designed the enclosures for his automobile collection himself. He knew all the little intricacies involved in his car collection garages. For instance, he knew the overhead door to the Charger's storage unit often stuck when lowered to about two feet from the ground and stopped.

Finding the door jammed and the keyless entry box smashed, Burns unwisely shimmied under the door, sliding his injured leg behind him.

Once inside the garage, Burns used the door frame to help him stand. A cordless mini projector, perched on the roof of the Charger, cast a video against the rear wall of the enclosure.

Burns stared in disbelief at the projection.

It featured a black Mercedes aggressively tailgated by an orange Dodge Charger with a *The Dukes of Hazard* custom package.

Burns recognized the Charger as his own.

The video ended when the Charger forced the Mercedes off the road. After a slight hesitation, the video looped back to its beginning, *The Dukes of Hazzard* theme song was playing in the background.

Looking closely at the Charger in the garage for the first time since entering its storage unit, Burns saw the shadows of people inside.

Raising the Ruger, levying the watchman's flashlight to provide illumination, he slowly approached the vehicle from the right side, the silhouette of someone sitting in the passenger seat becoming clearer with each step.

Inching forward until he drew parallel with the Charger's closed window, Burns found himself slightly relieved to recognize his youngest son.

Lowering the pistol, he snatched the passenger door open, "What are you doing here, Charley? You're supposed to be in school!" he yelled.

Charley's lifeless body fell out of the car and into Burns' arms.

Burns screamed.

Father and son fell to the garage floor with a thump, Burns' pistol skidding under the vehicle. Trapped under Charley's weight, intoxicated and confused, Burns lay on the floor until suddenly all the mansion's lights flashed back on and the garage door rolled completely open.

The lights and the garage door were controlled by police officers, several of whom rushed in with guns drawn, screaming "*Freeze!*"

Burns' security team had wisely escaped notice and left the property.

Chapter Fourteen: Sterling Frisbee

Tina was in the residence of Mister Hughes when there was a knock on the front door of the Hughes Home. She hurried to open the door to find a handsome man carrying a briefcase.

His appearance, his slight nervousness, and his briefcase made her think he was one of the attorneys from Hughes' firm.

When he cleared his throat and apologized for arriving unannounced, Tina fell in love with the gentleman with the deep southern accent. However, when he introduced himself as Seargent Sterling Frisbee of the Pittsburgh homicide department, Tina's demeaner changed dramatically.

The man noticed the frown embedded on Tina's face. "I am not attempting to deceive you, ma'am. I identified myself at the door and will identify myself again so there is no confusion about my status. I am detective Seargent Frisbee of the Pittsburgh Homicide Department. I would like to speak with Mister Hughes."

"Mr. Hughes is receiving his physical therapy right now," Tina answered after swallowing her sudden fear of the southern man. "He is in his gym and unavailable."

"Perhaps I should go to him," said Frisbee as he advanced in the direction of Hughes' gym, startling Tina with his sudden movement.

Tina had eschewed wearing sensible shoes, a decision she was regretting as her heels caught in the heavy nap of the living room carpet.

She began to fall, but Frisbee moved quickly and prevented her from hitting the floor. Unfortunately, he latched onto her wrist with his right hand in the process of saving her. His touch caused her to scream loudly, as if he were burning her.

She followed her scream with a right cross that knocked Frisbee to the ground, just as Hughes returned from his morning workout with the new physical trainer Tina hired.

"I do not allow visitors in my gym. Nurse Tupaz was correct in stopping you. Although I do not approve of her excessive use of force; I witnessed your attempt at turning her into a submissive pawn. I hope you have learned your lesson," he added, chuckling.

"Now, I must ask you who you are before I turn Mister Day on you for breaking into my house and assaulting my employee," Hughes continued, without a chuckle.

Day stepped away from Hughes' wheelchair, looking with unbridled anticipation at Frisbee.

"Ah am Detective Seargent Frisbee from the Pittsburgh Police Homicide Department," he said in a very deep southern accent. He slowly pulled his ID out of the inner pocket of his jacket.

"Please, stand down, Roger," Hughes said to his new trainer.

Then, he addressed Frisbee. "You will keep your hands off my employees."

"Which brings me to my first question," Frisbee said after watching Roger Day flex his massive arms. "You referred to the young woman as Nurse Tupaz, Mister Hughes." Frisbee directed everything he said at the most impressive member of the group, Roger Day's muscles notwithstanding. "Would she be the same person as Christina Tupaz, the woman who witnessed your accident?"

"Tina did not witness the accident, sergeant. She arrived at the scene after the crash, but she did get there in time to save my life. Shall we move on to another topic?" asked Hughes, clearly annoyed.

"How well do you know Attorney Joseph Burns, Mister Hughes?" Frisbee asked.

"I spent a couple of evenings at the same charity dinners as Burns, but never said much to him other than to suffer through introductions."

"Did your wife have anything to do with Burns?"

Hughes sighed. "Victoria hated everything Burns stood for to the point of resigning from any committee Burns's wife de jour was involved in. She hated him personally for the clients he represented and professionally for the same reasons. Why are you asking these questions about Burns, detective?" Hughes' curiosity was piqued.

Frisbee glanced in Roger Day's direction, catching a pointed stare Roger aimed directly at the detective's forehead.

He quickly decided to answer Hughes honestly and directly. "I introduced myself as a member of the Pittsburgh Police Department's Homicide Division. I think y'all are bright enough to figure out my appearance here has to do with homicide. In particular, the homicides that took place at the Burns residence last night."

Frisbee was prepared to say more, but his cell phone sounded at just the right time.

Without announcing his intentions, Frisbee left the room to take the call.

He returned a few minutes later, excused himself, and headed for the door.

As he was leaving the residence, Frisbee paused. He seemed to think things over for a moment before he announced, "Burns owns the Dodge Charger that caused your daughter to crash." He then left the speechless group at the Hughes residence, got in his car, and drove away.

There was a moment of awkward silence before any of them could bring themselves to speak.

"Did Frisbee's actions during his departure remind you of anyone?" asked Hughes, scratching his head in contemplation.

For her part of the drama, Tina held her breath until she could no longer hear Frisbee's car, before she walked quietly skulked off to the kitchen.

Both men heard Tina uttering curse words in both English and what they assumed was her native language.

Even though she had managed to calm herself down, both Bill and Roger simply stared at the floor and stayed out of Tina's way until her temper had abated.

Chapter Fifteen: Police Headquarters

Following the disastrous incident at the Burns residence, Decker had wisely accepted retirement with full benefits, instantly becoming a civilian. Burns had enough sway and power to convince the powers that be the warrant was actually unwarranted and Decker allowed his goons to inspect the Charger without probable cause. Of course, that meant Decker would have to choose between retirement or termination.

Officially a non-worker, he now spent his mornings sitting alone at a coffee shop's elevated table, gazing at a plate glass window, where he found he could study the reflections of the other patrons.

He watched the reflection of a beautiful woman with shoulder-length blonde hair. He studied her with undisguised interest.

She was dressed in tight jeans and a vintage rock T-shirt.

He watched her closely as she entered the shop and looked around the small café, her eyes eventually settling on him.

The blonde smiled and began walking across the room with the obvious intention of joining Decker.

She stopped several feet away, hesitating slightly before speaking. "How are you doing, captain?"

"I'm no longer a captain, Caroline," replied Decker.

"I never realized you knew my first name." Carlisle laughed.

Decker sighed. He didn't think ignoring her would make her go away. "What brings you here, Carlisle? I haven't been gone long enough for reminiscing."

"Did you ever think of becoming a private investigator?" asked Carlisle, getting directly to the point.

"What? No!" scoffed Decker. "I'm a career police officer, not some rent-a-cop."

"Beats sitting around doing nothing, captain."

Decker stared at Carlisle, quietly waiting for her to continue.

"The new boss asked me to help out the Pittsburgh police with a murder investigation," said Carlisle, filling the awkward silence.

"Why would they ask for you, Carlisle?"

"The murder has connections to a case I'm currently working on," Carlisle proudly replied.

"I know all the cases you're working on, Carlisle. None of them have a connection to a homicide."

"Burns' family was murdered last night," said Carlisle, no longer able to control herself.

Decker choked, spitting coffee onto the table.

"What?" Decker exclaimed, gingerly wiping up the spill. "It sounded like you said Burns' family was murdered last night."

"That's exactly what I said."

Decker paused in thought, coffee-stained napkins in his hand. "Burns?"

"He was spared."

"Damn," muttered Decker. "How did you get involved, Carlisle?"

"The OIC, a Sergeant Frisbee, called me from the crime scene early this morning. He asked if I would be willing to assist in the investigation and cleared it with my boss. I'm on loan to the Pittsburgh police for a month," Carlisle replied. "I told Sergeant Frisbee you had overseen the original investigation and asked if you could join us. He agreed immediately."

"I'm retired," Decker grumbled.

"Which is why you can't be an official member of the investigation. You would be a consultant, especially since your recent run-in with Burns may make you a suspect."

"Normally, it would," Decker said, "but since I attended a function at the governor's mansion last night, I have an airtight alibi."

Carlisle smiled. "That's great, captain. It saves me from having to ask if you can account for your whereabouts. If you agree to the consultant gig, we can head over to police headquarters, get your paperwork signed, and bring you up to speed in time to observe the interview Sergeant Frisbee has scheduled with your old friend Burns."

"You'll have to drive, Carlisle," said Decker, sauntering toward the exit. "I walked here."

The desk sergeant at police headquarters knew Decker personally, having worked with him on several occasions. They spent time trading war stories before determining Decker's clearance paperwork unnecessary.

Awarded visitor's badges, he and Carlisle passed into the depths of the Pittsburgh Police Department.

Frisbee met the pair outside the interview rooms.

Following quick introductions, Frisbee accompanied his new partners into the adjoining observation room, handing each of them an official crime scene report.

"This report doesn't address what happened at the Burns residence before the police arrived, but it does describe what they found," Frisbee said by way of explanation. "We invited Burns to join us in the hope he can fill in the missing information.

"Y'all will have a clear view from here," added Frisbee, indicating the one-way mirror.

"Any idea when they will arrive?" asked Carlisle.

"Burns was taken to Shadyside Hospital early this morning to be treated for various scrapes and bruises," Frisbee replied. "His attorney met him here and escorted him to a private conference room to discuss his potential interview."

As if on cue, Burns, accompanied by his attorney, stepped boldly into the adjacent interview room.

The trio of police watched them through the one-way mirror as they both calmly sat behind the steel table.

"Huh," barked Frisbee, gently shaking his head in wonder as he left the observation room. "Two hours late, and he walks into the place like he owns it! You must admit, the guy really has a pair."

Seconds later, Frisbee appeared in the interview room next door, sat in a vacant folding chair, and introduced himself to Ms. Monica Chang, Burns' personal attorney.

Tall and willowy, wearing a Ralph Lauren business suit that cost more than Carlisle's monthly salary; she looked more like a runway model than a criminal attorney.

"My client is here voluntarily," Chang said. "He has agreed to be interviewed but will answer only questions aiding in the arrest and conviction of his family's killers."

"Thank you, Ms. Chang," said Frisbee. "Mister Burns, I would like to ask a few questions about last night, if that is agreeable."

"I'm here, ain't I?" Burns growled.

"Thank you, Mister Burns. I am under legal obligation to inform you these proceedings are being recorded. Do you agree to the recording of your statement today, Mister Burns?" Frisbee asked with a friendly smile.

"Get on with it, you jerk," Burns replied.

"Thank you, Mister Burns," Frisbee said as his patience began to dissolve. "Your CCTV cameras have all been wiped clean, but traffic cameras located at a traffic light outside the entrance to your property indicate you arrived at your Fifth Avenue residence at approximately 1:00 a.m. May I ask where you were last night before that time?"

"You can ask, but I ain't gonna tell you," Burns sneered. "That has nothing to do with what happened at my house."

"Perhaps we should be allowed to determine if your earlier activities have any bearing on what transpired at your home," Frisbee retorted.

"My client has decided to defer on that question," Chang said. "If you persist, we shall terminate the interview."

"Thank you, Ms. Chang." Frisbee took a deep breath. "Mister Burns, can you tell me, in your own words, what transpired after you arrived home?"

Burns looked to his attorney for permission to answer the question.

Chang nodded, slightly.

"Guillermo let me out at the front door before taking the car to its garage."

"Excuse me, Mister Burns," Frisbee interrupted, "who is Guillermo?"

"He's my driver and bodyguard! If you continue to interrupt me, I'm outta here!"

"Sorry, Mister Burns," Frisbee muttered. "It won't happen again."

Burns continued without acknowledging Frisbee's apology. "The house was dark, so it took me a few minutes to find the keys. When I finally opened the door, Princess, my puppy, came charging out, knocking me down the steps."

Frisbee typed a few notes into his laptop as Burns continued his statement. "I walked over to the carriage house. We had taken the Maybach, and its bay was wide open. Noises were coming from the Charger's unit. I figured Guillermo was in the next garage, but when I went to check, I found my Charger with bloody bodies in it. The upholstery is ruined."

Burns ended his narrative by crossing his arms and leaning back in his chair.

"I have a few follow-up questions, Mister Burns," Frisbee said. "Let's begin with an easy one. Where is Princess?"

Burns showed emotion for the first time since the interview began. He looked down at the table and shook his head.

"Princess was found in the front garden when the police searched the grounds. She was taken away with the rest of the family," Chang said.

"Thank you, Ms. Chang."

His reward for thanking the attorney was an alarmingly beautiful smile.

"I would like to get a statement from your driver, Mister Burns. Specifically, why would he drop you off at a darkened home, and what he might know about several homicides?" Frisbee was clearly having difficulty keeping his temper under control.

"The chauffeur is not available at this time," Chang calmly replied.

"I am from Hong Kong, Detective Frisbee, where an innocent victim of a crime would not be subjected to an inquiry. I believe this interview is over," Chang added, collecting her briefcase, and motioning to her client they were leaving.

"One moment, Ms. Chang," Frisbee called out, jumping to his feet.

"Are you charging my client, detective? I assure you that would be a very foolish move." Chang gave Frisbee a look she reserved for something she found on the bottom of her shoe.

"I want to know where your client was at the time of the murders," Frisbee retorted, unfazed.

Chang smiled, sweetly. "I knew you would ask eventually."

She slowly retrieved a piece of folded notepaper from her lacy bra and gently handed it to Frisbee. "I have taken the liberty of transcribing a young lady's name, address, and phone number on this piece of paper. My client was with her from 6:00 p.m. until 12:30 a.m. The young lady will be happy to provide a sworn statement attesting to that fact."

Chang cooed and moved close enough to Frisbee their bodies almost touched. She reached out and gently caressed Frisbee's cheek.

"Goodbye, detective," Chang purred. She then turned and walked away.

Frisbee stood, motionless, watching the very sexy attorney Chang walk away.

Momentarily unable to speak, Frisbee motioned for his new associates to follow him until they reached a seldom-used conference room in a remote corner of the station.

Frisbee stood, motionless, watching the very sexy attorney Chang walk away. Afraid to speak, Frisbee motioned for his new associates to follow him until they reached a seldom-used conference room in a remote corner of the station.

Chapter Sixteen: Searching for Clues

Once they were back at the station, Frisbee ordered pizza, and the team dug right into the murder files.

A uniformed officer wheeled in a portable whiteboard for the detectives to use to display evidence. The first crime scene photo mounted on the board was a coroner's photo of Burns' Charger with three mangled and bloody bodies.

"Why didn't Burns call 9-1-1?" Carlisle asked.

"Burns has his own protection. He would call them long before he would call any of the local police," answered Decker.

"If Burns didn't call 9-1-1, who did?" pondered Carlisle.

"The anonymous 9-1-1 call came from a burner cell phone," replied Frisbee. "There has been no activity on that phone before or since. A positive identification of Mrs. Burns and the two boys was made prior to Burns' statement. We're still waiting for autopsy and toxicologist reports before the official cause of death can be determined, but the video playing at the crime scene gave me an idea.

"I asked the ME to compare the injuries of the Burns family with those suffered by the hit and run accident's family. If the incidents are connected, the preliminary crime, on-site, examinations of the injuries will be identical."

"Identical or simply similar?" asked Decker, his curiosity piqued.

"We won't be certain until the autopsies are completed," said Frisbee. "But the ME gave me her best guess on the victims' injuries."

Frisbee opened his notebook, reading the preliminary medical examiner's report, "Burns' twenty-year-old son from his third marriage, riding in the passenger seat, suffered several injuries consistent with a collision with a concrete abutment at a high rate of speed."

"What about the other two victims?" asked Carlisle.

"A thirty-five-year-old white female, Burns' present wife, was found lying in the back seat of the Charger; she also showed injuries consistent with a high-speed vehicular accident.

"The final victim, a twenty-four-year-old male, Burns' son from his second marriage. The body was found in the driver's seat. The ME's preliminary examination indicates the body also suffered from a high-speed collision and was decapitated."

Carlisle shook her head. "This is Pittsburgh, for goodness sakes. The only time you should see violence like that is when the Steelers play the Baltimore Ravens!"

"She's got a point, Frisbee," Decker said with a slight chuckle. "Do you have any idea who could have done this, and why they are mimicking the car accident?"

"Not really, and the only fingerprints on the car belonged to Burns," Frisbee replied. Then, he slapped his forehead with the palm of his hand. "I forgot to follow up on my interview with the hit-and-run victim and his staff this morning!"

"What staff?" asked Decker.

Frisbee looked at his new partners, "You are aware the man is in a wheelchair?"

The pair nodded.

"A former boxer is working with him on strength conditioning every afternoon. I ran a quick check on the boxer. He fought professionally as a welterweight, amassing an impressive win/loss ratio, but not good enough for a shot at a title. He's retired from boxing, but stays in fighting shape, complete with bulging muscles and an intimidating glare."

"One washed-up pugilist doesn't make a staff," said Carlisle.

Frisbee smiled, "Right. Pugilist. Good word, Carlisle. There are also nurses. The accident victim signed a contract with a company named Best Home Health, guaranteeing the provision of twenty-four-hour in-house nursing services. That includes three nurses on swing shifts, a charge nurse, and a nurse assigned general duties."

Frisbee paused for effect. "The administrator of the entire program is a beautiful Filipina."

"What are you telling us, Frisbee?" asked Decker.

"I knew you were going to like this part." Frisbee grinned. "Christina Tupaz is Hughes' administrative nurse!"

Decker slammed his fist on the table. "I knew that woman was dirty! I could smell something wrong the minute I saw her in the victim's hospital room. You could sense it, too, couldn't you, Carlisle?"

"Honestly, boss, she just seemed like a scared, confused kid to me."

"Carlisle!" Decker shouted. "She has you fooled, too. Just like that union broad she had on her side. What do you think, Frisbee?"

"I haven't formed an opinion yet. The only person in this entire case I am currently familiar with is Burns. Burns' arrival necessitated me putting the hit-and-run victim on hold. Although I didn't get a chance to talk to either of them, I did get to do some research, and I got the impression they shared a secret. You know, like close friends."

"I'll be damned," Decker snarled. "I'll bet Hughes and that little Filipina piece of work are in this together."

"He came close to dying in that accident, captain," Carlisle reminded her old boss.

"What if he wasn't supposed to be in the car, Carlisle?" asked Decker. "What if he was supposed to meet Tupaz someplace else and the accident was meant for just the wife and kids?"

"I'm not buying it, captain," Carlisle said with conviction. "His family meant everything to him, and I don't think he knew Tupaz before the accident. Something else is at play here."

"I'll tell you what's at play, Carlisle. The man's parents were killed in a hit-and-run two years ago. He inherited a small fortune, and I think he was behind the accident. Now, he has a new partner, and he did his wife and kids the same way."

Frisbee stood, interrupting the conversation. "Whatever the answer may be, it will have to wait. I'm due at the morgue, in …" he glanced at his watch, gasped, and broke into a severe southern drawl. "Forty-five minutes ago!"

"I'll keep y'all posted on the medical examiner's findings," Frisbee said, practically running out of the room. "In the meantime, if y'all would be so kind as to find out who this Guillermo is, and where he has gotten himself off to, I would greatly appreciate it. Bye."

He left, and the door swung shut behind him.

"Have you noticed his accent gets cute when he's stressed?" asked Carlisle, dreamily.

"You are scheduled to get married soon, Carlisle, try to keep your pants on." Decker ducked as a pizza box flew by his head.

Chapter Seventeen: Doctor Hua

The Allegheny County Medical Examiner's Office officially opened for business in 1884, but the first group of autopsies were not handled by the office until the arrival of the victims of the Homestead Steel Strike of 1892. Using handwritten documents as records, local physicians added their barely legible cursive longhand to the death records of the sixteen men who were killed during the ensuing riots.

Since the Homestead incident, forensic investigations of all questionable deaths in Allegheny County have been handled at the Pittsburgh Medical Examiner's Office.

The newer building, opened in 2004, contained several large autopsy rooms designed with the corner and his assistants in mind.

Frisbee did not like autopsy rooms. He claimed seeing death first-hand at crime scenes sufficed, but Charlotte Hua, the assistant medical examiner, did not agree. She made a point of meeting him in the operating theaters.

Hua was occupied with sewing up the chest cavity of her latest cadaver when Frisbee rushed into the autopsy area.

Even with her assistants hustling in and out of the room, carefully carrying marked containers of organs and fluids, she was able to perceive his movement outside the viewing windows surrounding her work area.

Hua looked up to see Frisbee's hurried shuffle toward the room.

She continued to watch while he slowly donned hospital scrubs, boot coverings, and a surgical mask.

"It's not like you to be late, Sterling," Hua said as soon as the detective entered.

Hua also came from the south, South Korea, that is. She met Frisbee while she was a pre-med student at Duke University in North Carolina. Frisbee had studied law at UNC. Unable to fit into the usual social cliques, they found common ground and became best friends. Hua lost her accent and grew from the proverbial ugly duckling into a beautiful swan, never losing her love and dependance on Sterling.

"I'm truly sorry, Charlotte. This case already has a great many facets; I allowed myself become distracted."

"Are you okay, Sterling?" Hua looked carefully at her old friend.

"I'm fine, Charlotte. I haven't slept in over twenty-four hours, and I may be a bit punchy." Frisbee smiled. "Tell me what you've found."

Charlotte removed her protective headgear and moved around the corpse to stand next to Frisbee and hold his hand. "It would be a lot easier if you weren't such a sissy about the autopsies, Sterling," she said with a slight giggle. "I thought you were going to faint."

"I don't like it here, Charlotte. When I see the bodies on the street, they're still human. After you start cutting them up, they just become slabs of meat." Frisbee faked gagging and then laughed. "Can I take this mask off now?"

"Not yet. I want to show you a few things." Hua moved away from the body she had been suturing.

"Who is that?" Frisbee asked as Hua covered the body.

"This guy? Probably a drug-related killing. He was found in a dumpster before the rats had a chance to completely devour him. Don't waste your time, Sterling. Some other homicide detective landed this case."

"Okay," Frisbee said, averting his eyes from the slab. "Tell me what happened with the Burns family."

"You were right." Hua walked across the room toward the refrigeration units where bodies were stored. "The deaths mirrored the accident victims almost one hundred percent." She stopped in midstride, a puzzled look on her face. "Except for Princess."

"Who?"

"Princess. You know, the Irish wolfhound brought in with the Burns family."

"You autopsied a dog?" Frisbee whispered in disbelief.

"She isn't just any dog. She is an actual *princess*, an AKC-registered champion Irish wolfhound. By the way, she wasn't dead, just in a mild coma. She refused to leave her family's side, so I kept her here until she was able to move on her own. Then, I sent her back to the Burns residence."

"Thank you, Charlotte," Frisbee said, uneasily. "Can we get out of here and go up to your office? I would like to be able to think clearly when we discuss the bodies brought in today."

"Do you mean the Burns family? Each victim of last night's murder suffered injuries that corresponded almost exactly to injuries suffered by the victim's family. Minor differences can be attributed to the methods the killer used to mimic the impact of a high-speed collision. Before you ask, I don't know how the killer was able to mimic the impact."

"Did you attend the identification process?"

"You know I always talk to the relatives of the person I'm autopsying, Sterling. It helps me with the process."

"What did you think of Burns?" asked Frisbee.

"Who?"

"Burns? The father of the two murdered boys and husband of the murdered woman were brought in this morning? Husband of the female victim? You know, the group found in the garage in Shadyside?"

"Oh, a woman came to identify the bodies. I think she was a housekeeper. She cried a lot but seemed happy Princess was okay."

"I feel a headache coming on." Frisbee turned and headed out the door of the autopsy room, peeling off his scrubs as he walked. "Thanks, Charlotte," he called over his shoulder. "Messenger those reports to me as soon as you can. I owe you lunch."

After he left, the door swung shut behind him.

"Damn right you do," Hua muttered to the empty room.

Frisbee dialed Carlisle's cell phone as he headed out the building.

Decker answered on the first ring.

"Hey, Deck. Y'all have any luck finding Billy Boy?"

"Frisbee," Decker grumbled, "who is Billy Boy?"

"Y'all know Guillermo is Spanish for William, right, Deck?"

"Yes, detective, I am aware of the translation," Decker huffed. "In answer to your question, we have found no record of Burns having a driver in his employ, let alone a driver named Guillermo. And please, don't call me Deck."

Frisbee stifled a laugh. "Very well, captain. It appears we may be onto something."

Frisbee studied his fingernails, saying nothing, until Decker finally broke the silence in a huff, saying, "All right, detective, I'll bite. What are you talking about?"

Frisbee brushed imaginary dirt off a wrought iron bench located outside the main doors of the MEs' building before gingerly sitting down.

"There is no reason for you to get your knickers in a knot, Deck. Why did you answer Carlisle's phone? Is she there with you?" Frisbee asked when he heard someone sniggering in the background.

"Yes, she is, detective."

"You've got me on speakerphone and didn't tell me! You are a sneaky devil! I'm likin' you more all the time, Deck!" Frisbee said with a laugh. "How you doin', Caroline?"

"I'm fine, Sterling," Carlisle answered. "We've tried everything we can think of to locate the driver. Pennsylvania doesn't require a CDL to operate as a chauffeur, but many employers do. That was the first place we looked, but we found nothing. We tried all Captain Decker's contacts but have struck out so far."

"Not everyone has gotten back to me yet," Decker added. He wanted to tell Sterling not to call him again, but he figured he would let it slide this time.

"I wouldn't count on learning much more," Frisbee said. "Guillermo disappeared right after the Burns family was massacred. He's probably our killer."

Frisbee filled them in on his visit to the morgue.

"I need more facts," he continued, silently watching as Hua exited the building.

"I am going over to the victim's residence to speak with him now. Perhaps we will know more in the morning," Decker answered.

"You know what, Deck?" Frisbee said, "It's been a long day. Why don't we put this thing to bed for tonight and meet in my office tomorrow morning at seve—"

Hua firmly shook her head.

"Eight?" Frisbee mouthed at the ME.

Hua shook her head again.

"Nine?" he mouthed, receiving a reluctant nod.

"What I meant to say was why don't we meet at my office at 9:00 a.m. for a fresh start?"

When the call ended, Decker stared bullets at Carlisle.

"When did you and that weirdo get on a first-name basis? You haven't even known each other for twenty-four hours!"

Carlisle blushed. "You know what, captain? Thanks for agreeing to help. This case is going to eat up a lot of my time, and I doubt I'll be able to think of anything else. Let's go grab a couple of beers and talk about it."

"He's really cute," she added under her breath.

Chapter Eighteen: Caroline Carlisle

Arriving at police headquarters shortly before his crew, Frisbee began his day by staring intently at one of the hit-and-run files.

He was pleasantly interrupted when Carlisle knocked on his office door. Frisbee found himself so enthralled by Carlilse's appearance he was momentarily at a total loss for words.

She was wearing a light blue summer dress and high-heeled cowgirl boots. She had her long blonde hair tied into a ponytail. With makeup highlighting the Carolina blue of her eyes, Carlisle looked like a young woman on her way to a club instead of joining the hunt for killers.

"Caroline," Frisbee sang out, following a deep swallow. "How are you this morning?"

Without waiting for an answer, Frisbee jumped to his feet. He moved folders cluttering the two chairs situated in front of his workspace, placing them on the already hazardous pile of paperwork on his desk. "Come on in; come on in. I've cleared a place for you to sit."

Carlisle looked around the room before cautiously sitting down on the recently cleared chair.

Frisbee's office could be considered quaint, but compact, barely large enough for a compact desk and two chairs. When several reams of paperwork were added, it became claustrophobic.

Fearing an avalanche of printed materials, Carlisle sat on the edge of her seat, prepared to escape. She peered cautiously at the piles of paperwork that could spell her doom.

"Love what you've done with the place," Carlisle remarked, sarcastically.

"I have my own filing cabinets, but the boss won't allow me to use them. He wants me to share cabinet space with the other detectives, but they don't understand my system," replied Frisbee, grinning sheepishly.

"You have a system?" Carlisle asked, incredulously.

"Yes!" proudly exclaimed Frisbee. "I know exactly where everything is. I've cataloged every case I've worked on since I moved to Pittsburgh."

"Is your partner hidden somewhere under this rubble, Sterling?"

"Very funny, Caroline." Frisbee leaned against a small section of his desk clear of paperwork. "We have a lot of work to do. I'm ready to get started if you are."

Carlisle stood, moving toward the door. "Do you mind if we work out of a conference room, Sterling? I don't mean any offense, but your office frightens me."

"It has that effect on a lot of people." Frisbee smiled. "May I suggest using the same conference room we used yesterday? It has a great view of the parking lot."

"I have one thing I have to ask you first, Sterling." Carlisle seductively leaned against the doorjamb. "What does your apartment look like? Do you need someone to straighten it up?"

"My house is immaculate," he replied, confused by the question. "I have a service that comes in once a week to do the dusting and fine-tune cleaning, but I take care of the rest. Why would you ask something like that?"

"No reason." Carlisle sighed and looked cautiously at the pile of papers.

Frisbee carefully transferred the folders from under his arm to the table. "I would like for us to review the autopsies and medical records of the Burns family, as well as the victims of the hit and run, looking for similarities in injuries and cause of death."

"Sterling, I need to ask you something before we get too involved in this." Carlisle pointedly looked away from the folders. "How did you get your hands on the files so quickly? I realize the coroner's department falls under police jurisdiction, but I thought you required a warrant and time to get the records."

"Normally, it takes about a week, but the video playing footage of the Hughes accident told me the two incidents were connected, making the coroner's notes an integral part of a murder investigation. I couldn't sleep, so I went to Judge O'Connor around 2:00 a.m. to request a warrant. He reviewed the evidence, agreed with my assessment, and issued the proper paperwork. The ME had copies of both sets of autopsies on hand, making them immediately available. The warrant is on file. Let's not waste time on trivialities." Frisbee snatched a folder off the top of the pile and began to read.

"By the way, Caroline, you look exceptionally lovely today," Frisbee muttered, his eyes never leaving the folder.

"Wait a minute; you woke Judge Andrew O'Connor at 2:00 a.m. to get a warrant? The same Andrew O'Connor who refused to grant a warrant to a SWAT team last year during a hostage crisis because they misspelled a street name?"

Frisbee sighed. "That's what you took away from my coroner's records explanation?"

"Well, Judge O'Connor has a reputation as a hard ass." Carlisle laughed. "Don't tell me you are friends with him."

"Judge O'Connor and I have mutual respect for the letter of the law. As a result, he approves the occasional off-hours warrant for me. When I show a significant need, of course." Frisbee's accent was becoming thicker with each word. "Besides, it is vitally important all spelling and grammar be correct in a legal document."

"Sterling, you crack me up!" exclaimed Carlisle, laughing loudly. "By the way, thanks for the compliment. I didn't think you even noticed me."

Frisbee—partly insulted, partly confused—took a deep breath, handing Carlisle two folders. "These are the files for two of the latest victims, along with the coroner's notes," Frisbee said, his accent now really noticeable. "What Ah would like you to do is compare the autopsies of the two victims for similarities, if you can control yourself, of course."

Frisbee stopped when Carlisle sniggered. He rolled his eyes and sighed, causing Carlisle to cover her mouth and giggle.

"Really, Caroline!" Frisbee said, his southern drawl now so thick you could cut it with a knife. "If you're goin' to insist on actin' like a schoolgirl, we are nevah going to catch this heah killah. Ya hear?"

Carlisle couldn't take it anymore. She lost control, laughing hysterically.

Frisbee watched for a moment and then joined her. The two investigators were completely lost in the moment.

Wiping tears from her eyes, Carlisle noticed Decker standing in the doorway. She kicked Frisbee in the shin to get his attention.

"The duty officer told me I could find you here, Frisbee," Decker said with undisguised disgust. "I apologize for being late. There was a multi-vehicle accident with fatalities on the parkway. Traffic was backed up for miles."

He stepped into the room, taking a seat next to Carlisle. "I saw some troopers I knew, so I found a place to pull off and offered my help. While you two were back here playing, I was investigating a crime. I miss my job." Decker sighed.

"That's understandable, Deck, you were a top cop for a long time," Frisbee said.

"It was time for me to retire, and don't call me Deck," he paused a moment. "You have a strange reputation in this building, Frisbee."

"Which reputation is that, Deck?" Frisbee asked, his curiosity piqued.

"The one about your history with partners. How you always work alone," Decker answered, a little miffed at Frisbee for continuing to call him Deck.

"I don't *have* to work alone," Frisbee said, defensively. "I've had partners. They just can't seem to get along with me. Because I have an almost one hundred percent success rate, the boss allows me to bring in consultants when I need them."

"That's right," Decker said. "Special consultants for each case. New case, new consultants. So let's get to work on this case so you can find a new crew."

"Is that true, Sterling?" Carlisle asked with a slight hitch in her voice. "You just bring in consultants just long enough to solve a case?"

Glaring at Decker, Frisbee said, "I keep hoping I will find people who will stay, Caroline."

Embarrassed, he continued, "But for now, Deck is right. We need to solve this case."

Frisbee handed Decker two folders. "These are the forensic files for victims of both the hit and run and the killings in Shadyside. Caroline has the rest."

Resting his hand on the two remaining folders, Frisbee continued, "I have what we will call victims one. Caroline has victims two. I want you to look at victims three. I propose we go through the files to compare each victims' injuries."

Decker, handling his files gingerly, asked, "Have these files been obtained legally?"

"He got warrants from Judge O'Connor," Carlisle said in a stage whisper.

"Thank you, Caroline," Frisbee said with a smile. "May I continue?"

Decker nodded.

"Preliminary findings indicate several similarities in the injuries suffered by the victims in the Burns murders, and their counterparts in the motor vehicle accident. I have paired the victims according to the locations they were found in their respective vehicles. If my theory is correct, each pair of victims should have the same injuries and cause of death."

The team took up their respective files, working in silence, pausing only to turn pages and make notes.

"This is amazing," announced Carlisle, "I've covered about one fourth of my records. The list of injuries is extensive, and so far, identical for both women."

"I'm running into the same phenomena," Decker said. "The main difference is the type of injury. The accident victims have injuries due to the trauma of a motor vehicle accident. The murder victim's injuries are performed with medical precision."

"Good catch, Deck. I may have seen something similar, but missed the significance."

Frisbee dove back into his files and retrieved several pages of notes. "Here it is!" he said triumphantly. "The same results can be found in the comparisons of the decapitations of Ashley Hughes and Christopher Burns. We are definitely on to something, my friends."

Frisbee rose and began pacing about the room. "For some reason, the killer is mirroring every injury suffered by the victims of the hit and run. He ran into a problem when he could match the types of injuries, but not the cause. We need to find what he used to sever the body parts."

Carlisle, squirming in her seat, broke Frisbee's train of thought.

"Caroline," Frisbee said. "You're fidgeting like an excited schoolgirl. What is it?"

"The broken and crushed bones," answered Carlisle.

"Yes, what of them?"

"The broken and crushed bones. The bones!" she exclaimed as her partners stared at her in confusion.

"*The bones!* How did he break the bones? He didn't wreck the car against a wall! How did he break the bones? Not just how, but where?" Carlisle held up her notes. "The victims suffered a multitude of fractures, ruptures, and dislocations. Easy enough at 130 miles an hour when your car is suddenly slamming into a wall. How can it be accomplished when the victim is standing still? And presumably alive?" She whispered that last question.

The team returned to their reports with renewed enthusiasm, reviewing the orthopedic specifications on each of the victims, as well as the differences in the manner of how the damages occurred.

"I'm going to find Doctor Hua and get her professional opinion on your discovery, Caroline. I believe the differences in the cause of the injuries are significant. Good work!"

Frisbee snatched up the files and hurried out of the conference room.

Carlisle, a broad smile on her face, gazed out the door as Frisbee left.

"Why the hell are you grinning, Carlisle?" Decker asked. "The guy is weird!"

"He may be weird, but he has the highest conviction rate of any detective in the state, and he complimented *me*."

"Come on, captain," she continued, snatching her laptop off the table, and jumping to her feet. "There's a bar around the corner where the local police hang out. I'll buy you a beer."

Chapter Nineteen: James Doe

Shortly after arriving at the bar, Decker joined some old friends to swap stories, and Carlisle found a deserted corner where she could have more privacy.

Ignoring Decker, her cell phone, and several men who attempted to pick her up, Carlisle spent the next four hours digging into every police database and social media forum she could find, eventually locating two solid leads.

The first concerned Burns' automobile collection. Carlisle learned Burns had personally performed much of the restoration of the antique cars he purchased. In many cases, the process required custom-made replacement parts.

Carlisle resorted to back-door research, finding receipts from vendors and construction workers detailing the sale and installation of an aluminum extrusion press in a seldom-used building located behind the carriage house.

Burns also produced his own wine. He converted a building formerly used as servant's quarters into a vintner's dream, complete with all the tools necessary to decant and store barrels of wine, including a large grape press.

Excited about her findings, and perhaps a little intoxicated, Carlisle called Frisbee to share her thoughts, none of which had anything to do with the fact the bar had closed an hour before.

Frisbee answered Carlisle's call on the first ring, almost as if he were expecting her call.

Excited about the positive direction Carlisle's research provided the investigation, he made himself presentable and showed up at Judge O'Connor's front door by 0430.

Sitting on the judge's porch swing, Frisbee patiently waited for O'Connor to begin his day, the swing slowly swaying back and forth, its chains squeaking out their need for a few drops of oil.

Judge O'Connor finished his simple breakfast, filled two mugs with black coffee, and joined the detective.

Frisbee presented Judge O'Connor with the paperwork for his warrant requests. He explained his position, clarifying the specific evidence linking the murders to one or both specialized tools he expected to find on Burns' property.

Before leaving O'Connor's home, search warrant in hand, Frisbee called Decker and Carlisle. He left voicemails asking them to meet him at the Burns mansion at 7:00 a.m. on Monday morning for what he called a "crushing good time."

Early the following morning, a convoy of police vehicles navigated their way along Millionaire's Row on Fifth Avenue in Pittsburgh's Shadyside area.

The convoy turned in to the Burns residence and rolled silently past Burns' palatial mansion, finally coming to a halt in front of the carriage house, now often referred to by law enforcement personnel as "Decker's Last Stand."

Taking great care not to block access to any of the units, the police officers sat inside their vehicles with the motors quietly idling.

Frisbee's unmarked car brought up the rear of the convoy.

He remained in the driver's seat for a moment before turning off the ignition and exiting the sedan.

He walked briskly toward the mansion, coming to an abrupt stop a short distance from the marble steps.

Dressed in a gray flannel suit, white shirt, and a blue and white striped campaign tie, he also donned a pair of highly polished, handmade black wingtips.

His feet planted firmly at shoulder width, Frisbee stared straight ahead, moving only to sip hot green tea from a large travel mug adorned with a Pittsburgh Steelers logo.

A hot pink Jeep Wrangler, with Carlisle behind the wheel, cruised through the open gateway, coming to a stop directly behind Frisbee's unmarked car.

Decker stepped out of the Wrangler's passenger seat, warily approaching Frisbee much in the way he would a stray dog: slowly, at a small distance from the side, making certain the detective could see him and not making any sudden moves.

Staring at the entrance, Frisbee said in a soft voice, "What are you doing, Deck?"

"You are a weird man, Frisbee," Decker said. "I'm just being cautious. And stop calling me Deck!"

Carlisle, who had stayed in her Jeep until she heard Decker's explanation, stepped out of her Wrangler and faced the two law enforcement officers she idolized the most.

"Gentlemen," she harrumphed before stomping toward Frisbee.

"I am exactly fifteen feet from the marble steps, Caroline," Frisbee murmured. "Please don't go any closer."

"Why don't we serve the warrant and start the search?" asked Decker.

"We are awaiting Mister Burns' attorney of record, Ms. Monica Chang," replied Frisbee, taking a sip of his tea.

"How does Chang know we're here?"

"I called her before heading out of the station. You don't ambush somebody like Burns, Deck. He has too many friends in high places who can ruin your life. We wait."

Decker huffed but stood his ground.

Carlisle smiled.

Moving next to Frisbee, both officers stared passively at the mansion's front doors.

A bright red Audi TT rolled onto the winding driveway, its high-performance engine emitting a low, menacing growl.

The sleek German sports car came to a rest in front of Frisbee.

Following a dramatic pause, the driver's door opened, and Monica Chang, wearing a sinfully short, form-fitting black ESCADA mini dress, slowly and sensuously folded herself out of the Audi.

"Good morning, Sterling," Chang breathed as she stepped up to Frisbee, gently taking his hand in both of hers. The three-inch heels of her black ESCADA pumps defined her curves while providing her with the extra height she needed to lean into Frisbee and whisper into his ear. "I believe you have something for me."

"Ah hope you will find everything in order, Ms. Chang," said Frisbee in a raspy, deeply accented voice. His hand shook as he presented Chang with the warrant.

Quickly scanning the document, Chang treated Frisbee with a bright smile. "The warrant is exactly what you told me to expect, Sterling. Shall we proceed?"

"The aluminum press is in the workshop on the far end of the carriage house, and the grape press is in the vintner's cottage behind the mansion," Chang said as she strolled seductively toward the line of police cars with Frisbee and Carlisle at her side.

Decker walked a few paces behind, alert to any sudden changes in Chang's attitude.

The group strolled to an ivy-covered Quonset hut standing behind the far wall of the carriage house.

Chang unlocked the entry doors to reveal a small, immaculately clean, manufacturing plant with an extrusion press in its center.

Frisbee's technicians entered the building, moving about the plant with machinelike efficiency, looking for any indication of the press being used for nefarious purposes.

"Ms. Chang, the technicians will perform their tasks to the highest level of perfection, with or without our supervision," Frisbee said. "I am certain your client's interests will be protected here while we move on to the winery with the remainder of my team."

Chang readily agreed.

Leaving the Quonset hut behind, the rest of them walked toward the rear of the main house, until a small brick structure came into view.

Frisbee sensed something was wrong. He stopped, drawing his service weapon with his right hand, simultaneously reaching out with his left, signaling Chang to stop.

"Hand me the keys, Monica," Frisbee said, his eyes glued to the padlocked door of the building.

"Really, Sterling? Is all this drama necessary?" asked Chang, petulantly.

Frisbee turned to face her. "I have an ugly feeling about this place, Monica. Due to bad policework, this building didn't get searched the night of the incident. I can't verify its safety, so for your protection, I need you to move away from the scene."

"I'll have someone accompany you," Frisbee added, signaling the two police officers closest to Chang.

"I don't have time for all this macho stuff!" Chang exclaimed, reluctantly handing Frisbee the keys.

Her police escort close behind, Chang turned and stormed toward her car.

Frisbee took a moment to inspect his team. "Four uniformed officers, Carlisle, and me; not bad odds."

He turned his gaze to Decker and the .357 magnum the old policeman held in his hands. "I'm sure you have all the legal permits to carry that cannon, but you're a civilian."

Decker holstered his pistol, walking away without a word.

"On the other hand, Caroline, as my partner, I need you to work with me. That is, if you don't mind, ma'am."

Carlisle looked briefly in the direction of her old boss and then moved to take an offensive position next to Frisbee, her weapon drawn.

The team began a slow, careful approach to the building, reaching the door without incident.

Frisbee positioned himself with his back against the wall closest to the lock. He quietly reached out, unlocked the door, and gently pushed it open.

Carlisle rushed inside, followed closely by Frisbee.

Keeping low profiles, they covered each other's moves like they had been partners for years.

As soon as the adrenaline rush of the entry died, the smell of death hit the detectives like a runaway truck.

Originally constructed as living quarters for permanent kitchen staff, the openings where beveled glass windows once faced the garden had been filled in with opaque glass blocks. The inner walls of the cottage had been gutted, leaving one large, poorly lit, poorly ventilated room.

The detectives observed a large man standing against an exterior wall. He appeared to be wearing a form-fitting, multicolored bodysuit.

Frisbee identified himself, commanding the man to freeze.

Moving with caution, breathing through their mouths because of the horrible odor, Frisbee and Carlisle inched closer to the silent, unmoving figure.

When the detectives moved within three strides of the suspect, they holstered their weapons.

The unidentified man—naked, tattooed, and dead—no longer posed a threat.

Frisbee stepped outside to notify the proper agencies, leaving the remainder of the search to the forensic team.

Photographs were taken of the crime scene, the body, and the position of the body in respect to the interior of the building.

The unidentified victim was tagged as *James Doe* and loaded into the coroner's van to take a short ride to the morgue.

As the van pulled away, the CSI team began working in earnest.

Marking the area into a search grid, they carefully combed the scene for anything that might be construed as evidence.

Banned from the scene as possible contaminates, the detectives took Decker to an extended lunch, returning more than two hours later.

The trio found a table and chairs set up on the mansion's lawn, safely outside of the olfactory range of the outbuilding's open door.

Howard Davidson, the head of the CSI team, having spotted the trio when they returned, rushed to join them.

"We have definitely found where the killer processed the victims," Howard said, enthusiastically. "Although we haven't located the tools he used to make the incisions; we know he butchered them inside the winery. We discovered a vast amount of blood, as well as a modified bone saw with human tissue in the teeth."

The technician moved closer to the police in a conspiratorial manner. "What is extremely interesting is the method with which the killer modified the winepress. It is highly unusual to find a privately-owned press large enough to accommodate a full-size human, so the killer modified the press in a manner that would allow him to operate the machine with his victims partially inside, providing him with the ability to crush only the areas of the body that he wished to destroy."

"I mean, really, this guy is a genius. Too bad he's crazy." Howard straightened an errant lock of golden hair. "Any questions?"

"Did you find any fingerprints?" Carlisle asked.

"Absolutely none. The killer wiped everything down with rags he found in the shop. He destroyed the rags in a wood stove used to heat the winery during occupancy. The only interesting discovery was in the ashes."

The detectives waited for a moment, allowing Howard time to continue. When he began to walk away, Decker broke the silence.

"What did you find in the ashes?" Decker queried.

"Oh, that. The killer disposed of his bloodied gloves in the fire. We found remnants of nitrile gloves mixed in with the cloth and wood ashes. I'd love to talk longer guys, but I gotta go."

Howard practically skipped with joy as he made his way back toward the crime scene, while Carlisle and Decker set out to canvas the neighborhood for witnesses.

Chapter Twenty: A Man with an Arm Tattoo

Frisbee headed to the morgue, placing a call to Monica Chang on his way, hoping to convince her of the importance of having Burns join them to identify bodies.

By the time Frisbee suited up and entered the autopsy theatre, Hua had performed a thorough external exam, taken blood cultures, removed the vital organs, and opened James Doe's skull.

With her back to the door, she greeted Frisbee, saying, "Hello, Sterling. Please, mask up."

"Why do I need a surgical mask around the deceased?" Frisbee asked, wondering how Hua could know whether he wore a mask or not with her back turned to him.

Deciding discretion outtrumped valor, Frisbee reluctantly tied on his surgical mask, circling the operating table to face Hua.

"Talk to me, Charlotte. Was the victim we found today processed like the others?"

"He appears to have met a much less violent end, Sterling. The victim is male, late twenties, and Latino. Healthy heart, liver, stomach, and lungs. No obvious cause of death, but there is something I want to bring to your attention. Please, step closer and take a good look at this man's skin."

Frisbee scanned the body for a moment. "I'm not sure what you want me to see, Charlotte. All the tattoos this guy has make it difficult to see his skin."

"I swear, Sterling, you are the best detective in this city, but you seem to lose all of your abilities when you walk in here!" Hua exclaimed. "Think about what you just said."

"You meant I'm supposed to be looking at the tattoos?" Frisbee answered with a sudden flash of understanding. "What about them?"

"You're kidding, right?" Charlotte sighed deeply. "Haven't you been keeping up with your reading? Many of these are gang tattoos."

"I've worked on a couple of homicides that involved the local gangs. I don't recognize any of these tats."

"They're from the new guys in town," Charlotte said as she moved Frisbee to the other side of the slab, directing his attention to a tattoo on the victim's shoulder, depicting a feathered dragon.

"Sterling, I would like you to meet Quetzalcoatl, Aztec god of the wind and the planet Venus. He was also the ruler of the legendary city of Tollan. Lately, Quetzalcoatl has been used as a symbol by a gang of drug dealers that have come to us from Nicaragua."

"Any ID?"

"Absolutely nothing. We took fingerprints and sent them to the different databases with no hits. The dentition is intact, so we did dental X-rays and sent those off, but they take longer. To tell you the truth, I don't think we're going to get a hit on the dental."

"Why do you say that?"

"Since you were running late, I took the liberty of shooting this guy's fingerprints and mug shot through all the databases, CODIS, VICAP, NCIC, even Interpol. We got nothing. Not a single hit," Hua said.

"Have you spoken with Mister Burns about coming to the office to look at the remains? He may be able to identify them," she continued.

"I spoke to his attorney on my way over here. She was present at the beginning of the search but took off when it looked like things were getting hairy. Since we found the latest body on his property, Burns has agreed to accompany her for the viewing. They should be arriving soon. While we wait, is there any other information connected to the Burns case you can share?"

"I received the toxicology report on Princess this morning. It wasn't what I was expecting, and I don't get surprised very often," answered Hua before turning her attention back to James Doe.

She began roughly stitching up the chest cavity, her attention quickly distracted by Frisbee. "The reports are all on my desk, Sterling. Why don't you go read them while you wait for Burns? That will give me a chance to finish up here and provide him with a clean corpse to view."

Happy to have a reason to leave the lab, Frisbee muttered a quick "Thank you" and charged out the door, before Hua had the opportunity to change her mind.

Seconds later, a very animated Frisbee rushed back into the operating room.

"Mask, Sterling!" shouted Hua.

Frisbee redonned his mask.

"What could possibly bring you back in here?"

"Gloves, Charlotte!" Frisbee exclaimed, waving a gloved hand in the air. "What are these gloves made of?"

"They're common nitrile gloves, Sterling. You can get them at almost any drug store, and hospitals have replaced all their latex products with them. They're hypoallergenic."

Frisbee spun on his heel, darting out of the room. He took the stairs to the top floor of the building, practically running into Hua's office.

Four times the size of Frisbee's office space, the coroner also enjoyed a river view through an outside wall of glass.

Completely uncluttered, the room was dominated by a large antique desk, hand-carved from an enormous black walnut tree.

The desk, given to Dr. Hua by Frisbee's father when she graduated medical school, had a significant historical and emotional background.

Ignoring the facts surrounding the magnificent piece of furniture, Frisbee focused on a stack of folders carefully placed in the center of the otherwise empty desk.

A page of printer paper with Frisbee's name written on it in large block letters lay on top of the pile.

Frisbee scooped up the stack of folders, sat in one of the four armchairs fronting the desk, and began to read.

Less time than half an hour passed before Hua joined Frisbee.

She quietly entered the office, seating herself in the captain's chair located behind the desk. She watched silently as Frisbee completed studying the reports, her elbows propped on the desk and her fingers steepled.

"I could use some clarification here, Charlotte. Why did you include the John Doe found in a dumpster in the Burns case?"

"Curare," Hua said. "John Doe died from an overdose of curare, as I believe did James Doe, and Princess was dosed with it. Curare, when used properly, causes temporary paralysis. It was once used by South American tribes to stop small animals long enough for the hunters to finish the job. It takes a large amount to kill a human, and even then, it needs to be injected directly into the bloodstream.

"Curare causes a weakening, or paralysis, of skeletal muscles by interfering with the transmission of nerve impulses between the nerve axon and the contraction mechanism of the muscle cell. Specifically, the alkaloid interferes with the activity of acetylcholine at the surface where it functions, thereby blocking the neuromuscular junction. The horror of curare poisoning is the victim is very much awake and aware of what is happening; they can feel the progressive paralysis but cannot call for help or even gesture. In plain English, the stuff is nasty."

"Additionally, it is an extremely unusual substance to be found in Pittsburgh," Hua added, almost as an afterthought. "A lot of it comes from South American countries."

"What do you mean, Charlotte?"

"Curare is extracted from plants that aren't found anywhere near Pennsylvania."

"This was used on the dog, too?" Frisbee asked.

"The dose of curare injected into Princess was not strong enough to kill her. It did paralyze her and cause her a great deal of confusion and fear. John Doe had enough curare in his system to bring down a water buffalo.

"That would be understandable if curare were a local, common substance, but it isn't. Obtaining enough curare to kill a man should get someone's attention. Especially since James Doe is showing the same symptoms as John Doe."

"What about the Burns family?"

"They were sedated with heavy opioids available at any hospital pharmacy."

"Charlotte, you mentioned curare needs to be introduced directly into the bloodstream to be fatal. Do you have any clues how the poison got into the Doe boys' bloodstreams?" Frisbee chuckled slightly at his unintentional pun.

Hua didn't get it, but there were a lot of things about Frisbee she didn't get.

She took a deep breath before answering. "I performed a thorough search of John Doe's body, looking for any sign of an injection site, but the fact he spent several hours in a dumpster after he died has made the task difficult. Rats and other vermin chewed on any area where fresh blood was exposed.

"After your appointment arrives, I will have more time to go over the body of James Doe for signs of injection points." Hua glanced at her watch. "It's a task I sometimes leave for my staff, but with the number of tattoos, I feel I should handle this one myself."

"I know I've already said this, Charlotte, but I do appreciate you and all the work you do." Frisbee gently took Hua's hand in his and looked into her eyes. "We need to meet Burns and his attorney. Monica Chang is seldom late," Frisbee whispered in a deep southern twang.

He dropped Hua's hand and turned toward the door.

"Monica Chang?" Hua asked, sheepishly, but Frisbee had already left the room.

Frisbee could hear Burns loudly haranguing the hapless receptionist long before he reached the lobby area.

"Is there something wrong, Mister Burns?" Frisbee asked, hurrying across the lobby to rescue the public servant. Separated from the public for safety, the design of the receptionist's office reflected the fears of today's society. Unfortunately, the office, surrounded by Plexiglas designed to repel small-caliber bullets, offered no protection from Burns's large-caliber insults.

Chang stood apart from the action, ignoring everyone.

"This mistake for a human being refused to allow me access to the main building," Burns said, his face beet red.

"Access to the building is restricted during non-business hours, Mister Burns," Frisbee said. "That's why I agreed to meet you in the lobby and escort you to the viewing rooms."

"I am an officer of the court!" Burns exclaimed. "This building should never be restricted to me! When I push a button for an elevator, an elevator should arrive, but that little freak behind the glass will not open the doors for me! Do something about him, Frisbee, or I will!"

Before Frisbee had a chance to react, Hua strode over to Burns with her hand extended. "I am Deputy Coroner Charlotte Hua," she said as she shook Burns' hand. "You must be the famous attorney, Joseph Burns. I am sorry for your loss, and I apologize for not being present during the identification process of your loved ones. I can only imagine how difficult this is for you."

Frisbee's amazement grew as he watched Hua play Burns. He knew Burns hadn't come to the morgue to identify his family.

"The day you came to identify your family, Mister Burns, was during regular business hours. Our staff was at full strength, permitting the public easy access to the building. As you know, the world is a dangerous place, so for security purposes, during non-business hours, a staff member must accompany visitors."

Hua flashed her ID card over the reader outside the elevator doors, lightly brushing her hand against Burns' arm. "We can go anywhere we would like now, Mister Burns." Hua rewarded Burns with a sultry look.

Moments later, Chang was formally introduced to Doctor Hua and joined them in the elevator.

The quartet whisked themselves to the sub-basement.

Hua arranged to have both James and John Doe on gurneys in the viewing room, their cover sheets pulled back to expose their faces and upper torsos.

"I am not sure what is going on here, but I know both these boys. The one farthest away from us is my driver, Guillermo," Burns said, indicating the gurney containing the body of James Doe.

Dr. Hua had someone push the gurney containing John Doe closer to the viewing window.

"I take that back! This one is Guillermo!" exclaimed Burns, quickly turning his head.

"Are you certain, Mister Burns?" Hua asked. "Please, look again."

Burns reluctantly turned and pointed in the general direction of Guillermo. "That is my driver, Guillermo Escobar. I don't want to look anymore. You people are messing with me!"

He turned and scowled at Monica Chang, who, standing away from the rest of the group, was engrossed with her smartphone. "You're here as my representative, Chang, not so you can be catching up on texts! Why the hell did you allow these jerks to ambush me?"

Instead of answering, Chang positioned herself next to Burns and showed him the message she had been reading.

Burns visibly stiffened.

"Doctor Hua, Detective Frisbee," Chang said, nodding to each in turn. "My client has nothing further to say. We will show ourselves out."

She took Burns gently by the arm, pocketed her cell phone, and exited the room.

Frisbee and Hua were left staring at an empty exit door.

"What do you suppose that was about?" Frisbee asked.

"Sterling, you associate with a lot of weird people," Hua said, ignoring Frisbee's question.

Grinning, she gently leaned against Frisbee's shoulder.

Briefly frozen in time, they were two ordinary people staring at a vacant doorway.

A moment later, Frisbee took Hua by the hand and led her out of the morgue.

Chapter Twenty-One: Bad Fortune

According to Webster's dictionary, *...fortune telling is the forecasting of future events using methods that are usually considered less than rational.*

There is evidence of forms of fortune telling being practiced as far back as 4000 BC, when interpreting dreams and the utterances of witches "speaking in tongues" played important roles in ancient religion, medicine, and politics.

Katie Daugherty believed fortunetelling was just another form of scam.

She told her friends as much when they went to visit a palm reader as part of Katie's twenty-sixth birthday bash. Katie went along with it because her friends paid the fortune teller in advance, and she thought it would be, "a hoot."

The reading took a little more than an hour. The fortune teller asked Katie questions, gazed intently at Katie's palm, and described, in detail, the nuances of every line. The palm reader finished the session by telling Katie all her dreams were about to come true.

Later that night, as she lay in bed telling her husband, Patrick, about her night, Katie began to cry. "It wasn't just the fact the fortune teller wasn't dressed all in black or had a mysterious foreign accent," she told Patrick, letting her disappointment out. "She ended my session with a generic announcement anyone could have come up with."

The following Monday, Patrick received a promotion and substantial raise at the Ford dealership where he worked as a mechanic.

The next day, Katie received a plaque recognizing her as the assistant manager of the year for the bank where she worked, along with a fat bonus check. Katie wrote the promotions off as a coincidence. She and Patrick worked very hard. They deserved to move up professionally, and no phony medium could have claimed to predict that.

The following morning, Patrick won a contest held by a local radio station by answering the trivia question, What is Alice Cooper's real name? The grand prize? "An all-expense paid trip for two to an exclusive Puerto Rican resort!" exclaimed the announcer.

Not only did he know the answer, Vincent Damon Furnier, but he also knew Cooper's birthdate, marital status, his progeny's names, and birthdates, and most importantly of all; *why the singer's name was Alice.*

Patrick surprised Katie on their fifth wedding anniversary with the church wedding she had always dreamed of, complete with a renewal of vows, a huge reception, and a second honeymoon in Puerto Rico.

That was when Katie began to believe in fortune telling.

The day the couple returned from Puerto Rico; long-awaited medical test results awaited them. As Patrick read the medical report, he began to realize one of their greatest dreams was coming true. After four years of failures and disappointments, Katie and Patrick were pregnant!

Katie set up appointments with realtors, arranging for several viewings of potential homes throughout the following week.

Of course, with her new attitude and her newfound certainty fortune telling was real, the very first house Katie and Patrick viewed was perfect.

Located in Pittsburgh's eastern suburbs, it had everything Katie dreamed of: a large fenced-in yard, an easy commute to the city for work, plenty of room for a dozen kids, and an award-winning school district.

She called every one of her friends to thank them for taking her to the fortune teller.

Katie placed her final call to her mother.

She arranged to meet her at a shopping mall in Pittsburgh's North Hills, a short drive from I-279. Katie planned to take her mother to a baby clothing store in the mall, dropping the good news at just the right moment.

Enjoying the crisp, beautiful spring afternoon, Patrick and Katie drove carefully along Interstate 376, the most direct route into the city from its eastern suburbs.

Ordinarily, during weekday rush hour, I-376 was a commuter's nightmare.

It was practically empty on an uncommonly clear and sunny Saturday spring morning. Wildflowers were blooming along the sides of the road.

The couple's four-year-old Ford Escape rolled along the freeway, negotiating a series of wide rounding curves designed to make the three-mile drop into Ohio River Valley effortless as the highway bottomed out to run parallel to the Monongahela River.

The couple enjoyed the view of Pittsburgh, nestled in the middle of the river, with a light fog settled at its foundation, surrounding it in a living, moving mist, towering over the valley like a modern-day Oz.

Patrick cautiously merged onto I-279 for the next leg of their short journey.

Concentrating on the highway construction just past the Veterans Bridge on-ramp, Patrick failed to notice the Exxon tanker truck merging into traffic, or the pickup truck careening along the freeway behind him.

The pickup, driven by a drunken construction laborer named Harold Sharpe, sped along the freeway, swerving from lane to lane as he struggled with the darkness enveloping his world.

Sharpe had begun partying the evening before, celebrating his first paycheck at a new job. He bar-hopped Friday night, picking up coworkers and friends along the way.

Saturday morning, Sharpe and his newfound friends had managed to fool the door man at an all-night club into allowing them entry.

Once inside, they quickly learned they did not have the necessary funds to partake in the club's activities.

Sharpe decided the party should continue at his home in the North Hills, necessitating a drive along I-279.

They staggered to Harold's pickup, determined to continue the festivities.

Lacking a rear seat, three passengers squeezed themselves into the front of the pickup with Sharpe. His male passengers quickly passed out, leaning against the passenger door, one sitting on the lap of the other.

Sharpe's third passenger found herself riding in the middle of the truck's seat, concentrating on lighting the joint hanging from Sharpe's mouth.

Unsteady, and half asleep, she hung on Sharpe's right arm to steady herself while she tried in vain to connect the flame of her lighter with the end of the joint, adding another distraction to Sharpe's already uncontrolled vehicular maneuvering and his general inability to notice what was directly in front of his face.

Sharpe's pickup, traveling at approximately ninety miles per hour, reached the construction merger point at the same time as Daughertys' Ford.

Sharpe sideswiped the Daughertys' vehicle, sending it careening uncontrollably along the freeway.

The Ford Escape's tortured motion stopped when it collided with the tanker.

The force of the impact caused the trailer to jackknife and roll onto its side. It slid along the freeway until coming to a stop against the concrete Jersey barrier separating the north and south lanes of the freeway.

It slammed into the Jersey Barrier with enough force to dislodge a section of the barrier, at the same time, allowing the center portion of the trailer to become impaled on the broken concrete. Fortunately, the broken section of the concrete barrier acted as a plug, preventing fuel from escaping.

However, when the SUV collided with the tanker truck, its airbags deployed, temporarily blinding Patrick.

He instinctively yanked his steering wheel to the left to avoid further impact with the tanker, glancing off the rear bumper of Harold's pickup. Reacting to the contact on his left, Patrick overcompensated, forcibly turning his Ford Escape to the right, causing it to crash into the underside of the upended trailer.

His head struck the steering wheel, knocking him unconscious.

The second impact of the vehicle with the gas tanker ripped the tanker loose from the plug formed by the barrier, resulting in a major fuel leak.

The couple had nowhere to go.

Katie sat motionless, staring at the love of her life and thinking fortunetellers suck.

Gasoline fumes formed a cloud around the tanker and found an ignition source.

The top half of the tanker disappeared in a ball of flame.

The explosion could be felt miles away.

Katie's mother, standing in the mall parking lot with a fresh bouquet of flowers in her hand, felt a dark cloud pass over her heart at the exact moment the ground shook beneath her feet.

Sharpe's pickup momentarily spun out of control after Daughertys' vehicle collided with his rear bumper, coming to a stop a hundred yards past the tanker.

Sharpe looked around at the carnage he had caused. He guided his truck onto the freeway and sped away from the scene.

Chapter Twenty-Two: The Murders and the Drug Cartel

Carlisle and Decker arrived at Frisbee's tiny office a few minutes before the usually scheduled 7:00 a.m. meeting time.

To their surprise, they found the room was dark and unoccupied.

"Would you like to sit, captain?" Carlisle asked, turning on the lights.

"No, thanks, Carlisle," Decker replied, looking nervously around the small office. "I may need to make a quick getaway."

Frisbee arrived moments later, looking much worse for wear.

"Are you okay, Sterling?" Carlisle asked. "You look horrible."

"Ah didn't sleep well last night, Caroline. New aspects of this case have come to light. They are quite troubling."

"Oh, multiple homicides mimicking an automobile accident isn't troubling enough for you?" grumbled Decker.

Frisbee acknowledged Decker with a nod and then quietly informed his team of the ongoing issues with the Doe boys. "I accessed all the databases, attempting to find information. I tried everything: names, fingerprints, tattoo records, known and unknown aliases, and facial recognition software. Nothing."

Settling into the worn office chair behind his desk, Frisbee continued. "Then, shortly before 0200, I got a visit from a handful of narcotics detectives. They indicated both gentlemen in question were acting as confidential informants and proceeded to warn me away from the investigation before I got their CIs in deep trouble. I informed them of the present status of their CIs. They agreed the time for caution may have passed. We traded information, but I seriously doubt they gave me everything they have."

"You didn't hold anything back on your end, did you?" Carlisle asked, sarcastically.

"No. I don't have anything to hide. We need to always cooperate fully with other departments, Caroline. Otherwise, they may refuse to share important information. For example, I learned John and James Doe are related, as we thought, and their actual surname is Jarquin, not Escobar. They worked for Alfonso Rosas. Rosas allegedly runs the largest drug smuggling ring in the eastern United States.

"Most of his product is smuggled from his home country of Nicaragua. The head of the narcotic's investigation told me Rosas has Burns on retainer. Burns is under contract to represent any employee of Rosas who might run afoul of the law, drug-related offense or not, including the recent allegations of Rosas companies and their addition to local pollutants." Frisbee looked bleary-eyed but continued his monologue.

"John Doe, AKA Raul Jarquin, was assigned to the area as an enforcer. The narcotics team says he arranged for Guillermo's job as Burns's bodyguard/chauffeur. The extra activity piqued the curiosity of narcotics. Believing Burns might be turning product, they took an interest in his activities."

"Do they still think Burns is selling drugs?" Carlisle asked, incredulously.

"No," answered Frisbee. "They believe he's dirty in other ways. The FBI is investigating him for money laundering and many of his associates for anti-pollution crimes. Results of the campaign against Raul and Guillermo yielded nothing until Raul got swept up in a vice raid.

"Vice was sweeping the north side of Pittsburgh, picking up hookers. Raul got nabbed for solicitation and was about to walk when someone looked in his Beemer and noticed the seven kilos of heroin the idiot had sitting on his back seat."

"I never heard about a drug bust that big!" Carlisle exclaimed.

"You probably never will," Frisbee replied. "Before vice could process Raul, narcotics seized the case, saying it was part of an ongoing investigation. They used the drug bust as a lever to turn Raul, and then they used Raul to turn Guillermo.

"Information provided by the Jarquin brothers has led to the arrest of over a dozen high-level drug producers and transporters. My contacts wouldn't say how much of a dent that's put in the network, but they said it's making a difference."

Carlisle let out a low whistle. "That would make the cartels want to kill a few people."

"That might give us clues about who killed the Nicaraguans, but why would they kill Burns' family?" Decker asked.

"That's the million-dollar question, Deck," Frisbee replied. "I presented all the information to my boss this morning. He wants us to pursue the Rosas lead. His theory is Rosas found out the Jarquin boys had narced on him and Burns was ripping him off. He went ballistic and wasted everyone his people could find that night. One of the narcotics detectives told me the Nicaraguan even has a history of using curare to torture his enemies as they die."

"So your theory says after Rosas found out about the Jarquin brothers and Burns, he sent a death squad to stage this elaborate murder?" Decker asked, incredulously. "Don't you read the papers, Frisbee? When these guys kill an informant, they want everyone to know what they did. They send a clear message. They don't hide it in some strange video. I think these are two separate cases, and we need to concentrate on the Burns murders."

Frisbee leaned across his desk. "I agree, Deck, but my boss thinks the Burns case is an isolated murder that can wait. He wants us to concentrate our efforts on the drug lord."

"I don't think that's the way to go, Frisbee. Let another homicide detective work on the Rosas case. We need to be looking at Tupaz and Hughes, and I really need for you to stop calling me Deck!"

"Whether or not the investigation into these murders becomes sidetracked due to its concentration on Rosas isn't the only issue we're facing, *Mister* Decker. If the local cartel punished Burns, he may be amenable to turning state's witness."

"Are you buying into that theory, Sterling?" Carlisle asked. "The way the Burns family was killed doesn't fit the MO of a cartel-sanctioned execution."

"I must follow up on Rosas. My boss is adamant. He wants me to work with narcotics to find out why two Rosas employees died in Pittsburgh," Frisbee said, calmly and clearly. "If you hate the prospect of looking at Rosas, you can walk out any time you like. I hope you don't, but I can't keep you here."

Decker tossed his visitor's pass on Frisbee's desk. "I'll send you a bill for my services. Gimme a call when your investigation needs some real detective work."

"Let's go, deputy. I'll buy you a beer," Decker said to Carlisle.

"I'm sorry, boss," replied Carlisle, "I think I better stay here and look after Sterling. He might need some help with the Nicaraguans."

Decker stared at his former underling in disbelief before storming away.

"You sure pissed him off," Frisbee drawled.

"I need to spread my wings. He isn't even a police officer anymore, yet he still acts like he's in charge."

Frisbee sighed. He pulled a file from the rubble on his desk and handed it to Carlisle. "The latest info we have on Rosas. It's a copy; it's yours."

He glanced at his watch. "The boss is holding a roll call in a few minutes; let's see if we can pick up any information."

Catching Carlisle's questioning look, Frisbee clarified his statement. "They have the best coffee in the entire precinct."

###

Arriving in the detectives' squad room too early for roll call, Frisbee grabbed a cup of coffee and disappeared into the chief's office.

Carlisle plopped herself down at the desk of a middle-aged female detective whose nameplate identified her as Heather Jones.

Engaged in a heated discussion on her desk phone, Jones didn't notice Carlisle until she had completed the call.

Having only caught half of the conversation, Carlisle found her curiosity greatly piqued.

As soon as the call had ended, Carlisle briefly introduced herself and asked her first question. "I didn't mean to eavesdrop, but I couldn't help hearing your conversation. Are you working the parkway explosion as a homicide?"

Jones looked suspiciously at Carlisle, not certain she wanted to share any information with the younger woman. Then, she shrugged, saying, "Yeah, a witness came forward with a description of the hit-and-run vehicle. She even had the license plate number. Turns out the guy has a record."

"Were you able to make an arrest?" asked Carlisle.

Jones nodded. "The witness identified a Dodge Ram pickup truck. We were able to match that, and the license number, to a nasty piece of work named Harold Sharpe. When officers served the warrant for Sharpe's arrest, he was passed out in his living room with a known prostitute."

"Did you bring him in?"

"Yes, they did," Frisbee said from behind Carlisle, in the general direction of the head of detectives. "The boss just filled me in on the case. Sharpe and a prostitute named Lucinda Garcia were brought in for questioning, but they lawyered up and were released within a few hours."

"Wow," Carlisle replied. "Who was his lawyer?"

"Monica Chang," answered Frisbee. "She received a text at the morgue yesterday afternoon and rushed off. I'd be willing to bet it was to make sure Sharpe kept his mouth shut."

Chapter Twenty-Three: Drinking Buddies

Heading out the door of Hughes' residence near the end of her shift, Tina received a text from Jordan, asking her to join him for a drink at a club they frequented in her neighborhood.

Tina parked in front of her house and walked the few blocks to the bar.

She found Jordan waiting at a table in a secluded corner, with several empty beer bottles in front of him. He slurred an effusive greeting, motioning to a nearby waitress to serve him another round and to include Tina's drink, as well.

"I'm so glad you texted me, Jordy!" Tina gushed, greeting Jordan with a kiss on the cheek. "You have no idea what happened at work!"

"Aunt Joan tells me everything. You oversee the Hughes job." Jordan faked a yawn. "Big deal."

Playfully slapping his hand, Tina said, "You creep! She doesn't tell you everything."

"Did you hear about the circus on the parkway Saturday morning?" asked Jordan.

Tina nodded. "Everyone's been talking about it. Did you get called out?"

"We sure did," Jordan slurred. "Hey, do you remember that young Officer Nelson from the Hughes accident?"

"Of course. He asked me some questions. Nice guy, I guess."

"Well, he's been cursed or something, because he was the first on this scene, too," Jordan slurred, conspiratorially. "People were calling in to report a terrorist attack. I talked to him after the excitement died down." Jordan was unable to stay on topic.

"A gasoline truck exploded, right?" asked Tina.

"Right, but it didn't just blow up accidentally. An SUV was pushed into it by another vehicle, causing the tanker truck to roll over and blow up the whole neighborhood!"

138

"You're kidding me!" exclaimed Tina, taking a large gulp of her drink.

"No, I'm not," said Jordan, looking at Tina sideways, attempting to focus. "Have you ever ridden your bike on the Eliza Furnace Heritage Trail?"

"I think so. Isn't it part of the bicycle rails to trails system that runs along the rivers?"

"Right. A lot of people ride their bikes to the trails from the north side. There were several cyclists out on Saturday morning."

"Trooper Nelson said one guy riding to town heard the original crash. He locked over in time to see a pickup truck racing away from the scene. Seconds later, the explosion blew him off his bicycle. After that, he was too busy saving his butt to get a license number or a better description of the truck." Tina giggled, her drink already taking effect, "That's not funny, and I don't know why I laughed. Is he okay?"

"He was treated for minor injuries and released," Jordan answered. "Five fire companies were called in to keep the blaze from spreading to nearby buildings. My team and six other rescue units were called in to handle the injured. The blast hit people traveling on the parkway, as well as pedestrians and vehicles on nearby streets."

Jordan ordered another round. "Franky and I were running victims to burn centers all day while other teams were patching up minor injuries on the spot. There were a lot of injuries. We ended up running casualties to all Pittsburgh's hospitals.

"Firefighters found the remains of a young couple in the SUV wedged under the tanker. Police figure it caused a leak when it was pushed into the trailer. It took the forensics teams several hours just to find enough pieces of the guy who was driving the truck to determine there was only one other body," said Jordan after guzzling the remainder of his drink.

"Oh, my God!" gasped Tina.

"The blast, and the inferno that followed it, damaged the existing freeway, the new construction, and most of the heavy equipment stored nearby," mumbled Jordan, shaking his head.

"You know, this accident happened near the spot of the Hughes incident. This time, everyone involved in the accident died, except for the driver of the pickup truck and his passengers. I doubt any of them are long for this world." Jordan's tone of voice indicated an air of mystery.

The friends sat in silence, each lost in their own thoughts.

After a few minutes, Tina broke the silence. "Did I tell you a detective came by the Hughes residence?"

"No. Why would the Pittsburgh Police be bothering Hughes?"

"The detective said they might have found out who ran Bill's car off the road, and the people who did it were murdered. I think we're suspects," Tina added, gloomily.

Then, after another moment of awkward silence, she asked, "Hey, how did you know the detective was from Pittsburgh?"

"Just a lucky guess. Since when are you and Hughes on a first name basis?"

Tina giggled, "I think you're jealous, Jordan Best. I also think I may be a little drunk. I'm glad I don't have to work tomorrow."

"Me, too, Tupaz." Jordan sighed, reaching for Tina's arm to help her to her feet. He missed. "Mind if I crash on your couch tonight? I had a few too many myself."

"Jordy, you are always the responsible one. Of course, you can sleep on my couch. And in the morning, you can go to mass with me!" Tina added, excitedly. "Then, you can have dinner with my family. They haven't seen you in ages!"

Jordan laughed. "Now I remember why we never dated. I ask to spend the night on your couch, and you have us engaged to be married. Two drinks are definitely your limit."

"Why are you so mean, Jordy?" Tina asked, pouting.

They walked the few short blocks to her house in silence.

Tina went straight to bed.

Jordan slept on the couch, making certain to be awake and on the road before Tina got out of bed.

Tina enjoyed her day off, even if Jordan was too much of a coward to join her. She spent the day with her family, exactly as she had described the day before to Jordan. No wonder he wasn't interested in spending the day with her.

It was boring, and she didn't report to work the next day until the afternoon shift. Afternoon shifts were generally very quiet.

As Tina drove to the Hughes residence the following afternoon, she thought about things she needed to do at the patient's residence. She certainly would not be bored.

Chapter Twenty-Four: Carlisle's Promotion

More than a week had passed since the discovery of Guillermo Jarquin's dead, naked body, and Frisbee had an important decision to make. He gingerly approached Carlisle, who was seated at the front of his desk bent over her laptop.

"Caroline, I have something I need to discuss with you," Frisbee stuttered.

"If you are going to start in about sharing your office again, Sterling, I already told you. I cleaned this place up, so I get to use half of it."

Frisbee chuckled, looking around his immaculate office. "It's not about sharing the office space, Caroline. In fact, I'd like it if you would consider making it permanent," Frisbee said, his drawl alerting Carlisle.

"What are you going on about, Sterling?" Carlisle batted her big blue eyes and swept her blonde hair back from her slender neck. "Is there something you want to tell me?"

Frisbee took a deep breath. "You did that on purpose, didn't you?"

"Of course, I did, Sterling. Look, we both knew my leave of absence from the Sherriff's Department was running out. I knew if I waited for you I'd be back in my old office pushing papers, so I filed the necessary paperwork. Chief Smith signed his portion, and my boss signed hers. The request was expedited, and I am officially your partner."

"That's wonderful news, Caroline," Frisbee managed to garble out.

"Now I am an official partner, I think we should get my name painted on the door," joked Carlisle, breaking out in laughter at the look on Frisbee's face. "Maybe we can wait until they get your name on the door first. All kidding aside, Sterling, are you sure you're okay with this?" Carlisle was still unsure of her connection with the strange southern detective.

It was all Frisbee could do to mutter an enthusiastic, "Yes, ma'am!" while nodding.

"Caroline, you are dedicated, bright, intelligent," Sterling drawled. He hated giving pep talks, but Carlisle had seemed down in the dumps lately, and he was determined to not be voted the worst boss in headquarters again this year. If it meant doing things he hated, so be it.

Frisbee stopped talking when a uniformed officer appeared in the doorway, moving into a "parade rest" stance.

"Chief Smith wants to see both of you in his office, immediately," the officer announced. "I have been instructed to escort you."

"Why doesn't he just call and ask us to come to his office?" asked Carlisle.

"I think he's afraid I wouldn't pick up the phone and just slip out the back. If he sends someone, then he has an eyewitness who can say I received the message." Frisbee sighed, theatrically.

Carlisle giggled. "There just isn't any trust in this world anymore. Why would he think you might sneak out?"

"It may have happened once or twice." Then, he addressed the officer blocking the doorway. "Shall we go?"

The police officer turned, gesturing for the detectives to proceed him.

He accompanied them to the chief's office, opened the door for the detectives to enter, and left without a word.

"Outstanding personality, that one," remarked Frisbee to no one in particular.

"I spoke to the district attorney while waiting for you," Smith said without preamble. "The DA told me it would give him great pleasure to prosecute the parties responsible for the violent murder of a prominent Shadyside attorney's family.

"Since I was certain we needed to blanket Rosas with our investigation, I don't hold you responsible for choosing the investigation's direction, Frisbee. Problem is, I was wrong." Smith tapped a file sitting on his desk.

"A few days ago, at 3:00 a.m., the fire department responded to a call in Brighton Heights." Smith paraphrased the report. "Upon arrival, they discovered a pickup truck had been driven into the front of a house and set afire. The house was a complete loss. When the blaze had been brought under control, the bodies of three men and one woman were found."

The chief paused. "The truck is registered to one Harold Sharpe. You might have heard Harold was arrested recently in connection with the Parkway hit and run. Thanks to his attorney, Harold was a catch and release.

"The discovery of bodies, along with the truck suspected of having been involved in the hit and run, caused a great deal of excitement. It was enough excitement for me to push for the rapid ID of the victims. The first one identified was our old friend, Sharpe."

"Excuse me, chief," Carlisle said. "If I remember correctly, when Sharpe was brought in, his alibi was a hooker. You mentioned a female victim was discovered in the house?"

"Yes, detective. A prostitute known as Lucinda Garcia. She has been identified as the female victim. The other bodies were badly burned and were sent to the morgue for ID. We believe they were passengers in Sharpe's truck the day of the incident."

"What makes you say that, chief?" Frisbee asked.

"Because" answered Smith wearily, "the weirdness doesn't stop with a burning truck and a house fire. In the bed of the truck, investigators found a fireproof safe with an eBook playing a video on a repetitive loop. You know what was on that video?"

"Footage of the hit-and-run accident." Smith continued, without waiting for a response. "To be more specific, the video shows the collision from several different angles and is detailed enough for facial recognition software to identify every person involved in the deadly crash."

"What about the collision itself, chief?" Frisbee asked. "Does it cover that?"

"Yes. It captures the point of the impact from several different angles. It shows the pickup hitting the SUV, the SUV impacting the tanker, and the explosion. If the video is real, there is no doubt concerning the driver responsible for the accident."

"Chief," Carlisle said. "You have an ID on Lucinda Garcia; is she originally from Nicaragua?"

The chief smiled for the first time since the detectives entered his office. "You are a sharp one, Carlisle. Yes, Ms. Garcia claimed to be a political refugee from Nicaragua, but that isn't the connection I want the two of you to follow. We are going to leave Rosas out of this for now. Find out who the other victims are, where that safe came from, and most importantly, where these videos are coming from."

"We should go to the morgue, Sterling," Carlisle said as they left Smith's office.

Frisbee stopped walking, with a "deer in the headlights" look on his face. "Ah, er, um; Ah can handle the morgue work on my own, Caroline," he said in a drawl thicker than turtle soup.

"Is there something wrong, Sterling? That may be the worst I've ever heard your accent," Carlisle said, smiling. "You must be worried about me. You are a sweetheart, Sterling, but I can hold my own in the morgue."

Knowing he didn't stand a chance of changing Carlisle's mind, Frisbee called Hua, asking her to meet them at the entrance to the medical examiner's building.

Carlisle jumped out of the car as soon as it stopped.

Grinning from ear to ear, she skipped across the parking lot to where Doctor Hua waited outside the building's entrance.

The two ultra-conservative professionals screeched some form of ancient greeting, understandable to only them, and perhaps a few canines.

They hugged each other warmly, crying in joy.

After several minutes of unintelligible muttering through tears, Hua caught her breath.

Holding Carlisle at arm's length to see her better, she smiled broadly and began to speak in a language Frisbee could understand. "Caroline, how nice to see you again! When Sterling mentioned he had a new partner, I expected a robot, not someone with brains, backbone, and a will of her own."

Carlisle smiled, "Charlotte, I've learned more from Sterling in the past month than I had in the whole five years I spent in the sheriff's office. But yeah, he is kind of set in his ways."

"What? How?" Frisbee said, mustering all the vocabulary currently at his disposal. Giving up the prospect of attempting to make sense out of Carlisle and Hua at the same time, he walked slowly across the lobby to the elevators, shaking his head and mumbling, "The whole world is stacked against me" as he pushed the call button.

Deciding to show some mercy, Carlisle explained her relationship with the medical examiner to a dejected-looking Frisbee. "I met Doctor Hua a few years ago. A young couple had been thrown from their motorcycle and struck by several passing vehicles before traffic was brought to a stop. The freeway was closed for hours while forensics looked for pieces of flesh that resembled body parts. Eventually, they were brought here.

"It was my first investigation, and a couple of the jerks were planning on playing games with the forensic evidence to make me sick. I found out about their little game before they could pull any stunts. I wanted to nail the jerks to the wall, but Charlotte heard what was happening and approached me with a plan of her own. We turned the tables on them and got them suspended for sexual harassment."

"Good for you, Caroline," Frisbee said. "I'll bet they think twice before trying something like that again."

"The investigation into the prank snowballed, turning up other issues. Eight deputies lost their jobs. The ringleader, the one who wanted to show me a lesson for trying to be a smart-assed girl in a man's world, ate his service revolver," replied Carlisle in a quiet monotone. "The only member of the force who would work with me after that was Decker. The good doctor and I continued our friendship and over the years; we have become very close. I am surprised she didn't tell you, Sterling."

Doctor Hua rolled her eyes and mouthed, "I told him several, times" to Carlisle.

"Before we enter the morgue, I think I should prepare you," Hua gravely announced when the small group exited the elevators.

"We have burn victims inside. When a body burns, the muscles contract, and the flexor muscles, being stronger, overpower the extensor muscles, thus giving rise to a pugilistic position of the body. This term arises from the similarity of the posture to that of a boxer in the ring. The arms are raised in a defensive position, and the hands are tightened into fists." Hua explained and demonstrated the position. "Quite often, the legs are bent into a defensive stance, as well. I haven't had the opportunity to perform complete autopsies on the victims, but we can take a look."

The team entered the operating theater.

Opening the nearest body bag, Hua rolled back the top half to expose severely burnt human remains. "According to the face recognition software available, this is a twenty-five-year-old white male. My initial finding for his cause of death is a shock from burns on over seventy-five percent of his body. Notice the pugilistic stance. Further ID will be coming shortly."

Hua covered the badly burnt body.

She moved to the next table. "This a twenty-three-year-old white male. Same cause of death as our previous victim, same ID."

Hua paused.

"Their dental records have been sent to the proper agencies for positive identification. Judging by the poor state of their health and dentition, my professional opinion would be both men were alcoholics and drug addicts. The only reason they have dental records at all is because they were wards of the state on numerous occasions. I'm certain detectives of your caliber have already deduced that," she added, winking at Carlisle.

"Are you okay, Sterling?" Hua asked as she moved toward the next table.

Frisbee, looking a little green, nodded.

"What can you tell us about the others?" Carlisle asked.

Hua held up her index finger, stepping to a computer workstation on a nearby counter. "Since you were so enthusiastic concerning the Burns family and the accident victim's comparisons, I assumed you would like to do the same with Daugherty-Sharpe." She opened a summary of the Daugherty autopsies.

"James Russell, the driver of the tanker truck, was from North Carolina. He was identified via company records. The force of the explosion separated appendages from Mister

Russell's torso, the ensuing fire destroying the smaller pieces. None of the victims from the Sharpe residence have been dismembered. That eliminates the first of the possible similarities."

"What about the severe burns?" asked Frisbee. "That's a strong indicator of the killer copying injuries of the Daugherty accident victims."

"I agree," Hua replied. "The two unidentified men suffered almost total bodily coverage of severe burns. That is a close approximation to mirroring the injuries of what was left of the truck driver."

"Which brings us to Sharpe and Garcia," said Carlisle.

"Right, you are, Caroline," Hua said, moving to the two autopsy tables on the other side of the room. "I've had enough time to perform autopsies on both Sharpe and Garcia, so I believe I will have answers to many of your questions."

"Did you also perform the autopsies on the accident victims, Charlotte?" Carlisle asked.

"I performed the autopsy on Katie Daugherty and supervised the others."

"Can you tell me how they died?"

"Of course, Caroline," Hua said with obvious pleasure. "I just don't want to spend any more time in the morgue than necessary. Sterling doesn't particularly like it in here."

"I'm fine," Frisbee said through gritted teeth. "Please, give Carlisle what she wants."

Hua sighed. "The Daughertys' SUV was wedged underneath the tanker. The front end of their vehicle partially collapsed, causing severe blunt force trauma to the upper thorax of both occupants. When the tanker exploded, the main force of the blast passed directly above them, sucking the oxygen out of the air as it did. Combined with their chest injuries, that resulted in the complete collapse of their lungs, causing what is known as a complete pneumothorax. I believe they would have lost consciousness, and suffocated within moments."

"Wouldn't it be rather unusual for both victims to suffer such extreme thoracic injuries at the same time?" Frisbee asked.

"Unusual, but not impossible," Hua answered. "I can check around with some colleagues for other opinions if you would like."

"Some other time," Frisbee muttered.

"So where does that leave us with Sharpe and Garcia?" Carlisle asked. "Are their injuries similar to those suffered by the Dougherty couple?"

"Yes and no," Hua answered, uncovering the body of Lucinda Garcia. "The first thing you will notice is, like Katie Daugherty, Ms. Garcia's body is not incinerated. Having been protected by the vehicle from contact with direct flames, Katie Daugherty's cause of death was suffocation and trauma. The extreme heat of the fire caused tissue damage, but not the severe distortions as seen on the other victims."

"Garcia looks like she wasn't touched by the heat at all," said Carlisle.

"There is some tissue damage due to extreme heat, but in a way, you are correct, Caroline. The killer could not replicate the BTUs generated by the tanker fire, so he improvised."

"What do you mean, improvised?" Carlisle asked.

"Notice the chafing on Ms. Garcia's wrists? Those are rope burns suffered while she was still alive." Hua turned her focus to the woman's midsection. "If you look at Ms. Garcia's thoracic region, you can see a pattern of bruising consistent with bludgeoning. I believe she was beaten repeatedly with a blunt instrument, probably a baseball bat."

Hua uncovered the body of Harold Sharpe. "You can see Mister Sharpe has also been spared tissue damage from exposure to high heat. He has rope burns on his wrists and appears to have suffered more bludgeoning than Ms. Garcia."

"Why would they do that, Charlotte?" Carlisle gasped.

"My guess, Caroline, is so they could mimic the trauma causing the dual lung collapse the Daughertys suffered when the tanker explosion pulled the oxygen from the surrounding air. Because the killer couldn't mimic the power of the explosion, he had to damage the lungs enough to cause them to collapse and then allow the victims to suffocate."

Carlisle closed her eyes before asking, "Were these victims sedated before being tortured?"

"I've seen no indications of it, but toxicology screens have been taken. It will be a few days before we have the results."

"Great work, Charlotte," Frisbee muttered. "Can we wrap this up now?"

"Not quite yet, Sterling. There is one more thing I must show you. Please, come closer."

Frisbee had been standing several feet away from the examining tables, as close to the exit as possible while still being able to participate. He slowly moved next to Doctor Hua.

With Carlisle on Hua's other side, the doctor indicated a spot located on Sharpe's left shoulder, and another on the outside of Garcia's right thigh. Both victims wore tattoos depicting Quetzalcoatl.

"The obvious connection to Rosas the multiple tattoos represent might explain why the court system treated the victims differently, but we aren't any closer to finding who killed them, or why."

Frisbee was both excited and frustrated because of that discovery. He turned, storming to the exit.

Pausing at the door, he began stripping off his protective clothing. "I'm sorry, Charlotte, I think I may have spent too much time in the autopsy room today. We must go. I'll call later." Frisbee exited the room and shuffled toward the elevators.

Carlisle and Frisbee rode back to headquarters in silence.

Chapter Twenty-Five: News Media

Finding the front doors overrun by media, they rounded the block, taking a restricted alley to the rear of the building.

Entering through the delivery bay, like thieves sneaking in during the night, the detectives were met by uniformed officers, their escort to Chief Smith's office.

"I've been trying to get hold of you for the last two hours, Frisbee," Smith said in a rage when the detectives entered his office.

"I'm sorry, chief," Frisbee said, fumbling with his cell phone. "I turned my phone off for a meeting in the morgue and forgot to turn it back on."

"Sit," Smith commanded, pointing at a chair. "Didn't your phone vibrate?"

"I turn off the vibrate function, sir," Frisbee replied, sheepishly.

"It freaks him out, sir," Carlisle said with a slight smile. "Detective Frisbee is extremely uncomfortable inside the morgue."

"Many of us are uncomfortable inside the morgue, Detective Frisbee," the chief said, "but we still need to remain in contact. Was your service radio off, as well?"

"Yes, sir," Frisbee drawled, slightly chagrined. "I'm not certain it works."

"Have it checked out, Frisbee. Don't let this happen again."

"Yes, sir."

The chief moved to the window, looking at the press gathered below. "What are we going to do about that circus outside?"

"Why are they here?" Carlisle asked.

"The press learned about the videos. I'd like to know how that happened." His words were soft and non-threatening, but Carlisle found herself squirming.

"I don't like what you're insinuating, chief," Frisbee said.

"I'm not insinuating anything, Frisbee," retorted Smith. "I didn't track you here to accuse you of leaking information. While you were hiding at the morgue, one of our IT people figured out where the videos originated. They've been compiled from traffic cams, dash cams, and even national satellites. She said whoever put it all together is a genius. *No one* has legal access to all that information, but the video's producer compiled all the imagery and came up with evidence we missed. The IT person also identified the fireproof safe found at the scene as coming from Home Depot."

"That is wonderful, chief," Frisbee answered. "Now, we can identify the perpetrator, or at least identify the purchaser of the safe."

"No identification was made of the purchaser at Home Depot. The IT person found a similar safe at her local store and made the connection herself."

"I need to know what you two have been up to while everyone else was doing your jobs!" the chief continued with a growl. "We need to make progress on our investigations so we have something to feed the media vultures!"

Frisbee took a deep breath and began reciting from memory, "We met with Doctor Hua and viewed each of the victims from the Brighton Heights incident. The dentition recovered from the bodies of two badly burned males have been sent off for positive identification."

"I hate when you do that," Smith grumbled. "You were there, Carlisle. Did you write things down?"

Carlisle briefly looked in Frisbee's direction before reading from the document she had typed and saved on her phone. "The bodies of Lucinda Garcia and Harold Sharpe, positively identified earlier, were also present in the lab. Doctor Hua believes Sharpe and Garcia were kidnapped, tortured, and murdered in a manner that would approximate the fatal injuries of the Daughertys. They were constrained, suffering repeated blunt force trauma to their thoracic regions, which resulted in broken ribs, punctured lungs, and asphyxiation."

"What kind of injuries did the Daughertys suffer?" Smith asked.

"Extensive damage to their thoracic regions due to the impact of the collision, coupled with the force of the explosion, caused them to suffer complete pneumothorax, otherwise known as collapsed lungs. The couple died almost instantaneously."

"Was there any other way for the killers to approximate the injuries?"

"Doctor Hua didn't have an opinion on that, sir," replied Carlisle as she looked up from her phone. "She did say Sharpe was beaten more severely than Garcia, most likely because his musculature was more developed."

Frisbee cleared his throat, "While we are on the subject of Garcia and Sharpe, Doctor Hua brought one other thing to our attention, chief."

"What might that be, Frisbee?"

"Both Sharpe and Garcia are sporting gang tattoos; more specifically, tattoos of Quetzalcoatl, the same as the Jarquin brothers. Everything's coming up Rosas, to roughly quote the gypsy."

"I don't care if one of the suspects is a gypsy," Smith replied after he gave Frisbee a strange look. "The Rosas case is secondary to these gruesome murders. Narcotics will be helping on Rosas. In the meantime, we must deal with the press."

"We?" Carlisle and Frisbee chorused.

"Yes, we," growled Smith. "The commissioner has been getting calls about the videos since early this morning. She wants it handled, right now. In about fifteen minutes, we will make our way downstairs for a press conference, where we will communicate as little as possible while making them think we are giving them the world."

"I've never done a press conference, chief," Carlisle said. "I have no idea what I should say."

"Don't worry, Carlisle. If Detective Frisbee had bothered to reply to me during the time you spent at the morgue, we might have had time to be better prepared. However, I have a prepared statement I'm going to present before introducing you. Frisbee will then step up to the podium and answer three questions by saying he can't give out that information due to the ongoing investigation. You, Detective Carlisle, will stand to the side and smile." Smith paused. "I'm heading for the men's room to freshen up before the press conference. Do you need me to return, or can I trust you to show up?"

"We'll meet you downstairs," Frisbee said.

"Okay, ten minutes," agreed Smith.

"Really, Sterling?" Carlisle said as soon as the chief left the room. "Channeling gypsy Rose Lee? What is wrong with you?" She grinned and shook her head.

Grabbing Frisbee by the hand, she led him toward the elevators.

"Multiple murders are big news, Sterling," gushed Carlisle. "Representatives from all the news branches will be there: television, radio, and print. If we hurry, we can get there in time to see everyone before the chief arrives."

Carlisle practically ran out of the lift when the elevator reached the ground floor, dragging Frisbee behind her like a reluctant dog on a leash.

A makeshift stage stood on the headquarters portico with a dozen microphones taped to stands in front of the podium.

Carlisle moved about the press, introducing herself to the most famous of them. She seemed to be having the time of her life.

Ten minutes before the scheduled press conference was due to start, uniformed police officers began filtering out of the building, forming a semi-circle between the stage and the building's entrance.

Precisely on time, the police commissioner stepped out of the building and walked to the stage, stopping occasionally to shake hands with supporters in the wall of blue.

Electronic flashes from dozens of cameras broke through the Pittsburgh gloom.

Once the photo ops were completed, the commissioner stepped onto the stage.

The first female police commissioner in Pittsburgh, Carmine Diulius, held the press, as well as much of the city's voting population, in the palm of her hand.

Diulius leaned slightly forward to center her position over the microphones. "I have often expressed my appreciation of the fifth estate's involvement in the daily operations of our city."

An accomplished speaker, the commissioner's gaze locked onto a friendly face for a second, and then moved on to the next, playing the gathered press like a violin.

"Thanks to your diligence and tenacity, many crimes have been brought to the public's attention that would have otherwise gone unnoticed. Such is the case with recent multiple murders targeting some of Pittsburgh's prominent citizens. Our investigators have missed the importance of public awareness. My detectives are professional, experienced, and proven crime solvers. They leave the publication of their heroics to you."

Diulius paused to allow for a spattering of polite laughter.

"The investigation into these murders is being led by our homicide department, under the direction of Chief of Detectives Malcolm Smith. Chief Smith will fill you in on the scope of the investigation." The commissioner turned to the wall of blue behind her. "Chief Smith?"

Chief Smith received decorations for extreme bravery three times during his career. He faced down a drug-crazed gunman holding three children hostage, he saved two senior citizens from a burning building, and he'd been seriously wounded when he foiled a bank robbery. He once poorly quoted Tennyson saying, "Guns to the right of us, guns to the left, we charged the guns!" There wasn't much that scared Chief Smith, except for public speaking.

Comedian Jerry Seinfeld once said, "According to most studies, people's number one fear is public speaking. Number two is death. Death is number two. Does that seem right? That means to the average person, if you have to go to a funeral, you're better off in the casket than doing the eulogy."

Smith stumbled up to the podium like a prisoner heading to the gallows.

Looking at a point just above the heads of the gathered reporters, he cleared his throat and began speaking in a monotone, just loud enough to be heard. "Good afternoon. Everyone should have received a packet containing a press release with complete information on the dates and probable times of murders perpetrated at the Burns residence on Fifth Avenue in Shadyside, as well as the Sharpe residence on California Avenue in Brighton Heights. The investigations into the multiple murders have been combined into a high-level task force led by Detective Sergeant Sterling Frisbee. Sergeant Frisbee is prepared to answer any questions you may have regarding the investigation. Thank you."

Smith stepped away from the podium, frantically motioning for Frisbee to take his place.

Then, Smith rushed across the portico and fled into the building, forcing Frisbee to scramble to the microphones.

Frisbee looked out at the assembled crowd of reporters. Thanks to the chief's unnerving behavior, instead of members of the press, he imagined he saw the group of townspeople armed with torches and homemade pitchforks as they stormed Frankenstein's castle. Frisbee shook his head to remove the visage, took a deep breath, and regained control.

"Good afternoon," he said, forcing a smile. "I am Detective Sergeant Sterling Frisbee from the Homicide Division of the City of Pittsburgh Police Department. As Chief Smith mentioned, I have been appointed to head the investigation of recent murders in Shadyside and Brighton Heights. I do not have a prepared statement, but I am ready to answer any questions you have concerning these cases."

Following a slight hesitation, the reporters all shouted at once.

"I'm sorry, I don't know your names. I will simply point," Frisbee said, indicating a female reporter at the front of the mob. "What is your question, ma'am?"

"Sergeant Frisbee, how long have you been with the Pittsburgh Police Department?" she asked.

"Just over eight years. Can we please keep the questions on task? Our time is limited."

"Thank you, detective," the reporter said. "But I asked the first question to provide background for my second question. What qualifies you to lead such a high-profile investigation?"

"I participated in several murder investigations in Raleigh, North Carolina and have successfully led over a dozen murder investigations in Pittsburgh. My qualifications are a matter of public record."

Frisbee smiled and pointed to a smartly dressed middle-aged man politely facing the podium. "Do you have a question, sir?"

"Thank you, sergeant. Kyle Franklin with Fox News. Videos were mentioned in the informational packets handed out before the news conference. Is there a possibility the videos could have been photoshopped?"

"Our IT professionals are investigating that possibility, Mister Franklin. Please remember the videos in question are a part of an ongoing police investigation. Their content cannot be discussed, but if they have been tampered with, our IT people will know."

"Your question is next, ma'am." Frisbee indicated a reporter seated directly in front of the podium.

"Thank you, Detective Frisbee. Suzi Charles, CNN," she said as she straightened her back to better show her posture and her thousand-dollar suit. "I understand there are other forensic aspects of the investigations. Will you elaborate on the unique causes of death the multiple victims suffered?"

Frisbee hesitated, certain only the killer and the investigative unit were privy to the details of the fatal injuries suffered by the murder victims.

"The cause of death for each of the victims has been provided in your handouts," he replied, deciding to stay on script.

"I have a couple of follow-up questions, detective," Suzi Charles said before Frisbee had time to call on another reporter. "The handouts provided by Chief Smith recount the minimal details of the fatal injuries suffered by Rachel Burns and her husband's sons, Christopher and Charles. However, we have uncovered information stating another body was discovered at the

Burns residence. Since you seem to have a very close personal relationship with Doctor Hua, I thought you could provide us with some insight on this additional victim."

Ms. Charles' question concerning Jarquin startled Frisbee. No one outside the department had been permitted to discuss the investigation beyond the known facts.

"I'm sorry, Ms. Charles," Frisbee drawled. "Any further evidence recovered at the Burns residence is part of an ongoing investigation. In addition, I have known Doctor Hua since college and have a strictly professional relationship with her."

Carlisle stood to the side of the makeshift stage, just within Frisbee's peripheral vision, attempting to get his attention by waving her arms and slicing her finger across her throat.

"I have one last question, Detective Frisbee," Ms. Charles said with a slight sneer. She glanced at her notes, pausing for dramatic effect. "What is the connection between the murders and the Rosas Crime family? Were the Burns' murders a message from the Rosas family? Was Sharpe a member of a rival gang? Is there an indictment planned for Rosas? Is Burns being moved into protective custody?"

Charles fired off her questions in staccato fashion, partly for dramatic effect, and partly to avoid being interrupted.

Her fellow reporters followed her tirade with rapt attention.

"Ms. Charles, Ah'm not certain where your information came from. Ah can assure you the Pittsburgh Police Department is not investigating the Rosas family, or any other family, and Joseph Burns does not require protective custody."

Carlisle, waving her arms wildly, maneuvered parallel to the stage.

Frisbee, as well as everyone else in Pittsburgh, finally noticed her.

"I want to thank y'all for attending today's press conference," Frisbee drawled. "Unfortunately, we are out of time. Y'all will continue to receive daily news briefings through our outreach personnel and will be immediately alerted of any breaking stories. Good day."

Frisbee turned, marching from the podium amid a chorus of, "Detective Frisbee!"

He stormed past Carlisle, gesturing for her to follow him.

They practically ran to the elevators, riding up to the third floor in silence.

"Can you believe that woman?" Frisbee exclaimed as they walked toward his office. "Where did she get her information? We appear to have a leak somewhere, Caroline! Something like this can ruin the entire investigation and jeopardize the safety of everyone involved in it!"

"I found out while I was speaking with representatives of certain press affiliations before the conference CNN was not the only news agency with the information. That means the leak could be coming from anywhere, Sterling. The chief asked narcotics to investigate the Rosas connection while we were at the morgue this morning, adding at least a dozen personnel with access to the files."

"We can't forget the other news Charles let out of the bag! You know, the part about your affair with Doctor Hua." Carlisle giggled.

"Our entire investigation is falling apart, and you are amusing yourself with unfounded rumors about my private life!" grumbled Frisbee. "We need to concentrate on finding murderers before the whole thing blows up in our faces!"

Frisbee came to a sudden stop at the entrance to the office.

Carlisle, who had been following closely behind so she could hear his tirade, collided with him.

"What the…" Carlisle said, rubbing her nose as Frisbee stumbled into the office.

Frisbee stepped aside to allow Carlisle a full view of the room, as well as of the man seated behind his desk, paging through the contents of a folder.

"Good to see you, Deck," Frisbee said. "Not sure you're authorized to be reading that file, but it is good to see you."

"I came to offer my help, Frisbee. You are quite obviously way over your head, and stop calling me Deck."

Carlisle moved past Frisbee so she could get closer to her former boss. Not to embrace him, but if he were the type of person who went for that sort of thing…

Decker held up a hand, "Carlisle, it has been a little while since we've seen each other, but you need to remember we are police officers, not sorority sisters. If you hug me, I might just have to shoot you."

Carlisle stopped, a wide smile on her face. "I'm glad to see you, Captain Decker. I've been worried about you. I've called several times and left voicemails, but you never call back. What have you been doing?"

"I've been looking for murderers while you and Johnny Reb have been off chasing headlines," he answered gruffly. "You threw away your career so you can join this clown while he rushes around, tilting at windmills. You're nothing more than the Sancho Panza to his Don Quixote."

Carlisle looked like Decker had slapped her. She stared at him for a moment, her eyes wide and full of tears. Then, she stormed out of the room.

"Nice going, Deck," Frisbee sneered. "The only person left on the planet who still likes you, and you manage to anger her!"

"She sees you as a father figure," Frisbee continued. "She stayed with the Sherriff's Department because of you. It wouldn't kill you to occasionally tell her she's doing a good job. You know something else, Deck? She's a very good detective. Her work is exceptional. She's now my full partner, and I consider myself lucky to have her."

Decker looked at Frisbee, wide-eyed, and then looked down at the floor. "I'm not very good with people, especially younger people. I guess I just don't know how to act," Decker quietly responded.

"Maybe you should get a dog," snarled Frisbee. "Get out of my chair. Carlisle made room for a work table for herself and two folding chairs for guests. You can have one of the folding chairs."

Carlisle walked purposefully back into the office before Decker could sit.

She avoided Decker's eyes, speaking directly to Frisbee. "Do you mind if I take the rest of the day off, Sergeant Frisbee? I think I need to go home. I'm not feeling well."

The formality shocked Frisbee. Carlisle had never referred to him by rank or asked for time off.

Before he could respond, Decker stepped forward and spoke in a soft voice. "Carlisle, I'm sorry if I let you down. I should have returned your calls, but whenever I had the time, it was always too late at night to call."

"You can call any time. You know that," Carlisle answered.

"I didn't want to disturb your fiancé," muttered Decker.

"He would understand if you called. You're practically family." Carlisle's eyes were beginning to tear up again.

Decker, afraid she might try hugging him again, quickly sat in the folding chair Frisbee had offered earlier.

He waited until Carlisle sat behind her work table before continuing. "Carlisle, I apologize for the way I treated you. I think it's great you've joined this team permanently, and I wish you the best of luck. That's why I'm here. I want to talk to you and Frisbee about the murders. The two sets of murders are related."

"How much do you know about the second set of murders?" Frisbee asked. "If you learned the information by reading my files…"

"Take it easy, Frisbee. I caught the call about the fire on the scanner. I had a feeling about it and followed up with some of my old connections. I might even have a few things to tell *you*!"

"What exactly is it you want to tell us, Deck?" Frisbee drawled.

"I received a report from a CI who had spotted Sharpe's truck approximately two hours before the fire. He believes Sharpe was moving product for Rosas."

Carlisle started to speak, but Decker raised a hand to stop her. "Please, allow me to have my say. I'm not getting any younger, and I'm likely to forget what I'm saying if I don't get it out right away."

Decker stretched his legs as far as he could in the small office. "Rosas is somehow involved with both Burns and Sharpe, but I seriously doubt he's involved in their deaths. Let me tell you what I've learned, and you can make up your own minds."

Frisbee's desk phone jangled, causing all of them to jump.

"I didn't know that thing still worked," Frisbee said, grinning. "Excuse me while I get this."

Frisbee answered the phone, and muttered a few yes sirs, followed by, "We'll be right there."

He then addressed Carlisle and Decker. "The chief has set up a meeting with the narcotics team charged with investigating Rosas. It seems he accomplished that before the press conference. I doubt he can do anything right now."

Frisbee stood, holding his hand out toward the door. "Shall we go? You can finish your story after the meeting, Deck."

Chapter Twenty-Six: Carmella Ruiz

Frisbee and his companions found the conference room already occupied when they arrived. At the far end of an oval-shaped table designed to seat twenty people stood a classically beautiful Latina with long jet-black hair, large doe-like eyes, and soft features. She was flanked by two plainclothes officers so similar in appearance they were often mistaken for twins.

"My name is Lieutenant Carmella Ruiz," said the Latina, sternly. "I am the lead in the Rosas narcotics investigation."

She paced toward the open door to the conference room, the "twins" closely behind.

All three agents wore matching blue windbreakers.

After a brief whispered discussion, the twins left the room, closing the door as they departed.

"Please, be seated," Ruiz said, smiling as she returned to the head of the table. Her fingers lightly brushed Frisbee's hair as she passed.

She casually removed her windbreaker, draping it over the back of an empty chair.

Moving like she owned the place, Ruiz slipped gracefully into the captain's chair at the head of the table.

Leaning slightly forward, she placed her elbows on the table, resting her chin in her hands.

"Judging by communications I've received from Sterling," Ruiz began, addressing the detectives like old friends, "it has become evident we are all digging in the same sandbox but not playing well together. Do you agree?"

"Yes, ma'am," Frisbee muttered in response.

Ruiz scowled. "In order to get this investigation on the proper path, we all need to work together as one team. I've already spoken with the police commissioner and have received her promise of complete cooperation. My associates have provided files pertaining to our investigations into the Rosas family. Sterling, I trust you've brought the files on the murders you believe involve Rosas."

Frisbee was speechless; he simply nodded.

"We're going to be here a long time," Ruiz said with a smile. "We'll need food. My department will buy; just let one of my associates know what you want. We are not leaving here until we have found a way to combine our forces and work this investigation as a team."

"Why are we even talking about Rosas? He is not involved with the Burns or Sharpe murders. It isn't the way he operates?" Decker said.

"I'm in charge now, Decker," Ruiz replied, still smiling. "You can follow my lead or get out of my way. Your choice."

Decker stormed out of the room, slamming the door behind him.

"Whew! I thought he would never leave." Ruiz chuckled. "Seriously, he is a great lawman, but he doesn't play well with others, and we need teamwork."

"What do you have in mind, lieutenant?" Carlisle asked, not hiding the suspicion in her voice.

"The first thing I would like, Detective Carlisle, is for us to treat each other as equals. We can start by using first names. My friends call me Mel," Ruiz said with a smile, standing, and extending her hand across the table. "Who knows, we may even become friends."

Carlisle stood, shaking Ruiz's hand, "My friends call me Caroline, but you probably already know that."

The women smiled at each other, simultaneously looking at Frisbee.

"What do you think, Sterling?" Carlisle asked.

"Ah should have seen this coming," Frisbee murmured as he rose and firmly shook Ruiz's hand.

"Mel, you've seen the reports," said Carlisle, "Do you think Rosas murdered the Burns family and the Jarquin brothers to send a message?"

Ruiz shook her head. "When Raul got busted with enough drugs to put him away for life, he was terrified of what Rosas would do to him, but he refused to talk until he knew Guillermo was safe from Rosas's retribution, as well as safe from persecution from us. Once we turned Guillermo, they became the best confidential informants I've ever had, providing us with information on Rosas's shipping schedules, leading to the largest drug confiscations in history. If Rosas found out the brothers were acting as CIs, he certainly would have wasted them, but he would have sent a clear message, the killings would have been obvious."

"Which is exactly what he did with the Sharpe murders," Carlisle said.

"I'm not familiar with that case. Would you mind filling me in?"

Carlisle summarized the details of the Sharpe murders and autopsy findings.

"Both Sharpe and Lucinda Garcia were marked as members of the Rosas crime family," Carlisle said in conclusion.

"What exactly do you mean by 'marked'?" asked Ruiz.

Carlisle opened her laptop to access the department's website, scrolling to the page titled Identifying Marks.

"Sharpe and Garcia had the stylized Quetzalcoatl tattoo shown here. The tattoo, detailed in an addendum to Doctor Hua's autopsies on the Jarquins, is worn by members of the Rosas family," Frisbee said.

"Why didn't you mention these tattoos earlier? When we agreed to exchange information, that meant all our information! I trusted you, Frisbee," Ruiz said quietly.

"Ah am so sorry, Mel," Frisbee replied, "Ah honestly thought y'all were aware of the markings."

Ruiz stood, speaking with a quiet enthusiasm, her eyes lit with an inner fire. "Have you ever heard of the expression, 'Left of boom, right of boom'? Its terminology was popularized during the terrorism age, indicating the before and after stages of a particular act. The left of boom is the investigative stage where, ideally, law enforcement would find the terrorist cells and prevent an attack.

"Right of boom is the aftermath of the attack where investigators gather all the information they need to nail the perpetrators to the wall. Hopefully, at the same time, they gather the information that will place them squarely left of boom in time to prevent the next incident.

"In narcotic's case, our left of boom is where we gather information on suspects and prevent drug-related crimes before they happen. Unfortunately, we don't have the funds, personnel, or quite frankly, the talent to carry that out. We commonly find ourselves to the right of boom, frantically trying to catch up to the bad guys and often missing important information. These tattoos were a very big miss."

Ruiz stretched, causing Frisbee to choke on his water.

"Recent budget cuts have only succeeded in making matters worse. We knew about the connection between Rosas and the Jarquins, but we didn't know anything about Sharpe. I'm still not convinced Rosas is responsible for the murders, but I'm prepared to spend the man-hours checking on these leads. If your theory is correct, we can nail him to the wall."

Ruiz leaned over the table again, her dark eyes burning holes in Frisbee's heart.

"You need to be one hundred percent with me, Sterling. You must give me every shred of evidence you uncover. I promise to do the same for you."

"That's a deal, Mel," Frisbee said. "It will be an enormous relief to have your folks covering the Rosas angle. We know Sharpe and his associates were not murdered at his house. The bodies were moved after the fact. With your team involved, my people will have the time to look for the actual murder site."

"The neighbors didn't see anything?" Ruiz asked.

"No," Frisbee said while shaking his head. "The truck was dumped early in the morning, then torched. All the neighbors remember seeing is flames."

Ruiz sighed and stretched again before turning to Carlisle.

"It was nice meeting you, Caroline," said Ruiz, exiting the room.

"It appears we have a new member of the team," Frisbee remarked when the door shut firmly behind Ruiz. "Three beautiful women and me."

Carlisle laughed. "If I hear you make one remark about 'Sterling's Angels,' I will personally castrate you.

Chapter Twenty-Seven: Funeral

Tina rotated her staff's shifts and scheduled herself for a Monday afternoon so each of her staff would have an extra weekend day off. She purposely chose days where nothing big was planned so she could catch up on paperwork and spruce the house up a bit.

Her plans were shattered when she found several unfamiliar vehicles parked in Hughes' driveway.

Drawn to the slightly muted conversation coming from the living room as she entered the house, Tina stepped lightly across the foyer and into the larger room beyond.

She found Hughes entertaining several associates from his office.

He pulled her into the conversation as soon as she entered the room.

"These wonderful people stopped to see me after attending a funeral. They've been asking questions about my prognosis, my physical therapy, and especially about this thing," Bill said, indicating his Halo device. "I told them you had all the answers."

Tina took a deep breath. She was nervous, her mouth as dry as a desert wind.

She reached into her backpack for a bottle of water, took a long sip, and began talking. "Please allow me to offer my personal gratitude for your visit this afternoon. Your interest in Mister Hughes' health is a sign of the high regard in which you hold him. The very best treatment for any patient is interaction with his peers. I expect to get to know every one of you quite well during the coming weeks, as I am certain you will become regular visitors.

"Mister Hughes said there were several questions about his Halo device," Tina continued. "It's designed to protect him from further injury to his cervical structure by keeping his upper torso in place. He is required to wear it for approximately one month."

###

Tina's elegantly spoken description of Bill's injuries and prognosis left little room for questions. However, Tina found their concern so heartening she answered questions for over an hour.

The guests, satisfied with the information they received about their friend, thanked her profusely and began to file out of the house, each handing her a personal business card as they said goodbye.

The senior partner of Bill's law firm, Edgar Snyderman, and his son, Carl, were the last to leave.

Taking Tina's hand as they stood in the doorway, Carl said, "Please, take good care of Bill, Nurse Tupaz. He's much more than a law partner. He's a part of our family." He gently kissed Tina on the cheek and departed, leaving her alone with an exhausted patient.

"It was nice of your friends to visit, Mister Hughes."

Bill sighed. "The reason for their visit wasn't a social call. At least not at first."

"What's up, Bill?" said Tina, suddenly concerned. "Are you in trouble?"

Bill paused to catch his breath. "Do you remember the horrible accident and explosion on the Parkway last week?"

"Of course."

"A beautiful young woman named Katie Daugherty died in that crash, along with her husband. One of my wife's cousins, a paralegal at my law firm, is Katie's mother."

Bill began to choke up. "When Katie had difficulty conceiving, Veronica and I put up the money for her in-vitro procedure. Katie learned the procedure was successful the day before she and her husband were run off the road, directly into a gasoline tanker."

Gently laying her hand on Bill's arm, Tina crouched down to wheelchair height to look directly into his eyes. "I am truly sorry, Bill."

"I haven't told you the worst part, Tina. The drunk who caused the wreck has gotten away scot-free. The perpetrator had an alibi for the time of the hit and run. His truck is missing. Probably completely stripped and repainted, destroying any evidence that might have been found."

"I want to kill the bastard who did this!" Hughes cried out, clenching his fists in anger.

"Bill, you are obviously distraught. Why don't we take a little walk in the garden? We can soak up some late afternoon sunshine and relax," Tina's tone of voice was calculated and calming, but her eyes were full of fear. She turned, pushing the wheelchair toward the back door.

Hughes sighed, the fight draining out of him.

They came to a stop when they reached the ornamental bridge spanning the fishpond.

Tina took a seat on the small bench overlooking the pond, Bill's chair beside her. A spell of contentment fell over the garden, and the overwhelming fear dissipated.

"Did you always want to be a nurse, Tina?" Bill asked as they watched dragonflies buzzing around the water.

"No, like most little girls, I wanted to be a princess."

"I think you may have succeeded," Bill said with a chuckle.

Tina smiled, sadly. "I was ten years old when my family moved here from the Philippines. I thought anything was possible in America."

"Did you like it here?"

"No, but I was excited to see snow for the first time," Tina said, grinning at the memory.

"We lived in the basement of a big house, which was owned by the wealthy couple who helped my parents emigrate to America. In exchange, we worked as their servants. I was a skinny, sickly little girl. About two months after our arrival, I developed a lung infection. The infection led to pneumonia and an extended stay in the hospital."

"That must have been rough on you and your family."

"It was hard on my parents, but I didn't mind. I didn't like the basement, but while I was in the hospital, I found my calling as a nurse."

"What do you mean, Tina?"

"I learned a good doctor provides medical miracles and moves on, but a good nurse provides love, along with miracles, and is still there the next day. Every nurse I encountered during my stay provided me with positive care and mountains of love. I knew I had to become a nurse," Tina concluded, proudly.

Bill chuckled. "It's unusual to find someone who knows what they want to do when they're ten years old. People like that usually end up on a roof with a rifle."

Tina punched Bill playfully on his shoulder. "I had my difficulties, like any other kid, Bill. I went to Oakland Catholic High School with one eye on nursing school and the other on the star quarterback. Well, any boy some days," she said, blushing. "I was a cheerleader, but I was also in the chess club."

"Where did you go to college?"

"I won a full academic scholarship to the University of Pittsburgh, where I carried a perfect 4.0 GPA. My academic achievements won me another scholarship to the second-degree program at Pitt, where I earned my BSN."

"Did you go straight to work at your present job?"

"No. After graduation, I took a position as an emergency room nurse for another hospital group. I was on call for any one of the ERs in their system. I eventually landed my present position, but I have every intention of joining the staff at a children's hospital someday."

"That will be Best's loss. You're a very good administrator."

"Thank you, Bill, but I became a nurse because of the way the nurses at the children's hospital affected me. I want to give some of that love back to the kids. The position at the ER was going to help me move to a posting at a children's hospital where I can do the best." Tears filled Tina's eyes. "Now, I've gone and blown it all on some stupid stunt."

"Oh, so now I'm a stupid stunt," Bill said with mock anger and hurt.

"You know what I mean."

Movement at the house caught Tina's attention. "It's gotten late, Bill. Time for your PT."

"After my healing is complete, I think I will become the administrator of a children's hospital and offer you a job," Bill said with a smile.

Tina laughed, pushing Bill's wheelchair toward the house.

Chapter Twenty-Eight: Proposal

Billy Hayes worked for the Florida FDA, inspecting cattle for disease. One bright March morning, he discovered a 1969 Harley Davidson Electra Glide collecting cobwebs in a barn owned by a man called Odell Jones.

Odell had a daughter named Jeanine.

Odell raised the girl by himself following his wife's death when Jeanine was only one year old. Unused to fatherhood, and girls in general, he raised an untamed, dark-haired, dirt-bike-racing terror.

When Billy approached Odell about the motorcycle, he agreed to sell Billy the Harley on the condition he restore it where he found it, not trusting a city boy with such an important job.

Every weekend for the next six months, Billy made the two-hour trip from his home in Tampa to work on the Harley. Odell supervised the work and occasionally offered help.

Billy slept in the barn; Jeanine often kept him company.

When he completed restoring the Harley, he owned a "chopped out" replica of the motorcycle ridden by Peter Fonda in *Easy Rider*, painted monster green in honor of "The Hulk," Billy's nickname.

The following morning, as Jeanine walked across freshly mowed grass on her way to the barn, a new Harley Davidson Sportster adorned with a pink ribbon blocked her path. She found a diamond engagement ring on the speedometer.

Billy stepped out of the barn in a suit Jeanine didn't know he owned.

He dropped to one knee and proposed.

Jeanine's best friend, Bobbie Sue Foster, thought the proposal belonged in a magazine of the most romantic acts in the world. No such magazine existed, but Bobbie Sue continued, unfazed in her conviction.

Bobie Sue's excitement extended to her running out to have her hair dyed in a color not found in nature. Surprisingly, her hair perfectly matched the color of her maid of honor dress.

Before the wedding, Jeanine and Billy had contacted a genealogy expert to learn as much as they could about their family histories. Jeanine's family had been in central Florida for generations, but Billy's family tree branched out like a weed, including a distant cousin living in Pittsburgh.

Their honeymoon plans of riding their bikes directly to Niagara Falls were slightly changed.

Following a storybook wedding, the newlyweds traveled north, reaching Pittsburgh's suburbs at sunset three days after the ceremony.

Following Interstate 376 for several miles as it wound its way through the rolling hills of western Pennsylvania, they crested Greentree Hill for the final two-mile approach to the city and the entrance to the Fort Pitt Tunnel.

Their timing couldn't have been better.

Psyched upon hearing stories of what lay ahead, Jeanine and Billy entered the tunnel and opened their throttles.

Cruising at sixty miles an hour, the roar of their Harleys echoing off the tunnel walls, they failed to notice the BMW 328I closing in from behind.

When Jeanine and Billy exited the tunnel, Pittsburgh appeared in what has been described by *The New York Times* as "the best way to enter an American city."

The city's magnificent skyline, illuminated against a backdrop of distant clouds, provided a heavenly backdrop to the spotlights highlighting Pittsburgh's two major sports arenas, and the incomparable Point State Park Fountain, located where the Allegheny and Monongahela Rivers converge to form the Ohio.

Jeanine and Billy were awestruck. Riding side by side in the right-hand lane, they slowed to enjoy the view before merging onto I-279 and opening their throttles.

The detour signs and alternate routes around the freeway damage created by recent accidents confused the couple slightly, and they cut back on their speed to regroup.

The BMW drew dangerously close.

The car's driver, John Rayburn, and his significant other, Melissa Friend, were on their way to a late business dinner. A habitual tailgater, Rayburn maneuvered his BMW to within a few feet of the rear tires of the motorcycles.

His cell phone sounded, indicating an incoming text.

Without hesitation, Rayburn grabbed his cell phone from the console, opened the text, read the message, and began to respond.

As with most people who drive while texting, Rayburn performed those tasks without looking away from his phone, unaware the motorcycles he'd been tailgating had reduced speed.

Still riding side-by-side, Jeanine and Billy were in the slow lane, approaching the I-579 on-ramp.

Billy continued riding on the inside lane, adjusting the position of his bike slightly to allow Jeanine a clear view of merging traffic.

The newlywed couple still hadn't noticed the BMW behind them.

Rayburn inadvertently pressed on the BMW's accelerator while responding to the text. He looked up from his phone, realizing he had gotten dangerously close to the motorcycles.

He panicked, dropped his cell phone, and automatically reached below the dashboard to retrieve it inadvertently mashing the gas pedal to the floor.

The BMW shot forward like a missile, quickly closing the gap between the car and the motorcycles.

Violently crashing into the couples' rear tires, the Beemer rapidly pushed the bikes ahead of it.

Jeanine's Sportster shot off to the left, slamming into the concrete Jersey barrier.

Thrown from her bike, she spiraled through the air like a gymnast, landing in the middle of oncoming traffic. She was struck by a Land Rover, which killed her immediately.

The BMW 328I is designed with a slightly sloped hood for aerodynamics. It scooped up Billy and his green Harley, the motorcycle lying on its side on top of the BMW's hood, pinning Billy down.

Billy looked through the windshield at Rayburn's shocked face.

Rayburn partially regained his senses, slammed on his brakes, and jerked his steering wheel sharply to the right. He hadn't even noticed his action, which killed Jeanine.

The Harley, still pinning Billy "The Hulk" Hayes underneath, slid off the hood of the BMW, striking the concrete on-ramp of the Veteran's bridge.

The bike and the car screeched to a halt along the steel and concrete barrier.

Billy was thrown over the guardrail, momentarily hovering over the edge.

His hovering ended seconds later when he was struck by a ten-ton dump truck that was speeding down The Veteran Bridge's on-ramp.

Chapter Twenty-Nine: Jordan's Surprise

The following day, Tina lounged comfortably on her deck, enjoying a rare morning off and an even rarer sunny Pittsburgh day.

Stretched out on her favorite lounge chair, totally engrossed in the latest Dean Koontz novel, she failed to notice the hooded figure sneaking over the railing behind her.

The intruder wore a ball cap pulled down low to hide his eyes, the hood of his dark sweatshirt pulled forward to further obscure his face. He moved forward, closing the few feet between them with the grace of a ballet dancer and the silence of a cat.

He pounced, throwing himself at Tina like a living javelin.

At the last possible moment, the intruder twisted his flying body to land loudly on the padded recliner lying open by Tina's side.

Tina screamed, threw her book into the air, and kicked the intruder in the shins. "Jesus Christ, Jordy! You nearly scared me to death! What is wrong with you?"

"You should have seen your face, Tupaz," Jordan said, laughing hysterically and gasping for breath. "Your eyes were as big as saucers."

"That wasn't funny, Jordy!" Tina fumed, standing up to retrieve her book and right the table she had knocked over. "How do you think your aunt would react if you gave her best employee a heart attack?"

"I wasn't anywhere near Richard," Jordan retorted, still chuckling at his practical joke.

"You're a jerk, Jordy," Tina said, taking a deep, calming breath before returning to her chair. "I wasn't expecting you to drop by today, Jordy. Aside from scaring the living daylights out of me, what else is on your little mind?"

"Honestly, Tina, it's the job," said Jordan, looking at the deck floor. "It gets to be too much sometimes, and I need to be around friends."

"I know what you mean, Jordy, but why now?"

"I'm not sure," Jordan slowly replied. "The everyday stress is bad enough, but then something happens that can set you off on a spiral to a dark side that can last for weeks. The spiral got worse after the crash that killed the Hughes family. You felt it, too, but Aunt Joan and Hughes helped bring you out of it. That's why what happened is so hard for me to talk about."

"You're scaring me, Jordy! What's going on?"

"I got called out on a crash near the spot of the Hughes accident last night. Some jerk in a Beemer was texting and slammed into two bikers, killing them both."

"That's bad, Jordy, but unfortunately, not all that unusual these days," Tina remarked, sadly.

"I know; please let me finish. The bikers were newlyweds, from Florida. They were on their honeymoon, traveling the country. They hit Pittsburgh after dark and came through the Fort Pitt Tunnel. They were planning on visiting a distant cousin in Pittsburgh before heading to Niagara, but that clown rearended them, pushing the bride over the Jersey barrier into oncoming traffic. The groom was thrown into a dump truck that was speeding down The Veteran Bridge's on-ramp."

Jordan closed his eyes. "It took me and Franky over an hour to scrape him out of the grill."

"That is truly horrible, Jordy, but it still isn't all that unusual." Tina grimaced at the thought. "Okay, maybe a little out of the ordinary, but I don't see how it would push you further than the horrors you endure every day."

"Because that incident has implications that affect someone I care deeply about."

"Oh, my God, Jordy! Did you know those poor people? Why didn't you say so?"

"No, Tina. Not me. It affects you. The cousin they were coming to see was Hughes."

"That can't be right, Jordy. All Bill's relatives are gone. You told me yourself."

"I guess I was wrong. The groom's mother has some distant cousins still living in Pittsburgh, and Hughes is one of them. The newlyweds planned on contacting him as soon as they settled into their hotel room."

"Are you sure that wasn't a scam, Jordy? Bill has a lot of money. People will do some rotten things to get money."

"They have a family tree proving the connection," Jordan said, softly. "The groom's parents will be arriving today from Tampa to collect the bodies. I expect they'll want to see Hughes when they do."

Tina's cell phone had fallen on the deck during Jordan's arrival. She stood, retrieved her phone, and started to dial.

"Who are you calling?" Jordan asked.

"Bill. I have to see how he's handling this news."

"Wait, Tina. I'm not sure he knows yet. The police only notify next of kin."

"Thank you, Jordy. You really are a good friend. I have to get changed and head out to Bill's house." Tina put the phone down and hurried into the house. "He's going to need someone with him when he learns about this. You're welcome to hang out here as long as you want. Just lock up when you leave."

Jordan watched until Tina closed the front door behind her, closed his eyes, and took a nap.

###

Twenty minutes later, Tina gently prodded Jordan with her foot. "Wake up, old deadbeat. A thought struck me while I was changing clothes. If only the next of kin have been informed, how exactly did you get the information, Jordy?"

"A woman I know keeps me informed," Jordan reluctantly answered.

Looking down at Jordan, her hands on her hips, Tina said, "Is she also telling you when there is going to be an incident in that area? It seems like you're there for every bad accident. It's getting very weird, Jordy. What's going on?"

Jordan blushed, "Nothing, Tina; I just didn't want to tell you the rest of the news."

"You better cough it up, Jordan Best," Tina said, sternly. "If I hear about it from someone else, you'll be in big trouble."

Jordan laughed quietly to himself at the thought of the tiny woman in front of him causing trouble. His bravado evaporated quickly, and he decided he had better answer. "I don't know what to say about the accidents. I get a feeling something is wrong near that intersection, and I zone out. The next thing I know, me and Franky are picking up bodies." His voice was barely loud enough for Tina to hear.

"One last thing. My source told me the driver of the Beemer was only charged with tailgating, and texting while driving. He faces a total of two hundred and fifty dollars in fines."

"What?" screamed Tina.

"They took him in for a blood test, and he passed with flying colors," replied Jordan, showing Tina his serious face. "The dude has no record. He doesn't drink, take drugs, or smoke."

Furious, Tina went on a tirade. "So he just gets away with killing two innocent people? *He* should be run over by a truck!"

"Don't say things like that, Tina! You never know who might be listening." Jordan said, mortified by Tina's outburst.

Whoever might be listening, Tina wasn't among them. She got into her car and drove away.

When Tina stepped into Bill's house, she found Hughes seated at the dining room table with a bowl of soup in front of him, but he wasn't eating. Instead, he was holding the spoon like a drummer would hold a drumstick.

He tattooed the tabletop with it in a staccato rhythm.

"What's wrong, Bill?" asked Tina.

Bill huffed in anger, "About an hour ago, I received a phone call from some pompous government employee notifying me of the death of my cousin, Billy Hayes. I informed him an accident destroyed my entire family, none of whom was named Billy. He said he was just doing his job, I'm on the contact list for this Billy character."

"Try to calm down, Bill," Tina said, attempting to ignore the rat-tat-tat of the spoon. "A friend came by my house today and told me the entire story. Billy researched his family tree and found you in one of the branches. He believed his relationship with you was legitimate and he was on his way to meet with you."

Bill continued to bang the spoon down on the table.

"Please stop banging that spoon!" Tina yelled.

"How do we know this family is legitimate?" Bill asked, carefully laying his spoon on the table. "I could have one of the firm's investigators look into the Hayes family, see what skeletons jump out of their closet."

"William Hughes!" Tina said in her most intimidating voice, "Don't you dare have someone investigate that poor family!"

Taking Bill's hand in hers, Tina slid the spoon out of reach while looking into his eyes, "Why don't we call Mr. and Mrs. Hayes? I have a feeling they are good people who need a friend."

On her drive over, Tina had learned what hotel the unfortunate couple had registered at. She placed the call without waiting for Hughes to reply.

Rachel Hayes quickly took control of the conversation. Within fifteen minutes, she and Bill agreed to meet for a late lunch to review Billy's research.

About that time, Roger Day showed up, and Bill began his regular physical training routine.

"It won't be long before you're walking without a cane, Bill," Tina said when Hughes returned to the dining room from his morning session.

"I owe it all to this guy," Bill quipped, clapping Roger Day on the back.

"You have a whole staff of trainers, Mister Hughes," replied Roger with a happy grin.

"Yes, but you have always pushed me the hardest. Are you ready for another round?"

"I'm sorry, Mister Hughes; that's all for today. You've already developed admirable upper body strength and great stamina. Like Miss Tupaz says, in a few weeks, you'll be walking unaided. Probably even jogging."

"Bill, stop procrastinating; you need to get ready for your guests," Tina remarked. "They'll be here soon."

Bill blew air through his lips, making an obscene noise, "I think I've changed my mind, Tina. I don't want to do this."

"Stop being such a baby! Surely, you can help comfort a long-lost cousin!" Tina said in her most officious voice.

Hughes looked dejected, "I don't think I can comfort anyone. I'm not certain I'm over the deaths of my own wife and children."

"I hope you never get completely over it, Bill, but helping other people is a primary recovery step. The rehabilitation process requires psychological healing, as well as physical healing." Tina gently placed a hand on Bill's arm. "You need this as much as they do, Bill."

"Okay, Tina. Everything you've asked me to do has ended up being good for me," Hughes grinned, adding, "After causing me horrible pain."

Tina smiled and rolled her eyes. She scooted Bill out of the kitchen so she could cook in peace.

Planning to serve traditional Filipino dishes for lunch had Tina exceptionally busy. She was concentrating on the presentation when Bill stepped out of his dressing room.

Tina wasn't aware Hughes had entered the kitchen until she turned around to find him decked out in an Armani shirt with matching slacks and Umbro shoes. He stood inches away.

"You look very nice, Mister Hughes, and you seem to have conquered your fears."

"I decided you were right. I need to generate a positive attitude before facing my new cousins."

Tina smiled, giving Bill a tight hug. "You are a good man, Bill Hughes," she murmured, resting her head against Bill's chest.

The doorbell rang, announcing the arrival of their guests.

Dressed in jeans and red flannel shirts, Frank and Rachel Hayes appeared comfortable, but sad.

Standing at the entry as Tina opened the door, Rachel tentatively extended her hand in greeting. "Hello, I'm Rachel Hayes. You must be Tina. We spoke on the phone."

Tina stepped past Rachel's hand, gave her a long, warm hug, and tearfully welcomed her. She held Rachel's hand, turning her to face Bill.

"William, I'm Rachel Hayes. This is my husband, Frank. We are dressed like twins because jeans and red flannel shirts were our son Billy's favorite clothes."

"Billy was coming to you with proof of our family ties. Frank has a copy of the family tree research Billy was carrying when he…" Rachel couldn't hold back her tears any longer.

Tina held her while she cried.

Hughes took Frank by the arm.

"Please, come in and have a seat," he said, leading them toward the dining room.

Tina served lumpia shanghai, pork adobo, rice, and sinigang soup as Bill's Florida relations told their story.

"Frank is a Florida native," Rachel explained, indicating her husband. Orig9nally from the central farmlands, he moved to Saint Petersburg with his parents when their family dairy farm was absorbed by a large conglomerate. I moved from Pittsburgh to Clearwater when I was a toddler."

Rachel smiled sadly before continuing.

"I met Frank in college, and we immediately fell in love. We got married right after graduation, and our oldest daughter was born just a little over a year later. We had two more girls before Billy was born. He's our only son," she said, stifling a sob.

"Both Billy's grandfathers were named William. It seemed only natural to name our boy William. He became 'Billy' before he even left the hospital," Rachel finished.

"Billy didn't have many friends growing up. He spent a lot of time with my mother, listening to her stories," Rachel sighed. "She passed when Billy was a senior in college. He met Jeanine a few years later and was happier than I'd ever seen him. When Jeanine came up with the idea of researching family histories, he was ecstatic. Billy eventually found every relative possible, six generations into Europe and four times removed. That's how he discovered you."

"Billy's research didn't end with family tree information," Frank jumped in when Rachel found she couldn't talk anymore. "When he learned of your recent tragedies, he told me he felt he had found more than just a distant cousin, he had found a kindred spirit."

"He was so excited about meeting you. For the three weeks before his wedding, when he wasn't talking about Jeannine, Billy was talking about you." Rachel ended the story, racked with sobs.

Tina led her to the hall washroom, leaving her behind to compose herself.

Returning to the dining room, Tina noticed the front door standing partially open. Assuming it had been left ajar during the confusion of Rachel and Frank's arrival, Tina stepped around the entry door, pulling it completely open to make certain the decorative storm door had been properly latched.

Then, she let out a blood-curdling scream.

Standing in the open doorway with a small parabolic receiver in his hand, and a recorder over his shoulder, stood the large, impressive figure of Aloysius Decker.

Chapter Thirty: The Killing Zone

Pittsburgh, Pennsylvania, once an industrial center with black soot roiling out of its dozens of smokestacks connected to the steel mills below, transformed itself into a thriving community consisting of hospitals and technology.

The city, led by men and women of supreme foresight, turned many of the abandoned mills into centers of the new technology.

However, not all the abandoned steel mills transited to the new economy.

Acting on a tip, Carlisle and Frisbee found themselves traversing the deteriorating parking lot of an abandoned factory.

Carlisle provided color commentary, doing her best not to complain about Frisbee's driving.

"Large steel plates were once manufactured in this factory," Carlisle said, her body shaking as Frisbee sped along the overgrown parking lot. "The building is approximately forty feet high and four city blocks long. The ventilation provided by the multiple rows of windows running along the top ten feet of the building stayed open year-round, but were never enough to combat the heat created by the furnace."

"Most of the windows are broken, Carlisle," Frisbee said, rolling over a large crack in the asphalt.

"The ones that aren't broken are on the top tier," Carlisle observed. "Must be too high for kids to hit with rocks."

"How long has it been closed?"

"Over thirty years," Carlisle answered. "The owners stripped the factory of most of its tools and equipment. They left the furnace intact because it would cost more to dismantle than it would be worth as scrap. I was born and raised in Pittsburgh, Sterling. My dad, my uncles, and all their friends worked in the mills. Everybody's life changed when the steel industry died."

Carlisle grimaced as Frisbee brought his unmarked cruiser to a skidding stop, mere inches from a large hole in the pavement. "Sterling, as your junior partner, I should be driving, you know, like your chauffeur."

"Are you trying to tell me something, Caroline?" Frisbee asked with a huge grin.

"I'm just trying to do my job, Sterling," Carlisle answered, stretching her back. "Of course, since you race around like a NASCAR driver everywhere we go, it might do us both some good for me to get behind the wheel."

"Not everyone from the south loves NASCAR," Frisbee said, tossing the car keys to his partner.

The screeching of a large door rolling open for the first time in years turned their attention to the abandoned building. Standing at the entrance, every strand of his blond hair in place and his white coveralls sparkling, was forensics supervisor Howard Davidson.

Behind him, forensics teams crawled around the old factory like an army of ants, the site experiencing more activity than it had seen in decades.

"Caroline! Sterling!" Davidson called as he walked up to the detectives, grasping Carlisle's hand and shaking it vigorously. "I am so glad you could make it! It is nice to see you again."

"Yes, um, well, um, it is a pleasure to see you, Doctor Davidson," Carlisle muttered.

"Please, call me Howie. Everyone does."

"Howie," Frisbee said in his best business voice, "can you bring us up to speed?"

"Yes, and no, Sterling," Davidson replied, finally releasing Carlisle's hand. "What have they told you so far?"

Before Frisbee could answer, a black SUV raced onto the lot, kicking up dust, heading straight toward their group at breakneck speed.

The trio watched as the SUV ground to a halt in a cloud of dust.

Ruiz, dressed in a black pantsuit with a black lace toreador jacket and black, high-heeled boots, stepped gracefully out of the vehicle.

"Lieutenant Mel!" Davidson gushed, "What a wonderful surprise! You look marvelous!"

Ruiz walked past the detectives, warmly shaking Davidson's hand. "It's been too long, Howie. I hope Rowena is doing well, and I suspect the twins are growing like weeds. We'll have to catch up when this is all over."

"Thanks, Lieutenant Mel. I know how busy you are. I was just getting ready to update my good friends, Sterling and Caroline, on what we've found." Davidson paused. "They're going to share their findings first. It may help prevent us from working at cross-purposes."

Frisbee cleared his throat, "We figured the bad guys must have had a place to cook their victims before dropping them off at Sharpe's house and asked the help of Pittsburgh's uniformed officers to locate it."

"We caught a break on the first night," Carlisle said, "One of our patrols picked up a pair of petty gang bangers for tagging a bridge abutment. The punks made a deal, a slap on the wrist for defacing public property in exchange for information. They told the arresting officers about a burned-out van in this factory."

"That's where my people come in," said Davidson. "Sorry to interrupt, Caroline, but we need to keep the ball rolling."

Facing Ruiz, Davidson continued, "My team had been on standby since the Brighton Heights Fire, and we were here in less than an hour. We sealed off the entire lot to prevent any further contamination."

"Don't get me started on indigenous wildlife," Davidson added in a stage whisper.

"Inspection outside the building led us to the discovery of several tire tracks leading to an accessible entrance on the south end, hidden from the road. We called for armed backup. It's the procedure."

"Howie always follows procedures," Frisbee mumbled.

"Thank you!" Davidson exclaimed. "The SWAT team arrived first. They found an older model, mid-sized Chevrolet panel truck about twenty yards inside the factory doors. They apparently didn't like what they saw because they backed off to wait for the bomb squad and accelerant sniffing K-9s."

"Always according to the procedure," chorused Frisbee and Carlisle.

"Of course," Davidson said. "The K-9s went directly to the van. Preliminary findings show the van had been incinerated using an accelerant consisting of liquid natural gas and jet fuel. I'm telling you, this guy is a genius."

"That's not a good thing, Howie," Carlisle said. "Good police could have died because of this so-called genius."

"I don't think so, Caroline. An experienced police team would never enter a danger zone without following the proper procedure," Davidson replied. "Doctor Charlotte will need to complete her examination of the van and furnace before we can finish our mission. Perhaps you would like to speak with her?"

"Doctor Hua is in the building?" Frisbee asked, sighing in exasperation.

"Didn't I tell you? Her whole team is inside. They got here shortly before you and started working immediately."

"What about the furnace, Howie? What did you learn about the furnace?" Frisbee asked, frustrated by Davidson's endless report.

"It's impossible to restart a coke-fired furnace of that size without proper material and experience. The Road Rage Killer had to improvise. He used the jet fuel and LNG combination he concocted to destroy the van, adding solid fuel cells of the same material to keep the fire burning longer. The K-9s marked it the moment they were released from the van."

"Thanks for all your hard work, Howie," Ruiz said before Davidson could start on another monologue. "We would like to go inside now."

"Of course, Mel. Follow me."

The detectives entered the rusty, old building, passing work bays cluttered with broken tools, walking silently along the ghostly aisleways. The area housing the work bays opened into an enormous room with a monstrous furnace filling the far end.

"Doctor Charlotte is over this way," Davidson said, heading toward the furnace.

"Howie," Carlisle said. "You called the murderer the Road Rage Killer. Where did you get that name?"

"A reporter used the name in an article I read. I like it."

"Hello, Howie," Hua said with a large smile as the group approached. "I see you brought the cavalry."

Davidson looked confused. "I think you know Detectives Frisbee and Carlisle," he said. "They are from the Pittsburgh Police Homicide Department. The other member of their team is Lieutenant Carmella Ruiz from narcotics."

Davidson hesitated for a moment. "None of them are with the calvary."

"It's okay, Howie," Hua laughed. "I'll take it from here."

"The forensic team has found evidence linking this site to the Brighton Heights Murders," Hua said as she guided the investigators to the furnace. "We believe the victims were 'processed' here before being moved to Sharpe's residence."

"There is something else I want you to see," Hua said leading the team to the charred opening on the far side of the furnace.

She pointed out two sets of shackles recently installed in the brickwork near the fire pit. "It is my opinion the two main victims were shackled against the furnace, suspended near the source of the extreme heat created by the jet fuel, LNG mixture. Their thoracic cavities were savagely beaten until the combination of trauma and searing heat brought about total lung collapse.

"I believe the van was used to transfer the bodies to the Sharpe residence. It was destroyed after it met its purpose. The pickup wasn't crashed and burned until everything else was in place. I'm afraid the extreme heat from the furnace, and the fire in the van, will have destroyed any DNA evidence," concluded Hua, smiling.

"What else do you have, Charlotte?" Frisbee asked. "I know you. When you smile like that, there's always more."

"We found these," Hua said, holding up a pair of used nitrile gloves. "Your killer is getting careless."

Chapter Thirty-One: Rayburn and Friend

John Rayburn and Melissa Friend resided in a luxurious townhouse overlooking the Monongahela River. Technically considered part of Pittsburgh, the townhouse and surrounding homes have their own personality.

Rayburn and Friend turned their home into their personal business space, wearing their MBAs from Pitt like sheriff's stars. Rayburn earned six figures as an investment banker while Friend had made a name for herself at Google.

They were on the fast track to success, until the collision with the motorcycles derailed their plans.

Rayburn contacted his attorney soon after being arrested.

His lawyer, having no experience in criminal law, referred him to the firm of Burns and O'Hara, where he retained the best criminal attorney in the business, Monica Chang.

Chang's fees were exorbitant, but within hours of taking his case, she had all criminal charges dropped, along with the possibility of being charged with vehicular manslaughter.

Unfortunately, Rayburn's conscience betrayed him.

After four days of insomnia, Rayburn obtained a prescription for a thirty-day-supply Ambien tablets.

Over dinner, he and Friend ingested two tablets each, split a bottle of wine, and fell into a deep sleep.

The following morning, a senior producer at KDKA TV News received an anonymous package containing a small computer storage device with one file on it.

In the process of checking for potential computer viruses, KDKA's IT team inadvertently viewed a compilation video of the accident that ended the lives of Billy and Jeanine Hayes.

As in the other videos, the record of the Hayes tragedy had been compiled from various traffic, weather, and dashboard cameras.

The compilation began with Rayburn's BMW exiting the Fort Pitt tunnel at a high rate of speed, less than ten feet behind the motorcycles.

The driver of the BMW could easily be identified as Rayburn.

The video showed Rayburn answering and replying to a text, followed by three seconds of complete blackness, something not included in the prior videos.

When video clarity returned, Rayburn was shown reaching for his dropped phone, with several different angles showing the impact of the BMW and motorcycles.

The video showed a graphic view of Jeanine being thrown into oncoming traffic, her body being tossed about like a rag doll.

A different camera angle caught the shock on Billy's face when the BMW struck his Harley, followed by terror as his motorcycle twisted maniacally and landed on the hood of the car.

The video ended with a graphic depiction of Hayes being thrown into the grill of a speeding dump truck.

After a thorough vetting, the IT department found no viruses, and copies of the video were sent to the senior vice president of the news department and the station's lawyers.

The producer wanted to run the video as a breaking news story, but their legal department convinced her to inform the police first.

She left a voicemail message for the Road Rage task force, informing them of the video, and then she summoned the news team to her office.

Chief Smith received notification of the message from the television station almost before it ended, the words Road Rage causing the usually cautious police force to jump into action. Patrol cars were immediately dispatched to Rayburn's address.

Smith demanded a copy of the video, sent a patrol car to the television station to retrieve the original, and called Frisbee.

Frisbee and Carlisle ran out of the building, jumping into their unmarked police cruiser within minutes of Smith's call.

With Carlisle behind the wheel, lights flashing and police siren wailing, the detectives rushed to Rayburn's townhouse.

The patrol cars arrived first.

Finding the exterior doors locked, house lights on, Rayburn's BMW, and Friend's Lexus parked in the carport, the officers decided to radio Frisbee with that information.

Deciding to continue to play it safe, the officers formed a loose perimeter around the building, keeping a close eye on the house until Frisbee arrived.

When he arrived, he quickly assessed the situation and enlisted the aid of two patrolmen and a portable battering ram to break down the front door.

They were met with a scene out of a horror movie.

John Rayburn and Melissa Friend were hanging from the ceiling of the open foyer, their nude, broken, and bloodied bodies swaying over the tiled floor like fallen angels.

A small projector displayed images of the tragic crash onto the bare wall directly below the bodies, Black Sabbath's music from *Paranoid* accompanied the looping video. It was the same video and music KDKA released as breaking news, ten minutes before the police broke down Rayburn's door.

###

Carlisle and Frisbee entered the forensics lab as Hua prepped Melissa Friend's body for autopsy. Doctor Karl Williams, Hua's boss, had already begun work on John Rayburn.

Hua began her work with a thorough examination of the deceased's body.

Melissa Friend had already been X-rayed. The films were on screens opposite Hua's.

Before bringing the body to the table, Hua's assistants weighed and measured her. Because Melissa's body had been nude when discovered, clothing protocol for a suspected murder victim could not be followed.

Hua began her investigation by removing the protective bags detectives had placed on Friend's hands. She carefully examined each of the dead woman's fingernails for traces of evidence, separately scraping each nail and preserving the findings.

Hua performed a thorough external examination next.

A certain protocol when performing an autopsy must always be followed. Though considered obvious, there were several things Hua's training and the autopsy protocol demanded before the official cause of death could be recorded.

Hua meticulously explored the remains, taking samples of any matter exuded from the body that might indicate drugs or poisons She took vaginal and rectal swabs to check for semen and performed a thorough examination of the conjunctivae on Friend's eyes for indications of carbon monoxide poisoning.

Utilizing a pre-printed form of the human body, Hua drew the position of all wounds, along with measurements and notes indicating X-ray verifications.

Although Ms. Friend was a petite woman, Hua requested assistance when repositioning the body, to eliminate the possibility of contaminating evidence.

Hua performed the process without conversation. The only sounds were the voices of Doctors Hua and Williams as they recorded their findings and the occasional buzz of a saw.

Hua stepped back from the table as her assistant moved up with a pail of soapy water and sponges. "Do you have any questions while my assistant cleans the body?" she asked.

"It looked like both bodies were cleaned before we got to the crime scene," Carlisle said. "Why do you have to do it again?"

"Just as you go over the evidence at the scene, we want to make certain nothing is missed," answered Hua.

The following step, the dissection of Friend's body using a "Y" incision to open the body cavity, provided Hua with access to Melissa's vital organs.

She carefully removed each organ, weighed it, bagged it, tagged it, and stored it along with other evidential items collected earlier.

Hua sighed as she closed the body and completed her oral report.

Turning off her microphone, she looked at Frisbee. "Are there any questions, Sterling?"

Frisbee looked over at the other table, watching as Doctor Williams finished his autopsy before answering, "If it's just the same with you, Charlotte, I would like to get out of here and meet in one of y'all's wonderful conference rooms to review the findings."

Carlisle and Hua sniggered at Frisbee's obvious discomfort, but after teasing him for a moment, Hua appealed to her boss for help.

Doctor Williams offered to host a meeting in the small conference room attached to his office.

Williams and Hua headed off to their respective locker rooms for a quick shower and a change of clothes.

The detectives grabbed a couple of cups of coffee, quietly taking the stairs to the third-floor conference room.

The room, designed for a maximum capacity of eight people, embodied all the comforts of home. A built-in set of oak floor cabinets with a granite countertop commanded the wall opposite Williams' office. Above the cabinets were a pair of dirty eight-inch television screens with connections for presentations and video conferencing.

Floor-to-ceiling windows lined the outside wall, offering a dark, overcast, and dreary view.

The trio sat in companionable silence, watching as a light misty rain covered the windows.

"Typical Pittsburgh weather," grumbled Frisbee.

"Watch it, southern man," Carlisle quipped. "I've lived here most of my life, and I love it."

"This is screwed up," said Frisbee, changing the subject. "What are these freaks doing? Why did they murder these kids?"

"There may not be clear connections, Sterling," Hua remarked, quietly entering the room, a briefcase in her hand, "This may be a case of the famous six levels of separation. Sorry for interrupting, but I heard you talking as I was coming through the door."

"That's okay, Charlotte," Carlisle said, rising to help Hua remove files from her briefcase. "You are a big part of the investigation and an extremely important member of our team."

"Thanks, Caroline. Doctor Williams won't be joining us, but he made certain I have the Rayburn autopsy. I also have Melissa Friend's autopsy, and the records of the other victims attributed to the Road Rage Killer," Hua said, sitting heavily in the chair opposite Carlisle and Frisbee. "I can tell you the latest two were similar but different from the first two groups."

"What do you mean, Charlotte?" Carlisle asked.

Hua handed a file to each detective and connected her laptop to the video screens. "The files I handed you contain the completed autopsies on the motorcycle accident victims, as well as Rayburn and Friend. Because the previous cases involved murderers mimicking the fatal injuries of the victims of automobile collisions, I hypothesized that latest murder would follow the same pattern. To prove that hypothesis, I set up a computer program which would automatically compare the injuries of the accident victims to those of the murder victims."

"That's amazing, Charlotte," Carlisle said. "Did it work?"

"Like a charm!" Hua said, projecting the files on the screen. "Let's begin with the file on the male accident victim. You will find a long list of broken bones, contusions, and lacerations, beginning with a shattered right clavicle. Do you have that?"

The detectives nodded.

"If you'll look at the spreadsheet I've pulled up on the screen, you can see the same list of injuries, almost identical in scope, for the male murder victim."

Hua clicked to the next page. "This is the comparison between the female accident victim and the female murder victim. As you can see, the injury lists are identical. They match right down to what is commonly referred to as road rash. Jeanine had several patches of skin torn off her body as she tumbled along the pavement. The murderers tore the skin off Friend in almost the exact same areas."

"Why was the skin torn in almost the exact places, Charlotte?" Carlisle asked.

"It was simply a case of size differential. Friend was petite while Hayes was a large woman. That would make it difficult to pinpoint the exact spots on both women. The killers got as close as they could."

"If I remember correctly, the female accident victim's cause of death was listed as severe trauma," Frisbee said.

"Yes," Hua replied. "She was declared DOA at the hospital."

"Can you tell us with any degree of certainty the cause of death for Melissa Friend?" Carlisle asked.

"The cause of death is identical."

"Was she at least drugged, Charlotte?" Carlisle asked.

"Having just completed the autopsies, we don't have any official toxicology results. However, we did make use of innovative mass spectrometry tests recently perfected at Carnegie Mellon University. The tests have allowed us to get a reasonable snapshot of the content of Melissa's lungs, as well as the chemical makeup of her blood at the time of her death.

"That might be very significant," Hua continued, displaying the test results on the screen. "The mass spectrometry shows an extremely high percentage of tubocurarine chloride, otherwise known as curare, in both her lungs and her bloodstream. In a woman the size and weight of Friend, the dosage of curare was strong enough to place her beyond help, perhaps even in a coma, before the murderer went to work on her."

"Could she have already been dead, Charlotte?" Carlisle asked, a note of hope in her voice.

"No, Caroline," Hua answered, softly. "The amount of blood loss and other indicators show her heart was still beating. However, even if she weren't in a coma, the number of toxins in her system would have made it almost impossible for her to have any nerve endings that remained active. I doubt she felt anything."

"What about Rayburn?" Frisbee asked.

"Doctor Williams found the same toxin, at the same levels, in Rayburn. I'm afraid he was alive, and even perhaps semi-alert, when he was attacked. The curare merely rendered him helpless."

"Am I missing something?" Carlisle asked. "On a cursory review of your reports, I haven't been able to find any mention of needle marks. How was the curare administered?"

"You guys are the detectives. You need to figure that out," Hua said with a grin.

"Their house is still sealed. We can start there," Frisbee commented.

"I can get a team there in an hour," Ruiz said as she entered the room. She had watched Doctor Hua's presentation from the hallway. "The curare loosely connects Rosas to this murder, so I can get narcotics personnel on it."

Carlisle smiled at Ruiz and then turned to face Hua. "What about the gloves you found? Will you be able to obtain any information from them?"

"No, the interior of the gloves were washed out with rubbing alcohol."

"The killer is thumbing his nose at us!" Frisbee snarled.

Carlisle's cell phone rang. She left the room to handle the call, but returned quickly, looking bemused.

"That was the boss, Sterling. Your phone is completely off again, and he wants us at his office right after we pick up Decker." Carlisle chuckled.

Frisbee frowned. "Okay, I'll bite. Where the hell is Decker, and why do we have to pick him up?"

"He's in the Allegheny County lock-up. He allegedly broke into Hughes' house, and he's been charged with criminal trespass. The magistrate agreed to release him into our custody."

Chapter Thirty-Two: Decker at the County Jail

A few blocks from the morgue, the Allegheny County Jail is located near Point State Park with a clear view of the Monongahela River.

Its modern architectural style and riverfront location received a great deal of bad press when it was originally constructed. However, following an open house tour of the facility, its opponents concluded no matter how attractive a jail is on the outside it is still a jail inside.

Not pleased to see his former partners when they arrived at the jail, Decker loudly expressed his preference for having anyone else as his legal overseer.

County personnel, obviously fed up with Decker's constant complaining, roughly handcuffed him and escorted him to Frisbee's unmarked police car.

To add insult to injury, the procedure required the cuffs to remain on during his transfer to police headquarters.

Once inside the building, they went directly to the chief's office, finding his mood had not improved.

"Sit," Smith said before the trio had a chance to completely enter the office.

Three straight-backed chairs were lined up in front of Smith's desk.

Decker took the middle chair, bookended by Frisbee and Carlisle.

"I'm going to deal with you first, Decker," growled Smith. "In less than a month, you have managed to tick off two different attorneys, both of whom happen to be close friends of the governor. The first time, it cost you your job. The second time, it landed you in jail. The only reason you are out is because Judge O'Connor and I took pity on you."

Decker began to respond, but a glare from the chief silenced him.

"In case you were wondering why this former paragon of the sheriff's department was languishing in our county jail," Smith said to his detectives, "he was caught inside the front door of the Upper St. Clair home of William Hughes. He was in the possession of illegal recording equipment, taping a private conversation between Hughes, Mr. and Mrs. Hayes, and Tupaz."

"What could you have possibly been thinking?" asked Carlisle.

"Carlisle, I'm telling you, those people are dirty," Decker said. "Hayes and Hughes are related. I heard them talking about it! And you know what? Hughes paid for the test tube baby the Daugherty girl was carrying when she died. You think his family died first, but it started long before that, back when his parents were killed. He and Burns hate each other—"

"Decker," Smith roared, interrupting Decker's tirade. "Your days on this team are way past over! Your theories and observations are not welcome!"

"A PFA has been filed against you by Hughes, Best Nursing, *and* Tupaz," continued Smith. "If you knowingly approach within one hundred yards their residences, their person, or any employee of Best Nursing, your bond will be immediately revoked, and you will be returned to the county lockup. This time in the general population!"

A knock came at the door, followed by the chief's barked, "Enter!"

Much to the surprise of everyone but Chief Smith, Deputy Nelson slowly opened the door.

"Judge O'Connor agreed, as a personal favor, to place you in my custody," snarled Smith. "He feels the same way as I do about cops who have gone sour. He wanted to put you in some damp dark cell so he would never have to see your crooked butt again. I managed to convince him that you weren't corrupt, just stupid.

"Your old boss and I have agreed, until this case is over, or at least until after your hearings, you will be accompanied by an officer of the court, beginning with Deputy Nelson. Now, get the hell out of my office," Smith concluded.

Decker wordlessly left the room, accompanied by Nelson.

At the last moment, Nelson turned to the room, saluted smartly, and closed the door behind him.

Smith smiled, Frisbee grinned, and Carlisle began to chuckle.

After a quiet moment, all three broke out in laughter.

Not at Decker's expense, nor at Nelson's, but as a release of the tension that had been building for weeks.

"What are we doing about the press?" Frisbee asked, still giggling.

"I was so physically and mentally drained after the last press conference I went straight home and didn't return to work for three days," replied Smith. "The commissioner decided it would be best if I no longer participated in press conferences, and if I don't have to be a part of that circus, neither do you. Considering this morning's broadcast, we should be extremely grateful."

"I'm not sure what you mean, chief," Carlisle said. "What broadcast?"

"Channel Two ran a film clip of the accident even before you had a chance to enter the victim's property. It contained all the accident information beginning with Rayburn exiting the Fort Pitt Tunnel, tailgating the motorcycles. It was immediately picked up by the national news services. Pittsburgh is, once again, known throughout the world, and not in a good way." Smith groaned.

"The video was delivered to the TV station by a local company. We have detectives searching for the delivery person." Smith paused. "Now, tell me what you learned at the morgue."

Frisbee quickly provided a summary of Doctor Hua's reports, concluding with the results of the mass spectrometer. "The presence of curare in the victim's bloodstream indicates Rosas may be connected to these cases, but we aren't exactly certain why. Ruiz arranged for narcotics to search the Rayburn residence. We hope to find a method of delivery for the curare. They will also be looking for any traces of drugs in the home or the vehicles."

"That is, if Monica Chang will let you near Rayburns's possessions," Smith said.

Carlisle snapped her fingers. "Thanks for the other connection, chief!"

Dumbfounded, Smith and Frisbee stared at Carlisle, waiting for an explanation.

"Attorneys! The other connection is attorneys," Carlisle exclaimed. "All of the murder victims were connected to Burns or his law firm!"

Chapter Thirty-Three: Road Rage

"The Road Rage Video (Rayburn Version)," as the media titled the video of the fated newlywed's collision with the stockbroker, had gone from major media to YouTube, to worldwide viewing in a matter of a few hours.

Pittsburgh, as Smith said, was famous again, but for all the wrong reasons.

KDKA News had somehow managed to obtain copies of the videos found in the first two crime scenes. Despite knowing the potentially harmful impact the recordings would have on the public, the videos became the focus of several special reports.

At first, Pittsburgh commuters reacted positively to the reports. They were extremely angry at the blatant disregard for basic safety concerns and the driving considerations of Pittsburgh drivers. At the same time, they became courteous, thoughtful, cautious, defensive, and safe.

Unfortunately, most of them quickly returned to their normal driving habits shortly thereafter. Aggressive tailgating, speeding, abrupt lane changes, and texting while driving once again became regular driving habits for those behind the wheel of a vehicle in Pittsburgh.

Some drivers, believing the occupant of the vehicle in the next lane might be the Road Rage Killer, pulled over to allow aggressive drivers to pass. Other drivers cut off speeders, spiked their brakes to catch tailgaters, and chased down other vehicles for imagined offenses.

Many drivers armed themselves, turning Pittsburgh's freeways into a war zone.

During a ten-day period, over forty incidents of handguns being brandished following a motor vehicle accident were reported. A dozen of those incidents resulted in a firearm being discharged.

Five resulted in fatalities.

The worst incident began in heavy traffic. Traffic was moving surprisingly well on I-279 during the Monday morning rush hour. A long line of cars, SUVs, vans, and tractor-trailers were flying along the freeway at an average speed of seventy-five miles an hour, with approximately ten feet between each vehicle.

Traveling too close to each other to see the new detours near the I-579 split, as well as the gridlock the freeway's configuration created for inbound travelers, the speedsters precipitated an incident that would capture the world's attention.

Commuters on I-279, blissfully unaware of the traffic tie-ups ahead, suddenly found themselves faced with a solid line of unmoving traffic.

Carl Wall, reviewing notes for a 10:00 a.m. meeting, led a pack of SUVs and German luxury cars speeding toward the bottleneck.

His attention was diverted; he didn't see the traffic jam, until far too late to avoid a collision.

He hit his brakes two seconds before plowing his Toyota RAV 4 into the vehicular barricade.

When Carl hit his brakes, the Audi tailgating him plowed into his Toyota.

A Mercedes Sedan, a Cadillac Escalade, A Jeep Wrangler, a Ford pickup, and a Lexus Convertible all joined the pile-up before the collisions ended.

Carl remained behind the wheel of his SUV, uninjured and furious, watching the other drivers involved in the pile-up as they exited their damaged vehicles to exchange insurance information and argue about responsibility.

Carl felt a dark cloud pass over his soul. His eyes turned black with hatred.

Muttering obscenities, he reached into a duffle bag on his rear seat, pulling out a purchase he had recently made for his gun collection, an AK-74 assault rifle and four extra magazines.

Stepping out of his SUV with the rifle locked and loaded, he aimed his fury at the drivers involved in the crash.

Once he felt satisfied they had been properly dealt with, he began taking potshots at other vehicles caught in the gridlock.

Police shut down the freeway and evacuated survivors.

SWAT teams formed an armed circle around the gunman and began a standoff lasting more than six hours.

Sitting in Frisbee's darkened office, brooding over their stalled investigation, the detectives didn't notice phones ringing on desks throughout HQ, or the sudden activity on police radios. Frisbee and Carlisle watched as several heavily armed officers rushed past.

Her reverie broken, Carlisle called out, "What's going on?" to a group of uniformed officers running by.

"Road Rage!" they replied in unison.

Wall ended the standoff by turning his rifle on himself. No one was going to take him alive.

Chapter Thirty-Four: Franky Tells a Story

As time passed, and his physical condition improved, Hughes' contract with Best Medical naturally expired. Although he wasn't psychologically prepared for the transition, his overnight nurse was completely cancelled, and his daytime nurse's schedule was revised to "as needed."

Joan Best personally thanked Tina for a job well done, rewarded her with a cash bonus, and gave her a week off with pay.

In celebration, Tina joined Jordan, Franky, and a few of their friends at their favorite club. One of the reasons it was so popular was the fact it was within walking distance of Tina's house.

Franky dressed for the club in his non-work uniform of black jeans, a long-sleeved black shirt, a long black cape, and black motorcycle boots.

His face was powdered deathly white, offset by black lipstick, black eye shadow, and black nail polish.

He added an other-worldly feeling to the bar, and he worked it with his storytelling.

With the Carl Wall tragedy fresh in everyone's mind, Franky looked sternly at his growing audience of bar patrons and began his tale. "I have chosen to tell a sad story of the foolish consequences of one woman's road rage. I had the dubious pleasure of overhearing a young woman report on the incident to the police while Jordan and I attempted to save the life of her mother."

Tina shut off her phone's ringer to keep from interrupting Franky's tale and placed it face down on the table.

"According to the victim's daughter," Franky began, "she and her mother were sitting in traffic at the Oakland exit off the Parkway East when a dude in a Toyota Corolla flew down the shoulder and cut in front of them without using signals. He weaved in and out of traffic and cut them off again a few minutes later.

"Mom laid on the horn, but the Toyota dude just flipped her the bird. That really made her angry. She got right up on his bumper and stayed on the Toyota guy's butt, honking her horn, until he swung into a parking lot and entered a corner restaurant.

"Mom headed for home. On the way, she called her son and told him she had been assaulted. She asked him to get her gun out of the closet and meet her in the driveway."

Franky paused for a sip of beer and a chorus of, "You gotta be kidding me!" from his audience.

"When Mom got home," Franky continued, "she wanted to drop Sissy off, but the girl hopped in the back seat, refusing to leave.

"With Junior riding shotgun and Sissy in the back, Mom hurried to the spot where she had last seen the Toyota. As luck would have it, the Toyota dude was just getting back in his car when Mom arrived. She slowed down, allowing the Toyota dude to pull out, resuming her horn-honking and tailgating until he flipped her off again. At the next stoplight, Junior came out of the car with this big ol' pistol and started screaming about respect.

"Sissy told me her mother believed that was going to be the end of it. They would scare some rude jerk and go home. They never imagined the Toyota dude would come out of his car with a bigger pistol!

"Junior nearly wet his pants!" Franky chuckled. "He wasn't ready for a gunfight. He jumped back into Mom's car, yelling at her to take off.

"Now, it was mom's turn to be chased around. Junior and Sissy kept their heads down while Mom drove around Oakland's one-way streets until she thought she lost the Toyota dude. But he was just hanging back.

"When Mom pulled into her driveway, the Toyota dude pulled right up behind her. He got out of his car, shot her three times, shot Junior twice, pulled out of the driveway, and hauled his butt out of there!"

The entire bar fell silent, except for Tina's buzzing cell phone.

She shut it off without looking at it.

Franky faced his audience with a hint of sadness in his eyes. "Sissy finally had enough sense to call 9-1-1. Jordan and I rolled when the 9-1-1 call went out, but we were too late. Both Mom and Junior were dead before we could get there."

"Did they catch the Toyota dude?" a member of the audience asked.

"In all the action and turmoil, Sissy never thought to get the license number of the Toyota," Franky said, sadly, shaking his head.

The gang at the bar fell silent, many staring at Franky, waiting for more.

"Funny thing happened to the Toyota dude after the shooting," Jordan said, joining in from his seat next to Franky. "He was so freaked out he sideswiped two parked cars. The owner of one of the cars wrote down his plate number and called 9-1-1. The Toyota dude was picked up in less than an hour."

Tina's phone buzzed again. Franky's story completed, she felt compelled to check her caller ID. She was shocked to see the call had come from Bill.

Checking her recent call history, she discovered there had been four other calls from him during the past hour.

Tina rushed outside to return Bill's call.

"Bill," Tina said as soon as he picked up. "Is everything okay?"

"No!" Hughes shouted in reply. "The night nurse never showed up. I'm here all alone."

"Bill, there is no night nurse. We discussed this last week. You've reached and surpassed all the rehab plateaus set for you. That requires a change in care."

"I remember talking about it; I don't remember agreeing to it," Bill said.

"It's in the contract you set up with Best Health," Tina patiently responded.

"I want to change the contract. I still need twenty-four-hour medical attention."

Tina sighed, "Bill, I suggest we meet with Joan tomorrow and see about setting up another contract. Your doctor will have to agree to the need for care, or your insurance won't cover it. It should only take a few days."

Not mollified, Hughes cried, "Tina! I am not talking about someone for next week! My heart is racing now!"

"Please, relax, Bill," said Tina quietly. "I'll be there shortly. We can set up a meeting with Joan tomorrow."

"Please, hurry," Bill urgently requested.

Tina returned to the bar to say goodbye.

An angry Jordan stopped her just inside the entrance. "What are you doing, Tupaz?" he demanded.

"There is a slight emergency at work. I need to go take care of it."

"This is your day off, Tina," Jordan said, stepping between Tina and the exit. "Can't you call someone else to take care of it? You're the boss, Tina. Delegate a little."

"This is my job, Jordy. I didn't become a nurse to call someone else when a patient needs help," Tina said, attempting to side-step Jordan.

He grabbed her tightly by the arm. "You're going to see Hughes, aren't you?" Jordan snarled.

"What has gotten into you, Jordy? You're hurting me! Let go!" Tina screamed.

Jordan released Tina's arm but continued to block the exit. "The first time we get together in weeks, and you go running off to be with some geezer old enough to be your father. I saw you duck into the alley to talk to him! Why are you doing this? Hughes is not only too old for you, but he's also out of your league! He just sees you as some little piece of ass to hold him over until he—"

Jordan had more to say, but the slap Tina landed squarely across his face cut him short.

"How dare you?" Tina shouted. "You have no right to say those things to me! You are not my friend, Jordan Best! If you were, you would know that I would never act inappropriately with one of my patients! I never want to see you again!"

Caught off guard by Tina's intensity, Jordan stepped aside.

Tina rushed to the exit, pausing in the doorway for a parting shot. "Do *not* follow me, call me, text me, Facebook me, or even snail mail me! If you try to contact me in any way, I will have protection from abuse filed against you so fast your head will spin! The man you just accused me of screwing is a very powerful attorney, so I may just take your license, too!"

Tina ran most of the way home.

Hurt, angry, and smelling of sweat, alcohol, and old bars, she decided to catch her breath and take a quick shower before driving to Bill's house.

Remembering a prescription for a low dosage of Lorazepam Bill had been prescribed for anxiety, Tina called him and advised him to take a dose of the sedative.

After a refreshing shower, a change of clothes, and fresh makeup, Tina felt ready to go. She called Bill to update him, relieved when he said the Lorazepam worked.

On the drive to her patient, Tina mentally replayed her fight with Jordan. She thought he'd been drinking a lot lately, but that didn't excuse his rudeness. She also came up with hundreds of retorts that would have made the argument better, or at least made her side of it better.

Tina parked on the street in front of Bill's house.

Looking around at the pristine neighborhood, she had a gut feeling something wasn't right.

Shrugging it off to the lateness of the hour, and a backlash from the fight with Jordan, she strolled unsteadily to the front door, her uneasiness growing with each step.

Tina nervously looked over her shoulder, her keys in hand, ready to unlock the front door and rush inside.

Reaching the entry, she lightly touched the door.

It swung open freely.

Taking a deep breath, Tina switched her grip to the can of pepper spray hanging from her keychain. She steeled her nerves, her hand holding the canister of Mace rock steady as she inched past the open door into total darkness.

Hoping Bill had turned off the lights and forgotten to lock the door after the Lorazepam took effect, Tina reached for the row of light switches just inside the door.

Activating all the controls at once, expecting the house to light up, Tina became frightened when only the two overhead lights in the foyer came on.

The overheads provided enough light to show the living room in a shamble, appearing to be ransacked.

Tina, her heart beating in her chest like a big bass drum, stepped completely into the foyer and called Bill's name.

Taking tentative steps deeper into the house, she reached into her pocket, pulled out her cell phone, and prepared to dial 9-1-1. She stopped when she sensed movement coming from the darkened living room.

Tina moved slowly. She took several steps in the direction of the living room, appraising the carnage in the once-immaculate home.

Placing one foot in front of the other, she moved to the center of the room.

She finally realized the movement that distracted her turned out to be Bill's head sticking out one end of a rolled-up Persian rug.

"What are you doing, Bill?" Tina exclaimed.

Hughes looked at her, frantically mumbling through duct tape covering his mouth, swinging his head around, his eyes wide in terror.

"I can't understand what you're saying with this tape over your mouth," Tina said, ripping off his gag.

"Ouch!" Bill hissed. "They may still be in the house, Tina! Get outside and wait for the police!"

"Are the police on the way?" Tina whispered in reply.

"Didn't you call them?" Bill asked, incredulously.

"No, I wasn't sure if you trashed the house in a fit of rage. I didn't want to get you in trouble."

"When have you ever seen me in a fit of rage?" Bill hissed, clearly aggravated.

"You didn't sound all that clear-minded earlier, and you are not winning any congeniality prizes right now, mister!"

"Tina! I am wrapped in this rug, and the jerks who did this may still be in my house! Will you please call 9-1-1?" Bill asked, clearly panicking.

Tina sat on the rug to make the call.

As she began giving the operator her location, as well as the state of the emergency, a series of gunshots rang out from behind the house!

Tina screamed and ducked behind the roll of carpet before reporting the new developments to the 9-1-1 operator.

The violent crime rate for Upper Saint Claire is 95.25% lower than the national average.

When the police dispatcher announces *Shots Fired* as part of the radio broadcast, the Upper Saint Clair (USC) police department jumps.

The first USC patrol car arrived on the scene less than four minutes after Tina called 9-1-1, with an emergency medical services ambulance directly behind it.

They found Tina stretched out on the living room floor, resting her head and shoulders on the rolled-up rug containing Bill.

Paramedics went to work immediately. They extracted Bill from his cocoon while Tina watched, making certain no extra damage occurred as her patient was unraveled from the expensive rug.

Bill and Tina were then escorted out of the house and across the street to an ambulance.

They sat together on the back of the emergency vehicle, covered with a scratchy blanket, arms entwined.

Lieutenant Ruiz arrived moments later.

Taking command of the incident, she ordered a thorough search and conducted a brief interview with Bill and Tina.

Bill had been hit from behind. Briefly knocked unconscious, he never caught sight of his assailants. When he came to, he found himself wrapped up in the carpet on the living room floor. He could hear someone trashing the rooms upstairs.

Tina made a much briefer statement, having arrived on the scene in time to call 9-1-1.

Bill made a lame joke about Tina continuously rescuing him.

Ruiz did not find it amusing.

The police searched the interior of the residence, looking in every closet, crevice, and corner.

Every room in the house had been ransacked, but the perpetrators were gone.

Once the police declared the house cleared of hazards, Ruiz allowed Bill and Tina to return to the living room, cautioning them to remain there until the local police completed a search of the grounds and gave them the all-clear.

Laid out in search grids of twenty-foot squares loosely marked with caution tape, a meticulous examination using K-9 units and klieg lights covered every inch of Bill's property, beginning with the front of the house and moving along the cordoned-off squares to the rear retaining wall.

Bill watched the progress of the search from the overstuffed cushions of his sofa.

Tina slept fitfully beside him, her head resting on his shoulder.

During the third hour of the search, a county police officer found the body of Aloysius Decker stuffed under the ornamental bridge spanning the fishpond.

As is customary, the police handled Decker's murder as if he were still an active member of the police force.

The vast, far-reaching, and terribly long arms of the law were stretched out to locate the person, or persons, responsible.

Chapter Thirty-Five: Edgar Snyderman

Route 28 winds along the north bank of the Allegheny River from rural Armstrong County to downtown Pittsburgh. Along the way, drivers pass through dilapidated "villages" whose sole reason for existence ended with the passing of the steel mills and the death of the coal industry.

Shells of abandoned steel mills turned to rust in otherwise vacant lots.

Edgar Snyderman traveled Route 28 on his way to Pittsburgh in his baby, a blue 1965 Corvette he purchased in mint condition at an antique car show in Florida.

He drove the car only on days when the weather forecast predicted clear, sunny skies, and never during rush hour.

Snyderman's mind wasn't on the feel of the Corvette as it purred along the highway. His thoughts were of his firm's future. He founded the law firm of Snyderman, Gould & Allen with the dream of running a prestigious law firm.

Gould and Allen struck out on their own after a few years, taking many of their clients, and Snyderman's dreams, along with them. High overhead costs, along with a few failed cases, left Snyderman in need of quick cash to keep his firm afloat.

In stepped Alfonso Rosas.

Because of the legal pitfalls of his industry, Rosas had a great deal of money he couldn't spend without the income tax agencies of several nations noticing.

He desperately needed financial representation.

He paid Snyderman's overdue bills, convincing him to bring Moe Greene and Francis Connelly in as full partners.

Green and Connelly were accompanied by several established clients. Some were friends of Rosas, and others were legitimate businessmen.

Snyderman's firm grew. He eventually added his son, Carl, as a full partner while keeping his association with Rosas secret.

He stored the records of every transaction his firm negotiated for the Nicaraguan.

Preparing to retire, and wanting to shake the skeletons from his closet, Snyderman contacted the FBI, agreeing to provide the feds with his files concerning the drug kingpin.

After negotiating a deal that would keep his firm afloat, he scheduled a meeting with his legitimate partners and the FBI. He intended to confess his relationship with Rosas and provide the feds with enough information to bury the cartel.

Driving his Corvette for what might be the last time, he mentally rehearsed the speech he planned for the meeting before handing his laptop with the encrypted Rosas files to the FBI and surrendering himself to federal custody.

As the city neared, Snyderman guided his Corvette across the Highland Park Bridge.

In typical Pittsburgh fashion, a Cadillac Escalade followed too closely behind him.

On the loop leading off the Bridge to Washington Boulevard, the Escalade accelerated, catching the much lighter Corvette on the right rear bumper.

Snyderman spun out of control, his car turning 180 degrees before it stalled.

The Escalade slammed into the front of the Corvette, pushing the smaller vehicle until all four wheels were off the road.

The driver of the Escalade opened his door and calmly stepped onto the roadway. He was a dark, muscular man, dressed in jeans and a tight white T-shirt. He wore mirrored sunglasses and a plain black baseball cap pulled low over his eyes. His arms were covered in tattoos. He carried a large automatic pistol.

The stranger stood in front of the Corvette, his muscles rippling as he removed a photograph from his T-shirt pocket, compared it to the face of the old attorney, and fired three rounds into Edgar Snyderman's head.

He calmly walked to the passenger door of the Corvette and removed Snyderman's briefcase and computer bag.

Seemingly as an afterthought, he tossed the photograph in Snyderman's lap. Then, he returned to his vehicle and drove away.

Chapter Thirty-Six: The Snyderman Case

Carlisle, denied permission to join the investigation into Decker's murder because of her personal history with him, received permission from Chief Smith to take three days off to deal with any psychological fallout.

She made it until noon on the first day.

No longer able to handle not being part of the investigation, she jumped into her Jeep and drove to headquarters.

She watched from the doorway to his office as Frisbee pounded away at his computer keyboard, answered his desk phone, switched to his cell, and frantically scribbled something on a notepad.

"You're going to blow a gasket, Sterling," she said, stepping inside the office.

"Caroline! When did you get here?" Frisbee drawled before returning to his task.

Reaching across the desk, Carlisle placed a hand on Frisbee's forearm, interrupting him. "Wait just one minute there, partner," she said in a poor imitation of Frisbee.

"Decker's murder has all of us worked up, but you aren't going to be any good to anyone if you end up going to the hospital with exhaustion."

"Wait, what?" That was Frisbee's usual answer when confused.

"You're working too hard on the Decker case!"

"I'm sorry, Caroline; apparently you haven't heard. I was never on the Decker case. They think I'm too close to…Well, you know. There was another shooting this morning. I'm working on that case."

"Why are you working on a shooting? Aren't they usually handled by uniforms?"

"Yes, but this is a special incident. It landed on Ruiz's desk right after the victim was identified, a white male named Edgar Snyderman. Since Ruiz caught the Decker shooting, I thought I would help her out with Snyderman."

"Edgar Snyderman," Carlisle said. "Isn't he the senior partner of Hughes' law firm?"

"Was, Caroline. Snyderman is the victim of a homicide. That wouldn't necessarily mean anything, but a witness saw a large man calmly walk over to Snyderman with a pistol and execute him."

Carlisle made a scoffing sound. "What makes the witness think it was an execution?"

Frisbee shared the witness's cell phone video of the shooting.

"Wow! Everybody's a filmmaker these days! Any idea what kind of pistol was used?"

"Not yet. The shooting took place at the Highland Park Loop. Uniforms closed it down to search the area but came up empty. Traffic tie-ups have been legendary. Doctor Hua is rushing the autopsy, so I'd better get to the morgue. Since you didn't take the day off, you want to join me?"

Noticing a look of abject terror on Carlisle's face, Frisbee quickly added, "Relax, Caroline, he won't be there. They sent Decker over to the Butler County ME."

"Do you know who is heading up the investigation?" Carlisle asked as they left the office. "I thought it would be you and hoped you would let me help find the creeps who killed him."

Frisbee took hold of Carlisle by both arms, saying, "Listen to me, Caroline! I've got two things I want to make perfectly clear. One, I know how hard it is to lose a partner and a close friend to some whack job, but the case has been assigned to personnel who have never been in contact with Decker. Even Ruiz has been pulled off.

"Two, you are in no way responsible for Decker's death. There was a PFA filed against him, prohibiting him from being within 100 yards of the Hughes residence. Ah don't know what he was doing, but his violation of the PFA cost him his life.

"Three, you are my partner now. We need to work together as a team, so as difficult as that may be, and as heartless as this may sound, someone else is handling the investigation into Decker's murder. We have a series of our own crimes to solve."

Carlisle sighed, "You said you had two things to tell me, but you told me three. Does that mean I can ignore one?"

"What?"

"You started what was probably the longest speech I ever heard from you, with 'I've got two things I want to make perfectly clear. Then, you went on to state three things. I just want to know if I can ignore one of the things you made perfectly clear?"

"What? No!" said Frisbee, confusion evident in his answer.

Carlisle couldn't keep herself from laughing. "You're probably right, Sterling. If we solve our end of this thing, we'll find Decker's killers."

She stood on her toes and kissed Frisbee on the cheek. "Thanks for looking out for me. I love you, too."

"What the hell? Don't do that!" Frisbee said to Carlisle's retreating form.

Already in the autopsy theater when the detectives arrived at the morgue, Doctor Hua looked up from her work as they entered the suite.

"Good afternoon," Hua called out cheerily as the two detectives entered her domain. "I haven't seen much of you lately, Sterling."

"I apologize, Charlotte." Frisbee replied, sheepishly. "I've been preoccupied."

"I assume this is Snyderman?" Carlisle asked, glancing at the body of an elderly man on the autopsy table.

"Yes, he's been identified as Edgar Snyderman, an eighty-three-year-old Caucasian male. The cause of death was listed as three gunshot wounds to the head. The shooter used a nine-millimeter handgun with copper jacketed rounds at close range. Ten feet, perhaps less. The first round created a fatal wound. The additional two shots were superfluous. All three rounds exited the back of the skull. As you can see, the damage was extensive."

Frisbee looked at the corpse, and then his eyes fixed on an object somewhere over Hua's left shoulder.

"Was there anything significant about the gunshot wounds?" Carlisle asked.

"The type of weapon used isn't unique. I checked the forensic databases and found a dozen reported murders in the US using similar weapons."

"Thanks, Charlotte," Carlisle said. "Anything of interest?"

"Snyderman had stage four stomach cancer metastasizing to other organs. I doubt he would have lived another six months."

Before Hua could continue, Doctor Williams entered the room, accompanied by two assistants pushing a loaded gurney.

The assistants moved a body bag from the gurney to an operating table.

"Doctor Williams?" said Hua, surprised. "I thought you were teaching a seminar today."

Recognition crossed Williams's face. He smiled.

"Charlotte!" he exclaimed. "I've never been so glad to see anyone in my life! I received a call from Commissioner Diulius concerning a body found in Highland Park. She wanted an autopsy performed immediately. I knew you were busy, so I came down here as soon as the body arrived. Do you think you can perform another autopsy?"

"I am always glad to help, sir, but why is this so important?"

"You've been working; you probably haven't heard the news. A dash-cam video of the shooting of Edgar Snyderman was delivered to the media, along with the location of another victim," answered Williams.

Ruiz glided into the room behind him. "I was on my way to join you when Chief Smith called, asking me to check on our latest victim," Ruiz said, indicating the body bag on the gurney. "When I arrived at the address in Highland Park, *so* conveniently provided to the media, I noticed the victim's prominently displayed Quetzalcoatl tattoo."

"Doctor Williams seems to have skedaddled," Frisbee said, watching the doors close behind the department head.

"Skedaddled? What kind of hillbilly talk is that?" Hua asked as she approached the body bag.

Carlisle giggled behind her mask.

Thank you for your patience," Hua told the lab assistants waiting next to the table. "Please remove the victim from the body bag. Take extra care in examining the bag to make certain nothing is left behind."

After the assistants removed the corpse from the body bag, they swabbed out the container for body fluids and bone fragments. They sealed the swabs in specially marked containers, processing them as evidence, along with the bag.

Hua carefully examined the victim's clothing before removing and sealing it. She meticulously swabbed his fingernails for any traces of evidence, adding the swabs to the growing pile of sealed forensic evidence.

Hua began a detailed examination of the victim, recording any abnormalities, identifying marks, or visible injuries.

Carlisle and Ruiz scanned the tattoos covering most of the victim's body.

Along with several jailhouse tattoos, the victim sported a prominent Quetzalcoatl tattoo on his chest.

Protocol demanded Hua perform an autopsy—complete with Y-incision, removal, and weighing of the victim's organs, as well as the collection of fluid, skin, and hair samples—even though a foregone conclusion of multiple gunshot wounds would be determined as the cause of death.

Hua left the "grunt" work to her assistants, quickly completing her part of the autopsy.

She nodded at Frisbee as she began removing her surgical mask, releasing him to head outside for a breath of dirty air.

Twenty minutes later, refreshed from her shower, smelling like fresh roses and armed with her laptop, Hua joined the team in Doctor Williams' conference room.

Without preamble, she sauntered to the middle of the room, plugged her laptop into the system, and activated the screens on the far wall. Hua smiled.

"While I showered and Sterling stepped outside, my assistants compiled a comparison of our most recent victim's gunshot wounds with the gunshot wounds suffered by attorney

Snyderman. A Glock G40, loaded with steel-jacketed nine-millimeter rounds, was found at the scene of the second shooting, pointing to the same weapon being used in both murders."

Hua changed slides to show a graphic of the entry wounds of both victims, side by side, with a measuring device showing the distance between each wound. "As you can see, the gunshot wound patterns are similar. Snyderman's wounds appear to be a little rougher and less well-patterned than the second victim's wounds, which may indicate Snyderman was moving when he was shot. The victim of the second murder was not. Snyderman was shot from ten to twenty feet. The second shooter was close enough to leave powder burns around the entry wounds."

"Why wouldn't an obvious stone-cold killer not defend himself from a gunman, especially one who is targeting him with his own gun?" Ruiz asked.

"Thank you, Mel, for that six-million-dollar question," Hua replied.

"Don't humor her, or we'll be here all day," Frisbee said, in a sotto voice.

"Really, Sterling. If there is no participation from the police in these discussions, how would we even know you are awake?" Hua said with a smile.

"There could only be two reasons why he didn't defend himself against his attacker. One: he was already dead, or two: he was unconscious. As you can see," Hua continued, flipping through crime scene photos as she spoke, "the amount of blood present at the scene indicates the victim was alive when shot, which brings us to the other reason he would not defend himself. He was unconscious. Since curare has reared its ugly head throughout this series of cases, I decided to use the mass spectrometer we borrowed from Carnegie Mellon."

Hua changed slides to show the results of the mass spectrometry test, indicating an extremely high concentration of curare in the most recent victim.

"I believe this tells us the killer was afraid of the victim," Frisbee said, interrupting Hua's monologue. "If I am interpreting the test results correctly, not only did they give him enough curare to be certain he was completely disabled, but they also injected enough to make sure it would kill him, just in case they failed to do the job themselves."

"Wait a minute! You went over the body with a fine-toothed comb and didn't find any evidence of an injection site," said Carlisle. "How did they poison him?"

"I'm glad you asked, Caroline," Hua replied. "I had Holly go over the body with a higher magnification setting on the equipment. She found two injection sites lost within the victim's tattoos. Ironically, one of the sites was in the Quetzalcoatl tattoo on his chest."

"Finally, we have this," Hua said, pulling up a video. "This is a copy of the dash-cam video sent to the Channel Two news team, showing Snyderman's execution."

Hua started the video, pausing, rewinding, and stopping the reproduction to properly show the murder, leaving no doubt who killed Snyderman. The question remained: Why did it only show Snyderman's execution?

Chapter Thirty-Seven: Theories

The detectives encountered a large crowd of protestors in front of headquarters. They detoured to the rear entrance of the building, hurrying straight to Smith's office.

They found the chief standing at his window, watching the crowd gathered on the street below, his back to the open door of his office.

Frisbee, followed by Ruiz and Carlisle, quietly entered the office and sat facing the desk.

When Carlisle cleared her throat, Smith turned to acknowledge the sound, seemingly startled to find people in his office.

"Frisbee, Carlisle, Ruiz! I had no idea you had returned from the morgue. I've been expecting your report, and I have some unfortunate information for you in return," Smith said, slowly moving to his desk.

"Are you feeling okay, chief?" asked Frisbee. "We can always come back at another time."

"No, no, no!" Smith said, sitting behind his desk. "I need your most recent reports."

"Yes, sir," Frisbee said, feeling concerned. "Carlisle and I followed up with Doctor Hua on her autopsy of an eighty-three-year-old white male. Shortly after our discussion began, another body was brought in, a thirty-something Hispanic male. Both men were killed by multiple gunshot wounds to the head. The unidentified Hispanic male has tattoos designating membership in Rosas's cartel. Preliminary findings indicate both men were shot with the same weapon. Hua has strong evidence showing the use of curare in the murder of the Hispanic male."

"Although there are similarities to the other murders, there are also some glaring differences," said Ruiz. "The video was just a dashcam; it didn't have multiple views, and it was a premeditated murder, not an accident."

"Thank you, lieutenant," Smith said, taking a deep breath before continuing. "A body found floating in the Ohio River has been tentatively identified as the man who delivered the original video to the TV station. The subsequent deliveries have been by snail mail. The delivery lead is another dead end."

Smith sighed. "As you know, the FBI took control of the investigation into Decker's murder almost as soon as the body was discovered. The feds believed we might mishandle the case due to the close relationship we all had with him. I'm not certain that is the real reason."

Moving almost in slow motion, Smith withdrew two manila folders from a locked desk drawer. Both folders had the word *CLASSIFIED* stamped on their covers in big red letters.

Indicating the top folder, Smith said, "This contains the findings from Decker's autopsy, performed at Forbes General Hospital in Monroeville by an unnamed FBI forensic pathologist."

"Isn't that unusual, chief?" Carlisle asked. "Won't we need the identity of the pathologist for future subpoenas?"

"Yes, it is odd," Smith agreed.

"The good news is our mystery pathologist was as thorough as Charlotte Hua," Smith continued. "The pathologist's report indicates Decker received four nine-millimeter gunshot wounds to the upper torso. He bled to death shortly afterward."

Smith paused briefly, looking at the folder in his hands. "Evidence discovered by the team investigating Decker's death indicates he was shot while standing on the flagstone porch attached to the rear of the house. He was transported to the fishpond and thrown into the water. After dumping Decker's body in the fishpond, the killers attempted to clean the blood from the flagstones, but the arrival of law enforcement caused them to leave the task incomplete."

"Any idea what Decker was doing on the property?" Ruiz asked.

Smith shook his head. "After Decker had been caught trespassing on Hughes' property, Hughes agreed to permit Decker's release on his own recognizance with the stipulation Decker be remanded to the custody of the police. To bolster the condition, Hughes obtained a PFA ordering Decker to remain at a distance of at least 100 yards from his residence.

"Deputy Nelson was assigned as Decker's first babysitter, followed by a series of junior patrolmen. The federal agents compiling this report believe the patrolmen did not check on Decker, leaving him free to return to the Hughes residence.

"An FBI electronics team discovered several listening devices during a targeted search of Hughes' house. The feds believe Decker planted the bugs before his arrest and returned to retrieve them, only to encounter someone else searching the house."

"Were the nine-millimeter rounds steel jacketed?" Carlisle asked.

Smith glanced at the report before answering. "It appears they were, Carlisle. Is there something you aren't telling me?"

"We may have the weapon used in Decker's murder. I believe ballistics tests will show it's the same gun used to kill Snyderman," said Frisbee.

"Get me the gun," said Smith, before changing the subject. "Information recovered from Decker's computer provides some interesting reading. Decker believed Tupaz and Hughes were behind the accident that killed Hughes' family. Decker's theory was Hughes and Tupaz were having an affair and wanted to get Mrs. Hughes out of the way.

"Decker was obsessed with Hughes. He was certain Hughes killed his parents for insurance money and planned a repeat performance with his wife. The plan backfired, catching Hughes and his children in the crossfire."

Frisbee scoffed. "Decker tried that 'theory' on us weeks ago. It didn't make sense then, and it doesn't make sense now. Why would Hughes put himself in such a dangerous position?"

"Why would he murder the Burns family and the other victims?" Ruiz added.

"Why have the killings been so violent?" asked Carlisle.

Smith shrugged. "Decker believed Hughes didn't want his children harmed, making the Burns murders an act of revenge. Decker also believed the other victims were signs Hughes was clearing out witnesses."

A young narcotics officer entered the room, handed Ruiz a folder, and exited without uttering a single word.

Frisbee looked at Ruiz, frowning in disapproval.

"They speak when they have something important to tell me," Ruiz answered Frisbee's unasked question.

"What did your assistant bring you?" Carlisle asked.

Ruiz scanned the contents of the file and smiled. "It seems our most recent victim was a very well-known and popular man."

Reading from the report, Ruiz said, "According to Interpol, the deceased was known as Jesus Garcia, a native of Cuba, and is listed as a suspect in at least six murders in Europe over the past ten years. CODUS processed the victim's DNA and determined he was a hired murderer from Colombia known as Pablo Ortiz. Ortiz is a suspect in eight murders in South America. The DEA and FBI have files on him that list ten aliases.

"His weapon of choice is a Glock G40, using steel jacketed nine-millimeter rounds. The same type of weapon I believe we will find was used to kill Decker, Snyderman, and Ortiz. The DEA has been watching Ortiz for several years due to his connection with various drug cartels.

Earlier today, Hua pointed out Ortiz's extensive body art, concentrating on the Quetzalcoatl tattoo on his chest."

Ruiz took a deep breath and looked around the room. "One of my contacts in Langley believes Snyderman has been in Rosas's pocket for years, but recently turned state's evidence in an FBI money-laundering investigation. The laptop removed from his possession when he was murdered held evidence that could cost Rosas millions."

"I guess that indicates Ortiz as the person who searched Hughes' house," said Carlisle. "When he didn't find any evidence of Snyderman's case against Rosas, he intended to ask Hughes about it but ran into Decker instead."

Smith's desk phone loudly rang.

"Aren't you going to answer it?" Carlisle asked.

"No," Smith replied, "It's the commissioner demanding I join her at a news conference."

"I thought she said you didn't have to attend news conferences after what happened last time," Carlisle said.

"She changed her mind." Smith's cell phone rang.

He gingerly answered the phone, listened for a moment in silence, muttered, "Yes, ma'am," dropped the phone in his pocket, and walked out of the room.

Frisbee watched as Smith disappeared.

He snatched the folders off Smith's desk, bolting out of the office.

He practically ran down the hall, looking into conference rooms as he passed them. Finding an empty conference room with a television set, he tuned in to Channel Two and made himself comfortable.

"What the hell just happened?" Ruiz asked, following Frisbee.

"Commissioner Diulius just happened," Carlisle answered with a chuckle. "Men, especially big bad powerful men, can't handle having an authoritative woman as a boss. It freaks them out and makes them act like idiots. The last time Malcolm Smith joined a press conference, he was out of commission for a week, but Diulius says she wants him at the microphone, and he hops like a stupid frog."

"As funny as that may be, we have to stop these clowns before they kill anyone else, and we can't wait for Smith to recover from his latest public speaking breakdown," Ruiz said.

"I agree, Mel," Carlisle replied.

The detectives quickly collected coffee, soft drinks, and questionable sandwiches from vending machines.

Munching on an ancient chicken salad sandwich, Frisbee led the detectives quickly back to the small conference room, determined to watch the televised press conference.

Carlisle reached over to the pile of folders Frisbee had taken from Smith's office, picking out the *CLASSIFIED* file housing Decker's reports.

She lifted the folder so her partners could clearly see the red stamp on its cover. "I doubt we were authorized to remove this file from the chief's office, but since we have, I think we should read it."

"Hold that thought, Caroline," Ruiz answered. "The mayor is stepping onto the stage."

Frisbee and Ruiz listened closely as the politicians spun the stalled murder investigation into something more positive. Smith stood at the edge of the stage, next to the commissioner.

"I wonder why they asked the chief to stand next to the commissioner," Frisbee said. "She looks like a midget."

"Smith doesn't look so good," Ruiz added. "If he faints from stage fright and falls in the commissioner's direction, the result could be disastrous."

While her partners watched television and made jokes, Carlisle lost herself in Decker's report.

At the press conference, the mayor ran out of pontifications and left the podium.

The mayor was followed by Commissioner Diulius, who made a statement praising the police department and turned to Smith for a wrap-up.

Smith read a short, prepared speech touching on the known facts of the investigation. He spoke of the possibility of a "person of interest" in the murders, whose identity could not be released at this time. He brought his statement to a close, told the gathered reporters he would not be answering questions, turned, and bolted from the podium.

Frisbee shut off the television, chuckling as he turned to his companions. "What a zoo! We probably won't see the chief for a week."

He noticed Carlisle with the files in front of her, furiously taking notes.

"What's up, Caroline?" Ruiz asked.

"I'm sorry, guys," Carlisle said. "I got bored waiting for the press conference to begin and started reading Decker's reports. I think he may have been on to something."

"You're kidding!" Frisbee exclaimed. "Hughes couldn't have committed the murders!"

"I'm not saying he did," Carlisle replied. "I'm saying Decker had some good ideas, and it's not at all what you're thinking."

Carlisle paused, "I apologize for not listening to what Chief Smith had to say. Did he hint at any suspects?"

Ruiz shrugged. "Not really."

"Good. That will give us a little more time before the real murderers feel the heat," Carlisle said, smiling.

Her partners looked at her strangely.

"It's all here in the reports," Carlisle continued, obviously enjoying her friends' confusion. "Of course, it helps if you have the information we've collected, too."

"Are you going to tell us what you're talking about, or do I have to kick your ass?" Frisbee said, half rising from his chair.

Ruiz and Carlisle laughed.

"Sit down, Sterling," Ruiz said. "Don't make Caroline embarrass you."

"Okay, but she has to tell us what the hell she is talking about because Hughes and Tupaz are simply not the killers," Frisbee said, wisely sitting down.

"I agree with you. I think we can find some answers, or at least some direction, by looking at what we've got right here," Carlisle said, indicating the pile of reports on the table.

"The media is ready to crucify the entire Pittsburgh police force if we don't come up with answers, soon," Ruiz said, looking at Frisbee.

"You ready to hear what I found?" Carlisle asked, patiently.

Reluctantly, Frisbee agreed.

"Decker first started to suspect Tupaz when she broke regulations to get next to Hughes at the hospital. His suspicions were doubled when Hughes employed Tupaz at his home."

Frisbee rolled his eyes. "How does Hughes hiring someone make them a suspect in the murder of his wife and kids?"

"According to Decker's notes, that was about the time he started to suspect Hughes and the nurse were in cahoots," replied Carlisle.

"You can tell someone has been hanging around Sterling too long when they start using words like cahoots," Ruiz said with a laugh. "Seriously, though, didn't we already determine neither Hughes nor Tupaz knew about the assignment before the time the nurse showed up at the door?"

"Right," Frisbee said. "We've already checked on that. The only person who knew Tupaz was going to work as head of Hughes' recovery team was Joan Best."

"Decker was privy to that information, but it didn't stop him from proceeding with his investigation," Carlisle said. "He was obsessed with Hughes and Tupaz and couldn't see any other possible suspects for the murders. Following the murders of the Burns family, he looked to Hughes as the likely suspect. The fact Mrs. Hughes was on a committee with Burns sealed Decker's suspicions. He started pursuing the possibility of an affair between Burns and Mrs. Hughes as a motive for both sets of murders."

"Was there an affair between Burns and Mrs. Hughes?" Ruiz asked, incredulously.

"No," Carlisle answered, "In fact, Veronica Hughes despised Burns and made no secret of it. Next came the Sharp/Daugherty Incident. When Sharpe was arrested for the Daugherty incident, his attorney turned out to be a member of Burns' law firm, and witnesses recanted their statements. The executions of Sharpe and Garcia, along with Sharpe's colleagues, added a new twist."

"I'm still not buying Decker's theory Hughes almost died trying to hide his affair with a nurse he never met," Frisbee said.

"Sterling," Carlisle sighed, "Patience, please, dear. I am simply trying to follow Decker's thought processes so we can determine what was driving him."

"Insanity," muttered Frisbee.

"Thank you, Sterling." Carlisle giggled. "Shall we proceed? Decker expanded his theory to include Burns as a second suspect, deciding the Hughes/Tupaz love affair didn't begin until after Hughes' accident. He concentrated his investigation on Hughes with the idea of finding the evidence to nail Burns would follow. Fate strengthened his resolve when shortly after the Sharpe murders Decker found a direct, close, personal connection between Hughes and the Daugherty couple."

"If I remember correctly, there was a connection between Hughes and each of the accident victims," Ruiz said, looking through the other files on the table. "There were also connections to Burns in all the cases."

"That's right, Mel! The icing on the cake, as far as Decker was concerned, was the relationship between Hayes and Hughes. Decker's illegal actions notwithstanding, he learned quite a bit by eavesdropping on Hughes."

"You're right, Caroline; Decker may have been onto something with Hughes and Tupaz," Ruiz said.

"Not you, too, Mel," moaned Frisbee. "I'm telling you, there is no way Hughes killed his family on that freeway. If Tupaz hadn't come along when she did, he would have died. No one would plan a murder with such a slim chance of survival."

"I agree on that point, Sterling," Carlisle said. "Decker did, too. He suggested Hughes set up the murder of the Burns family as an act of revenge."

"That's right!" Ruiz chimed in. "Then, Burns retaliated by having his boy, Sharpe, run the Daugherty couple off the road."

"How do you explain the tanker?"

"Sharpe was a drunken idiot," both women said at the same time.

"Who killed Sharpe?" Frisbee asked.

"Hughes couldn't have physically committed any of the murders," Ruiz said. "He was still wheelchair-bound for most of them and was incapacitated when Decker was shot."

"He could have hired Ortiz for the murders then popped Ortiz off in the end," Carlisle said, softly.

"We know Ortiz murdered Snyderman, and probably Decker. That would mean he was working against Hughes. Who took out Ortiz?" Frisbee asked.

"Tupaz killed Ortiz," Carlisle answered, emphatically.

"How did she get close enough to an experienced hitman to administer the curare?" Frisbee argued.

"Come on, Sterling," Ruiz said emphatically. "Have you looked at her? She could get close to anyone."

"Does proving Ortiz killed Snyderman mean he killed the Jarquins, too?" Frisbee asked Ruiz.

"I'm not certain, Sterling," answered Ruiz. "Even though we know Rosas sent a special killer to Pittsburgh to clean up his mess, I plan on hanging around until we find out who the Road Rage Killers are, and I think there are more than one. That might be the only way we find out who killed the Jarquins."

"I have to tell y'all something," said Frisbee, looking at the floor. "An old acquaintance from my hometown is in Pittsburgh. He believes the ghost of a Confederate colonel talks to him. He showed up at the Zone Four Station, looking for me, on the Saturday morning of the Daugherty accident. He became violent when officers approached him, and he was placed under arrest. He claimed I was his cousin, so the desk sergeant called me. They held him until I arrived.

"His name is Teddy Taylor. He isn't really my cousin, but my family looked after him because he seemed a little off. The Zone Four guys couldn't just let him go. They sent him to Western Psyche for a three-day observation, allowing me to drive him to the facility because we were 'kin.' On the way to the hospital, Teddy told me the Colonel sent him to warn me. He told me the only way we will be able to stop the *sorgina* is by waking a *mangkukulam*. I Googled the terms," muttered Frisbee. "A *sorgina* is a Basque witch. *Mangkukulam* is a Filipino witch with healing powers.

"First thing tomorrow morning, I'm going to send a patrol car to the Burns residence, and another to the Hughes residence. I'll ask the uniformed officers to politely request they join us for a brief interview. I'll have a unit pick up Miss Tupaz, as well, but I don't plan on asking her if she is a *mangkukulam*." Frisbee smiled.

Chapter Thirty-Eight: Burns Breaks

Burns arrived first, accompanied by Monica Chang.

He loudly proclaimed his intention of suing the City of Pittsburgh for police harassment.

They were quickly escorted to an interview room where Burns could continue his rant undisturbed.

Frisbee learned Tina assigned herself as Hughes' nursing contact in residence until a new nursing contract could be written up.

He requested Hughes and Tupaz arrive at the station separately, but they had other plans, causing repeated delays in their arrival.

Frisbee found himself forced to question Burns before he wanted to.

Frisbee asked Ruiz to join him in the interview room while Carlisle watched the proceedings from behind the one-way mirror in the observation room.

Chang nodded at Ruiz and Frisbee as they entered the room, nudging a daydreaming Burns to pay attention, like a parent waking a child up in church.

Burns suddenly opened his eyes. They immediately locked onto the beautiful Latina detective, following her every move like two guided missiles.

"Good morning, Mister Burns, Ms. Chang," Frisbee said, "Allow me to introduce Lieutenant Carmella Ruiz."

"Hey, Frisbee," Burns said. "Is this your new partner? She's even hotter than your little blonde!"

"I thought you were here to keep your client from making any mistakes, Ms. Chang," Frisbee said. "I believe he may have already angered Lieutenant Ruiz."

"I can advise him against conflicting with legal procedures, Sterling, but I can't stop him from being a pig," Chang replied.

"My client has generously given his time, only to be forced to sit in this dungeon waiting for you to saunter in at your leisure, Frisbee." Chang's tone of voice sounded evil all of a sudden. "Shall we proceed? Mister Burns and I have other appointments."

"We have asked your client to join us today so he can help clear up some questions we have surrounding the murders of his family, Ms. Chang," Lieutenant Ruiz said in the sweetest voice Frisbee had ever heard.

"It's about time somebody did something about the creeps who killed my boys!" Burns said. "Ask away!"

"Mister Burns," Ruiz continued, "we want to get to the bottom of this as much as you, but we need your help."

Burns appeared to be completely captivated by Ruiz. "Are you a local cop, Lieutenant Ruiz?" he asked with poorly concealed lust. "I only ask because I don't remember our paths having crossed before, and I would certainly remember you."

"I'm with the narcotics department, Mister Burns," Ruiz answered, her tone of voice moving from temptress to hard-nosed cop. "One of your clients has recently come to our attention."

Chang snapped alert at the change in Ruiz's tone. "My client is not prepared to discuss any interactions or conversations he may or may not have had with clients, nor is he required to do so. It is something known as an attorney-client privilege. They might not have heard of it in narcotics, but I think homicide is familiar with the concept. Isn't that right, Sterling?" she asked, facing Frisbee.

Frisbee leaned over the table, laying a pile of crime scene photographs in front of Burns. "The people represented in these photographs are all victims of the same murders. You may recognize some of them. Their demise makes their attorney-client privilege null and void."

As he spoke, Frisbee pulled photos out of the pile, beginning with the pictures of the Jarquins, followed by photos of the road rage victims, until two rows of photographs faced Burns and Chang.

"What are you trying to do, Sterling?" asked Chang. "The attorney-client privilege only ends when the attorney or client says so, the temperature of the client notwithstanding."

Ignoring Chang, Frisbee continued, "Do you recognize any of the people in these photographs, Mister Burns?"

Burns looked toward Chang, who nodded slightly, her way of indicating permission to answer the question. "Yeah, detective, I recognize those two guys," Burns said, indicating Guillermo and Raul Jarquin.

"Why do you recognize the Jarquins, Mister Burns?" asked Ruiz.

"Who are you talking about, sweetheart?" Burns replied.

"The two men you indicated are Guillermo and Raul Jarquin," Ruiz said. "What is your relationship with them?"

"Guillermo was working for me when he was murdered. I met Raul years ago in connection with a case, but when I knew them, they went by Escobar," Burns said directly to Ruiz. "You should come work for me, too. All the killing is over; you would be safe."

"Why do you say the killing is over, Mister Burns?" Frisbee asked, his adrenalin pumping.

Before Burns could answer, Chang placed a perfectly manicured hand on his forearm. "That was simply a figure of speech, Sterling," she purred. "My client can't possibly know for certain the murders connected to this so-called Road Rage Killer have ended. He is expressing his heartfelt hope they are."

"Thank you, Ms. Chang," Frisbee said. "Raul Jarquin was arrested several times, in several different jurisdictions, for sexual assault, battery, and rape. It is a matter of record, Mister Burns, you personally represented him in several of those cases. Raul is also a known member of the Rosas crime family. What is your connection with Rosas?"

Chang bolted to her feet, snarling as she rose. "You just crossed a line, detective! We are here to assist in an investigation, not to be harassed! If you have something you wish to charge my client with, then do so! We will not be answering that question." Chang said the last statement in a calm tone of voice.

"We have all been under a great deal of stress, Mister Burns," Ruiz said, sweetly. "I'm certain the detective just worded his question incorrectly. Are you familiar with the name Alfonso Rosas?"

"Of course."

"Were you aware both of the Jarquins were in his employ?"

"I suspected Raul may have worked for one of the cartels before he came to the US," Burns said before Chang could stop him.

Ruiz leaned forward on the table to seem more like a conspirator, and to allow Burns to stare at her cleavage. "What about Guillermo? The DEA has evidence that suggests he was also on Rosas's payroll. Were you aware of that?"

Once again, Chang tried to intervene before Burns could answer, but he blurted out, "Guillermo lived in my carriage house and drove my car when I needed him. What he did in his own time was none of my business."

Chang sat forward and spoke before Ruiz could ask another question. "I think this line of questioning has gotten out of hand," she remarked. "You are clearly on a fishing expedition, Lieutenant Ruiz, and my client is finished."

Chang rose and looked at her boss. "We need to leave now, Mister Burns."

"I would like to personally ask you a couple of questions before you go, Ms. Chang," Frisbee said. "If you don't mind, of course. It will only take a few minutes."

Chang sighed and slowly returned to her seat. "What do you want, Sterling?"

Frisbee separated the photo of Harold Sharpe from the lineup on the table. "Do you recognize this man?"

"He looks familiar, but I can't readily place him."

"That's odd, Ms. Chang. Your bio says you remember everything you see. The photograph is of a man named Harold Sharpe. You represented him during his arraignment for a hit-and-run accident that caused several deaths." Frisbee paused to look Chang in the eyes. "Do you remember him now?"

"As I said, Sterling, I can't readily place him," Chang said, sweetly.

Frisbee separated the photograph of John Rayburn from the pile. "What about this man, Ms. Chang? Do you recognize him?"

"No, I do not."

Frisbee blew out a frustrated puff of air.

"Ms. Chang, both these men were clients of yours." Frisbee looked Chang directly in her beautiful eyes. He felt faint.

"You represented both of them for the first time shortly after they were involved in fatal motor vehicle accidents. Each one was suspected of causing the deaths of innocent people. Both men were brutally murdered after you arranged for their release from police custody," continued Frisbee without breaking contact.

"What exactly are you insinuating, detective?" Chang asked, sweetly. "Do you have any idea how many indigents, drunks, and reckless drivers Burns and Gallo represent every year? How am I supposed to remember them all? Hell, I try to forget them!"

Chang casually inspected her fingernails, irritating Frisbee further.

He stood and snarled in frustration, "I would think the ones who were murdered shortly after you represented them would stick in your mind!"

"Sterling, I work for a multi-million-dollar law firm. I never see the bills, and I have no idea who the clients are. This interview is *so* over!"

Chang headed for the door.

"Wait!" Burns said, still seated at the table. "Just wait!"

The formerly powerful attorney slouched in his chair, resting his head in his hands. "What about my boys?" he said, quietly. "Are you going to find the animals who did this to my boys?"

"That's what we're trying to do, Mister Burns," Ruiz answered.

"Then, why are you treating us like suspects? I'm a victim!" Burns started to weep. "I lost my whole family! They were murdered in my garage, and you have the nerve to treat me like

I had something to do with it. I know I wasn't father-of-the-year material, but I loved my children! I would never have done anything to hurt them!"

Burns laid his head on the table, silently weeping.

Chang asked for a moment alone with her client.

Frisbee and Ruiz stepped quietly into the hall.

Less than a minute later, Burns headed to the men's room.

Chang remained behind, standing in the doorway of the interview room.

"He falls apart like that several times a week," Chang said to Frisbee. "He can't work. The other attorneys have been picking up his slack, but I don't know how long that'll continue. There's talk about a leave of absence or even a forced retirement. That's a long fall for a man who was so vital just a few weeks ago."

"I'm sorry, Monica. I didn't know," Frisbee said.

"He's been trying to keep it a secret. I didn't want him to come here today, but he insisted."

Chang looked appraisingly at Ruiz. "The way Burns was ogling you, I thought the old pig was going to come back, but even you weren't enough to make him forget what's happened.

"My client had nothing to do with any of the murders, Sterling. You need to keep looking." She smiled, placing a hand gently on Frisbee's arm.

Chang straightened her back, blew a kiss toward the mirror, said, "Bye, Caroline," and left the room.

Tupaz and Hughes arrived moments after Burns exited the building.

They were accompanied by an attorney Frisbee didn't recognize.

Frisbee planned to separate Hughes and Tupaz with Ruiz interviewing Hughes while Frisbee interviewed Tupaz in another room.

His plan depended on Mel's outstanding charms melting Hughes' heart.

Unfortunately, the uniformed officer in charge of the detail assigned to pick up Hughes stood in the middle of the hallway, blocking Ruiz and Frisbee's access to the interview rooms. He had information that would spoil Frisbee's plans.

"Thank you for getting this all ready, sarge," Frisbee said. "Were there any problems?"

"Problems, Frisbee? Let me tell you about problems!" replied the officer, angrily. "When I arrived at Hughes' house to pick him up, the female was already there, almost like they knew we were coming. Hughes advised me Ms. Tupaz would not require a ride."

Frisbee frowned, "I don't understand; I thought the delay was due to you needing to provide Ms. Tupaz with transportation."

"We waited, Frisbee, but not to give her, or Mister Hughes, a ride. Hughes asked us to wait inside the foyer, by the front door, until their attorney arrived. He said he was concerned for Ms. Tupaz's safety and was making a formal request for protection."

"Did something unusual happen?" Ruiz asked.

"That's just it, ma'am. Nothing happened. We sat there; nobody talked, and nobody moved. Hughes and Tupaz were reading books, so occasionally a page would turn.

"About fifteen minutes later, a limousine pulled up with a guy in a suit riding in the back. Hughes let him in the house, and they went into the living room to join Tupaz and whisper to each other.

"After they finished whispering, Hughes asked me to make certain it was safe for them to move to the limo. Once they reached the vehicle and the attorney and female were inside, Hughes asked me to provide a police escort to the station."

"What nerve!" exclaimed Ruiz. "Did you tell him to go to hell?"

"Not in so many words, ma'am, but I did express my concern my boss wouldn't approve. Hughes very politely said he understood and called Commissioner Diulius on her private phone. I was given direct orders to provide an escort. Once we arrived, we attempted to separate them, but Hughes shook his head and pointed to his phone. I escorted them to room one."

"Everyone is settled in," Carlisle said, walking briskly from the observation room to join the small group. "Hughes is reading something on his iPad. Tupaz is huddled up with an attorney, speaking in tones too low for the microphones to pick up."

"Why has Hughes been permitted to keep an iPad in an interview room?" asked Frisbee.

"The officer accompanying him tried to take it away, but when Hughes held up his cell phone, the officer backed off," Carlisle replied.

"I see," Frisbee said. He took a deep breath. "Let's go to work!"

Ruiz, armed with a file full of photographs, left Frisbee behind to thank the officer.

Overflowing with confidence, she strode into the interview room like a wild west gunfighter striding into the O.K. Corral.

Hughes jumped to his feet the moment Ruiz entered the room, effectively ruining her confidence.

"Separating Nurse Tupaz and me to gain the infamous 'tit for tat' confessions failed, Lieutenant Ruiz," Bill announced, calmly. "In addition, Nurse Tupaz has been instructed she is under no legal obligation to answer questions. My associate has accompanied us to make certain nothing untoward happens and no false claims are made."

"If you have no intention of answering our questions, why are you here?" Ruiz asked.

"To prove to you we have nothing to hide. I want you to find the people responsible for the murders. Badgering innocent people like me, Nurse Tupaz, and even Burns is a waste of precious time."

"As an attorney, you of all people should see the need for cooperation," said Ruiz.

Hughes sat, leaning his back against the wall. "I'll answer your questions, but Nurse Tupaz is completely innocent and will not be cooperating with you."

Ruiz sighed. "What do you suggest we do, Mister Hughes?"

"Now, we're getting somewhere, Lieutenant Ruiz," Bill said, slapping the table. "Make requests for our assistance; don't use force to try to make us do things."

Ruiz leaned back in her chair. "Okay, I get the point. I'm going to ask you once more: What can we do to gain your cooperation?"

"Nurse Tupaz is innocent of any crimes, as am I. We will answer your questions, but we'll do so as a team, not as suspects."

"If we are working as a team, Mister Hughes, then why do you need a lawyer?"

"Excellent question, Lieutenant Ruiz. You seem to have misunderstood what I said. Nurse Tupaz and I are a team. You, Frisbee, and everyone who attempted to place us in persons of interest status are not part of our team. We do not trust you. That, Lieutenant Ruiz, is why the esteemed Mister Snyderman will be present during our conversations." Hughes beamed, indicating the attorney seated next to Tina.

Frisbee quietly entered the room, taking a seat next to Ruiz.

"Mister Hughes," Frisbee said. "We usually don't permit our guests to dictate our interview process, but I have received communications from Commissioner Diulius, asking me to cooperate fully with your demands."

"I apologize for going over your head, Detective Frisbee. I didn't want you wasting your time on us when you could be out looking for the real killers."

"That is the sign of a true citizen, Mister Hughes," Frisbee said with a smile as he leaned across the table and whispered. "I want you to know I was on your side when Decker started going after you, but now you've made me angry. If you are even remotely connected to these murders, I will destroy you."

"Please, sit down, detective," Snyderman said. "I am making note of the threat you just made to my client. Any more such threats and I will advise my clients to leave."

"I have one last request before we continue," Bill said.

"What would that be, Mister Hughes?" Frisbee asked, incredulous.

"I would like the young lady behind the mirror to join us. If you feel you need backup in the observation room, you can borrow one of the homicide detectives I passed on the way in."

Frisbee sank his face in his hands and shook his head.

Moments later, Carlisle walked in the door, a stack of folders in her arms.

She plopped down in the last seat at the small table.

"I'm so glad you could join us, Caroline. I'm Bill, and this is Tina. Of course, you already knew that."

"Why don't we get things started? What exactly did you want to talk about, Sterling? May I call you Sterling?" asked Hughes.

"No, you may not," Frisbee fumed. "How the hell do you know so much about us?"

"Detective, what kind of an attorney would I be if I didn't thoroughly research my opponents?"

"Y'all consider the police your opponents?" Frisbee drawled. "Let me tell you something, Hughes…"

"Stop! Please, Stop!" Carlisle shouted, interrupting Frisbee's rant. She stood and leaned over the table. "Our time will be better served if we spend it sharing ideas and information rather than being engaged in some pissing contest!"

"Thank you, Caroline," added Ruiz. "Assuming you are telling us the truth. Mister Hughes, you are simply another victim of those killers. If you and Ms. Tupaz are here to provide information, then we need to work together. Let's start with some simple questions. Mister Hughes, you had some type of a connection to every one of the Road Rage accident victims, correct?"

"It appears so, Lieutenant Ruiz," Hughes answered, brightly. "We can't be certain there were no earlier incidents, but as far as anyone knows, the original Road Rage retaliation murders took place after the deaths of my immediate family. My connections to the Daughertys are slightly more distant. Katie Daugherty's mother was my late wife's cousin. My wife and I donated the money to help Katie and her husband achieve their dream of parenthood."

Taking a deep breath before continuing, Hughes said, "A family tree study indicates Mister Hayes could be my distant cousin. I am awaiting confirmation."

"The connection with Edgar Snyderman is relatively clear," Frisbee said.

"We were speaking of accidents, detective, not of a brutal, premeditated murder!" blurted Carl Snyderman. "Please, keep your questions in line, sir!"

"Are you okay, Carl? We don't have to stay," Bill said, concerned.

Snyderman shook his head. "I apologize, Bill. I just don't trust them."

Frisbee threw up his hands in disgust, and Ruiz glared.

Carlisle looked directly at Hughes and smiled.

"I think we can trust this one," Bill said. "Can we trust you, Caroline?"

"Yes, sir," replied Carlisle. "We are trying to catch a killer. If you help us, I promise you, we will find him."

Carlisle picked up a file.

Using the folder as a prop, she held it in front of her, asking her questions from memory. "Okay, let's say we agree the connection between you and the last two sets of accident victims was a coincidence. Your connections to the first set of victims most certainly were not. The Burns family was murdered shortly after your motor vehicle accident, intimately involving Burns in our investigation. Can you please explain your relationship with him?"

Snyderman began to speak, but Hughes intervened.

"I'll be glad to answer the question, Carl," he said to Snyderman, never taking his eyes off Carlisle.

"Caroline, I had no relationship with Burns before the accident and have very little to do with him now. I have some communications with his law firm and on rare occasions have spoken privately with Burns himself, but those communications are all legal. For example, I began legal procedures against Burns when I learned his vehicle was involved in the accident that destroyed my life. I ended the procedure when his family was murdered. I didn't have the heart to continue."

"You realize how bad that looks?" Carlisle asked.

"Of course, I do. It looks like I dropped my suit against Burns because I had already exacted my revenge. That pretext is totally absurd. I was still in a wheelchair when those murders occurred. I could not have possibly harmed anyone."

"According to our records, Mister Hughes, you made several financial transactions at the time of the murders," said Carlisle, glancing at the folder as if she were reading from papers. "You sold stock, closed accounts, and transferred large sums of money."

"My wife and children were killed in a major accident. I needed money to pay medical bills, and I closed my wife's accounts. I transferred funds to accounts that were still active. Every penny is accounted for."

Carlisle allowed herself a little smile. "I love working with attorneys," she said, her words dripping with sarcasm. "They always keep me on my toes. I just want to make it clear, you are saying no one in your family had any connection with Burns prior to the accident?"

"My wife and Mrs. Burns volunteered their time for several of the same charities. At least one of those charities held a ball as a fundraiser; others held dinners. Those events required the attendance of spouses. As a result, I spent a few social occasions in the same room as Burns. I may have even shared a few words with him. That hardly qualifies as a relationship."

"But you knew him," Carlisle pressed.

"Sure, I knew him. He's a high-profile defense attorney. He defends wealthy criminals. His firm represents drug runners, dealers, and murderers on the payrolls of drug lords. I kept myself and my family as distant from him as possible."

"Have you met any of his clients?" asked Carlisle as Frisbee and Ruiz sat silently watching the group across the table.

"I would have no reason to meet his clients."

"Mister Hughes, what is your relationship with Alfonso Rosas?"

"I have never met the man, Caroline." Bill held up his hands in mock surrender." I have nothing to hide. Please, have your investigators review my income as far back as they wish. You will find no discrepancies in my finances, no payments from criminal sources."

"I believe you, Mister Hughes. Your cooperation is noted, but unnecessary." Carlisle sighed. "As you are no doubt aware, the FBI named Snyderman Senior as a key player in Rosas's money laundering schemes. Our experts are already digging into your finances."

Hughes had nothing more to say, so Carlisle turned to Tina. "Ms. Tupaz, what is your relationship with Alfonso Rosas?"

Snyderman sprung up from his chair, placing his hand on Tina's arm, signaling her not to speak. "My client is not prepared to answer that question!"

"I have never met Mister Rosas," Tina said, ignoring her attorney.

Snyderman pointed an accusing finger at Carlisle, "That was uncalled for, detective! You pull another stunt like that and we're walking!"

Carlisle smiled sweetly at him, "Lighten up, Atty. Snyderman," she said, "These are friendly proceedings, remember? We're a team."

"Ms. Tupaz," Carlisle continued. "What is your relationship with William Hughes?"

Not sure what they were looking for, Tina huddled with her attorney before answering, "I'm his friend."

"I thought you were his nurse," said Carlisle.

"Look at him, detective," Tina answered, her voice soft and clear. "Does he look like he requires constant care?'

Snyderman pinched Tina's leg. Hard!

"*Ow!* Why did you do that?"

"You are not to say another word," Snyderman growled.

Carlisle lost none of her composure. "Ms. Tupaz, a body recently recovered from the fishpond on the Hughes' property has been identified as Aloysius Decker, a retired police officer you've had extensive contact with. Were you at the Hughes residence when Captain Decker was shot?"

"Decker was a bully. We filed a protection order against him, requiring him to stay at least 100 yards away from the house. I wonder why he just didn't obey the order," Tina said, speaking so softly Carlisle had to lean forward to hear her. "I was on the phone with the 9-1-1 operator when the shots were fired."

"That's right," Bill interrupted "Tina couldn't have shot Decker, but I'll bet the same guy who hit me did."

"Please explain, Mister Hughes," Frisbee said.

"I heard footsteps approaching me from behind. I turned to see someone in a stocking mask swinging at my head."

"Is that why you were acting so paranoid when the officers came to pick you up today?" Frisbee asked.

"I was attacked in my own home, my business partner has been brutally murdered, and a policeman was shot in my backyard. I am not going to take any more chances," Bill replied, absently rubbing the back of his neck.

Carlisle snatched a folder off the table. "According to this report, the FBI hypothesizes Decker was shot on the patio, taken to the far side of the fishpond, and dumped under the bridge."

"They…" Frisbee began, looked at Hughes sitting quietly on the other side of the table, and changed gears. "Mister Hughes, you and Ms. Tupaz are free to go. I don't believe we have any more questions for you today."

Chapter Thirty-Nine: Continued Investigation

When Frisbee arranged for a patrol car to take Hughes and Tina home, he also received clearance from Chief Smith to assign two detectives to watch the Hughes residence.

"Why did you dismiss them, Sterling?" Carlisle demanded as the detectives entered the conference room they commanded at the beginning of the investigation. "I wasn't finished questioning them."

"Yes, you were," Frisbee answered. "Didn't you hear what Hughes said?"

"What are you talking about, Frisbee?" Ruiz asked. "Caroline was doing a fantastic job. She could have gotten a lot more information out of them."

"Like what?"

"We could have looked deeper into their ties to Rosas," Carlisle said.

"They have no ties to Rosas," Frisbee answered. "You determined that during your interview. I believed them. Didn't you?"

"Yes, I guess I did." Carlisle hesitated a moment before continuing. "Burns certainly has connections to Rosas."

"He does, but Hughes has no real connection to Burns, and Tupaz claims she has never met Rosas," Frisbee pointed out.

"What now?" asked Ruiz.

"I'm surprised you asked that, Mel. It's right in front of us. Think about Caroline's reference to Decker's murder."

"What are you getting at, Sterling?" Ruiz asked.

Carlisle answered, "We've been looking for a group of killers seeking revenge for highway deaths, and a second killer connected some way to the Rosas crime family."

"We recently received ballistic reports positively connecting Ortiz to the Decker and Snyderman murders," Frisbee added. "The Road Rage Murders belong to another killer. I believe the Jarquins were also killed by someone other than Ortiz who was sent only to clean up the mess the elder Mr. Snyderman created. If an unconnected perpetrator, a freelance killer for lack of a better term, committed the murders, it changes the whole scope of the investigation."

"We need to review all the evidence, this time looking for the possibility of separate killers?" Carlisle asked.

"Caroline, do you happen to have the Burns file with you?" asked Ruiz, enthusiastically.

"Of course. What would you like to know?"

"Look for anything that would support our theory," Frisbee said. "Mel and I will review the other files, looking for the same thing."

Ruiz opened the Hayes/Rayburn file. "I don't see where it would make sense for Ortiz to kill Rayburn and Friend. Maybe, in an all-out war, he would take out the Burns family, and even the scumbags around Sharpe and Garcia, but Rayburn and Friend had no connection to Rosas."

"Rayburn was connected through Chang," Carlisle said.

"He hired an attorney after he killed someone with his car, Caroline," Ruiz retorted. "How many people hire low-life lawyers to cover their butts after a DUI?"

"We don't know that was his only connection, Mel. We could have overlooked something. I, for one, am going to look at the Burns file from a completely new perspective."

Carlisle moved to the sideboard and poured herself a fresh cup of coffee. "Can I get anything for you while I'm up?"

Ruiz stuck out her tongue while proffering her cup. "Sometimes, you make me gag, Caroline," she said in jest.

"I'll order pizza," Frisbee said. "I think this may take some time."

###

Two hours, two pizzas, and four pots of coffee later, Ruiz lined up several of the Rayburn crime scene photos. "I've been staring at these pictures for half an hour, and I think I found something my people overlooked. I would like you to look at these and tell me if you see something unusual."

Ruiz pulled electronic copies of the pictures up on her laptop, projecting the first of the series onto the monitor.

"These photos show the couple hanging from their foyer ceiling. We've seen these dozens of times, from dozens of angles," said Carlisle.

"We've been concentrating on Rayburn and Friend. Look at the ceiling," Ruiz answered.

"OMG! Hooks! Large hooks!" Carlisle exclaimed.

"I don't understand the significance of plant hooks in the ceiling. We're wasting time on this," muttered Frisbee.

Carlisle took his hand, "Not plant hooks, Sterling. No one would hang plants so far away from a window on hooks large enough to hold an elephant."

Ruiz smiled. "Right you are, Caroline, and if the hooks are connected directly to ceiling joists, they're in a perfect position for hoisting the bodies to the balcony, using a small block and tackle."

"Good work, Mel!" Frisbee exclaimed.

"I can send a CSI team to test the area for residue," Ruiz continued. "Maybe they can come up with clues about the origin of the block and tackle."

"I'm glad one of us is making progress," Frisbee said. "The more I go over the Sharpe file, the more it remains the same. The victims from Sharpe's crew were dosed with curare. I guess a single killer could have murdered them while they were all comatose."

"Caroline, have you discovered anything new?" Ruiz asked.

Carlisle had been texting while reviewing the Burns file. She patiently waited her turn, listening with rapt attention, as her senior partners discussed their findings.

"I'm not sure what it means, but there is a discrepancy in the Burns victims' toxicology reports. According to the results, Rachel Burns and the Burns boys were given large doses of a controlled substance identified as a sort of Valium/Xanax cocktail, effectively rendering the victims helpless. Curare wasn't used on them. I find the difference in MO troubling. Why would the killer use a prescription drug cocktail on the Burns family but use curare on everyone else? I texted Doctor Hua for some details not listed in the autopsy."

Frisbee's eyebrows rose. "What was missing from the report?"

"Don't get your nighty in a knot, Sterling," Carlisle said, grinning. "I'm not dissing your girlfriend. I needed to know if there were significant time differences between the victims' deaths, enough time to account for the different types of nerve blocks. Hua believes Rachel Burns was dead at least three hours before Guillermo was murdered, making our peripheral killer theory plausible."

"She's not my girlfriend," mumbled Frisbee.

After being given a ride home, Hughes and Tupaz remained in the squad car with the doors locked while police officers searched Hughes' house for any sign of intruders.

They were extremely thorough. The sun had set, and darkness surrounded the residence by the time they completed the search and gave an all-clear signal.

Tina turned on the lights as she entered the house, following Bill into the living room, where he stretched out on the overstuffed sofa.

Tina paced the floor, her temper boiling. "I've never been in a police car before. I'm angry and ashamed!"

"You have nothing to be ashamed of, Tina. You've done nothing wrong. The police didn't arrest you; they were only seeking information."

"They suspect me of murder!" Tina screeched. "In less than three months, I've lost my job, embarrassed my friends, and been arrested for murder. They're probably going to deport my entire family next."

"Please, Tina, don't be angry. The situation isn't anywhere near as bad as you're making it out to be. I know, I'm a lawyer."

"You think I need a lawyer?" yelled Tina.

"No, no," Bill desperately replied. "That's not what I meant."

Remembering how he handled situations when his wife or daughter lost control, Bill crossed the room behind Tina, carefully wrapping his arms around her waist, effectively breaking her purposeful stride.

Tina stiffened for a moment. Then, an overwhelming sense of safety coursed through her. She relaxed, resting her head against Bill's chest.

"Tina, I promise you; today's interview will not present a problem," Bill whispered, softly stroking Tina's hair. "I won't let anything happen to you."

"I'm your nurse. I'm supposed to be taking care of you, not the other way around," Tina said with a short laugh.

"You are doing a wonderful job, Nurse Tupaz," Bill replied. "I feel completely healed."

Tina took a deep breath, twisting her small body around until she faced Hughes. Eyes half-closed, her breathing labored, Tina wrapped her arms around his neck.

Bill, breathing a bit raspy, inhaled deeply.

"Oh!" Tina said, her voice hoarse. "Did I hurt you?"

Without answering, Bill bent his head to kiss the beautiful Filipina in his arms.

His kiss, tentative at first, grew more passionate as her welcome response emboldened him.

Bill pulled Tina tight to his chest, stroking her back, his hand inching toward her bottom.

Stopping to come up for air, the couple's eyes met.

Short of breath, ready for another kiss, they began pulling at each other's clothes, both certain what would happen next.

Much to the couple's surprise, something happened, but not what they were expecting.

The patio accessway exploded inward in a shower of glass and debris, leaving a gaping hole where the French doors once stood.

A masked man, wearing a black hooded sweatshirt, emerged through the freshly created hole, carefully stepping over broken glass and debris. He cradled a 6-shot 20 Gauge pump-action Mossberg shotgun.

He slowly threaded his way through the wreckage, loading the shotgun as he walked.

Bill and Tina dropped to the floor, hiding behind an armchair, but they were too late. The gunman moved toward the chair, raising the shotgun to his shoulder, aiming at Hughes' chest.

Tina shut her eyes, prepared for the worst.

The gunman rested his finger on the trigger, but before he could fire, the front door flew open.

The detectives Frisbee had sent to watch the house rushed in, their handguns drawn.

The intruder swung his rifle toward the detectives, squeezing the trigger.

The shotgun shells were loaded with pumpkin balls, round balls of soft lead that spread upon impact. His first round, fired as he turned, missed his target, disintegrating the doorjamb next to the nearest detective's head.

"Freeze! Police! Drop your weapon!" screamed the policemen simultaneously.

The gunman didn't hesitate to give warnings. He pumped in another round and fired, hitting the policeman closest to the door.

The detective's neck exploded as the round made contact, spinning him backward, blood spraying against the wall. Hands instinctively clutching his throat, he tumbled, landing with his head on the carefully fitted tile of the grand entrance, his life running out of his damaged body.

The second detective dove behind the kitchen doorway, blindly returning fire, hoping he would force the gunman to seek temporary cover.

Instead, the gunman rushed to the kitchen, firing three rounds as he ran, blasting plaster and dust into the air, forcing the detective to duck for cover.

The masked intruder rounded the kitchen opening and shot the policeman in the head, blowing his brains and pieces of his skull onto the side of the refrigerator.

Fortunately, the detectives had called for backup before entering Hughes' house.

The wail of approaching sirens told the gunman he didn't have much time to complete his mission.

Turning to dispatch his targets, it took him a moment to orient himself through the smoke and dust created by his gunfight.

Scanning the smoke-filled room, the gunman saw the couple hurrying away.

Tina remembered the master bedroom doubled as a safe room.

Latching onto Bill's hand, she ran them both to safety.

The gunman had time for one clear shot. He stopped, carefully took aim at Hughes' back, and slowly squeezed the trigger.

The hammer clicked on an empty chamber.

Pulling fresh shells out of his pocket, the intruder jammed them into the shotgun's chamber as he purposefully strode across the room.

Bill and Tina disappeared into the master bedroom, punching the button that lowered the plates of steel that covered the doors and the windows.

His targets out of reach, the masked assailant let out a low scream, bolted out of the house, and escaped across the darkened lawn.

Carlisle and Frisbee were at headquarters when they learned of the attack going on at the Hughes residence.

Moments later, they were on their way to Upper Saint Clare, with their siren blaring and lights flashing.

Tina watched from the safe room as the USC police arrived, drew their service weapons, and cautiously moved into the house.

She counted six officers, working together, searching each room, making certain to completely clear the room before moving to the next.

The USC police were still clearing the residence when the detectives arrived from Pittsburgh.

Carlisle brought the unmarked cruiser to a screeching halt in the middle of the street, jumping out of the vehicle in her rush to get to the house.

Frisbee followed closely behind.

Carlisle's first impression of the once beautiful home now saw nothing but its destruction.

At the front doors, she encountered blood splashed against the wall and an enormous hole blown out of the frame. The body of a young detective lay on the Italian marble. Shotgun blasts had shattered the plaster archway leading from the dining room to the kitchen.

In the kitchen, a second detective lay against the refrigerator, a gunshot to the head making his Kevlar vest obsolete.

Ignoring the bodies, the detectives moved purposefully to the master bedroom.

Frisbee looked directly into the camera mounted over the closed door, announcing the house and grounds had been given the all-clear.

Seconds later, Bill gingerly walked out of the room with his hands raised above his head.

Tina trailed a few feet behind.

The USC Police led them to the living room sofa.

A Red Cross volunteer provided them with blankets, and the couple perched on the edge of the divan, full of nervous energy and fear, a full cushion separating them.

Tina watched as Carlisle's line of sight tracked through the living room, past the large hole in the wall where the French doors once stood.

Bill kept darting looks around his ruined home, avoiding looking in the direction of the bodies. His right leg nervously jiggled in place. "It took a disaster cleanup crew an entire day to straighten up the last mess," he muttered. "They'll never be able to fix this." He dropped his head into his hands.

"Hello, Mister Hughes, Ms. Tupaz," Carlisle said, slowly approaching. "I know you've had a horrible experience tonight, and I am the last person on Earth you want to see, but I want to catch this guy before he hurts anyone else. May I have a moment of your time?"

Hughes sat up and shrugged.

"I'll take that as a yes," said Carlisle.

Frisbee snatched two chairs from the dining room, placing them in front of the sofa.

Tina scooted closer to Bill.

They moved closer again when the detectives took seats facing them. By the time Carlisle asked her first question, they were holding hands.

"Mister Hughes, what did you and Ms. Tupaz do after you returned home from our interview this afternoon?"

Hughes looked at Carlisle, his eyes wide with fear.

"By that I mean did you have a reason to visit any rooms in the house other than the living room?" Carlisle asked.

"No," Bill answered. "The patrolmen cleared the house. We moved directly to the living room and settled in."

"Mister Hughes, for everyone's safety, I think it may be wise if we continue this debriefing at the station," Frisbee said.

"I refuse to go back to the police station!" cried Tina, jumping to her feet.

"We cannot go to police headquarters," said Bill. "Unless you are placing us under arrest, I suggest we find somewhere else to continue our conversation. We already planned to move to a hotel room until my home is repaired. Perhaps we can meet there."

The detectives agreed on the condition Bill and Tina leave immediately.

Once the USC police deemed the area safe, the detectives made a beeline to the local Hilton where Bill had booked rooms.

Seated around a Formica-topped table in a well-lit corner of the spacious lobby, Bill spoke first. "I want you to know I booked separate rooms for the night. Tina and I staying in the same hotel may look bad, but she is still very shaken up and didn't want to go home."

"You owe us no explanation," Carlisle answered, turning to Tina. "I understand why you're upset, Nurse Tupaz. You could very well have been killed in tonight's brutal assault."

"Exactly," exclaimed Bill. "That jerk was trying to kill us!"

"He would have succeeded if it hadn't been for those poor detectives," Tina added, quietly.

"Can you start from the beginning and tell us what happened, Mister Hughes?" Carlisle asked.

"Anything you can add will be most helpful, Nurse Tupaz," she said, reaching across the table to lightly rub Tina's arm.

Thankful for the personal touch, Tina smiled for the first time that day.

Hughes recounted the harrowing story of the attack on his home, aided regularly by Tina's addition of details Bill had overlooked or forgotten.

They refrained from telling Frisbee and Carlisle about what transpired between them during the time that passed between their arrival at the house and the intruder exploding through the French doors.

Carlisle led the interview, Frisbee remaining uncharacteristically silent.

He sat in his chair, listening intently until the couple had completely recounted their take of the incident.

"Was there anything you found familiar about the assailant, Ms. Tupaz?" Frisbee asked.

"No, he was dressed in black, with a black hoodie, a black ski mask, and a very big black gun," Tina answered, quietly.

"Ah need to ask you, Mister Hughes, if you were aware of the senior Snyderman's involvement with Rosas," Frisbee stated.

"I had no idea of what Edgar was up to. We didn't share information on clients. It's unethical."

Frisbee let out a long breath. "Ah would like to thank y'all for your time. Please try and get some rest; y'all sorely need it. We'll be in touch with y'all tomorrow." He stood, walking leisurely toward the exit.

Carlisle said her goodnights before joining Frisbee outside the hotel door. "What the hell was that about? I wanted to at least ask a few follow-up questions before sending them off."

Frisbee held up a hand, signaling he wanted Carlisle to wait, infuriating her.

He quietly watched through the glass doors as Hughes and Tupaz boarded the elevator.

"My dear Caroline, we learned quite a bit tonight. Most importantly, the fact the assailant targeted Hughes, taking care not to harm Tupaz, speaks volumes."

"You may be right, Frisbee, but if you ever stick your hand in my face like that again, you will be pulling back a bloody stump," Carlisle growled, heading for the cruiser.

Chapter Forty: Additional Evidence

Quite often, Frisbee began his day before the sun came up. He was pleasantly surprised when he arrived at 7:00 a.m. to find a note from Carlisle stating she and Ruiz began their day early and would like him to meet them in the conference room.

"While the two of you were off babysitting last night," Ruiz began, sarcastically, "I was doing some real detective work. I met with the CSI teams investigating the murders for additional connections."

"What did they find, Mel?" Carlisle asked, her curiosity piqued.

Ruiz grinned, "All in due time, Caroline."

Carlisle huffed.

"Number one: Burns. All three members of the Burns family were heavily sedated, making them relatively easy to manipulate. They were systematically murdered in the winery, moved to the garage using a wheelbarrow, and placed in the Charger. The bodies were carefully positioned to mirror the Hughes accident victims. The wheelbarrow had been thoroughly cleaned and left behind the garage. Thanks to poor police work, it was ignored until yesterday afternoon. The application of Luminal identified the equipment.

"The body found on the premises, and the one located in the dumpster, were both victims of curare overdose, administered via a dart fired from a hunting rifle adapted to that purpose. A search of the chauffer's quarters uncovered an empty rifle case."

"I think that points to two different killers in the same place at about the same time. Jarquin's killer either knew the rifle, darts, and curare were there, or stumbled across them while hiding from the person killing Burns' family. It also explains the variation in times of death for them and the Jarquin murders.

"Number two: Sharpe, Garcia, and the other victims found at the Sharpe residence were dosed with curare prior to being murdered. Pliable, thanks to the poison, the process of murdering the victims became easier. The coroner believes Sharpe and his crew were murdered approximately an hour before the truck was driven into the living room and set afire. The CSI team surmised the van found in the abandoned factory was used to move the bodies to Sharpe's residence but were unable to verify their theory."

"You missed that one, Mel," Carlisle said with a grin.

"Number three: Rayburn and Friend," Ruiz said, ignoring Carlisle. "The team knew what to look for in the townhouse. The industrial-sized hooks were attached to ceiling joists above the open foyer. Both Rayburn and Friend were heavily dosed with curare before being murdered. They were hoisted up to the railings using a block and tackle liberated from the abandoned factory."

"Are you certain about the block and tackle?" Frisbee asked.

Ruiz nodded. "A partially restored pulley system was found among construction debris near the entrance to Rayburn's community. According to the experts at Grainger supply, it was a Gambrel and Pulley Hoist manufactured in 1937 by Campbell Industrial Tools; equipment that was commonly used at the abandoned mill. We think we found where Rayburn and Friend were killed and how they were transferred to their condo."

Carlisle reached across the table and gently pinched her friend's arm. "Give it up, Mel. What else did you discover while Sterling and I were heroically defending our star witnesses from the denizens of evil?"

Ruiz laughed. "There's a workshop near the townhouse, complete with any tool our bad guy would need to bust up a heavily sedated couple before dragging them onto an old golf cart for the drive back to the condo."

"Do you have anything to back that theory, Mel?"

"The tools in the shop, the golf cart, and the shop floor were sprayed with luminal. We have our slaughterhouse. Samples were taken for DNA testing, but it is unlikely any of the evidence belongs to our killer. He was wearing heavy gloves."

"Wait a minute," Carlisle interrupted. "One of the questions we had regarding the Rayburn murders was how the curare got into their systems."

"Great question, Caroline." Ruiz leaned back in her chair and smiled. "A small air pump was discovered in the same junk pile as the pulley. The team reinspected the air-conditioning unit and found evidence of tampering. We need to wait for tests to be completed, but it appears the killer poisoned the couple using their AC system."

"It's a good thing they didn't have any pets," Ruiz concluded with a smile.

"Amazing work, Mel, but it still doesn't lead us to a specific killer," said Frisbee.

"Wait, there's more!" Ruiz exclaimed. "I had a late dinner with your girlfriend. You know, Charlotte Hua."

"She's not my girlfriend," Frisbee said.

Carlisle giggled.

"Whatever! Over dinner, Charlotte told me several things."

Frisbee looked shocked.

"Don't worry, Sterling, we only discussed aspects of the case," Ruiz said with a smile. "Hua told me the cocktail of drugs given to the Burns family victims came from a hospital or pharmacy. It wasn't something a street thug could have gotten his hands on. One final thing. We caught up with Tupaz's brother. He said she left his house several hours earlier than she claimed."

"Why didn't I see this before? Decker was right about Tupaz!" Carlisle exclaimed.

"What are you talking about, Caroline?" asked Frisbee.

"Tupaz has access to the type of gloves and drugs the killer uses, and she's been connected to every one of the murders. I want to talk to her again."

Frisbee rolled his eyes.

"Think about it, Sterling," said Ruiz. "Rosas's empire was in deep doo-doo. The Jarquins were giving up information, and Snyderman was in bed with the FBI. Rosas needed someone to clean things up. Why not Tupaz? She's smart and beautiful enough to fool Hughes into letting his guard down."

"I know we seemed to exonerate Tupaz last night, but she could be playing us. Maybe we need to look a little closer," Carlisle stated.

Frisbee didn't look convinced. "Why the extremely brutal murders?"

"She wanted to send a message!" Carlisle exclaimed.

"We've been looking at the Hughes accident the wrong way," said Ruiz, her enthusiasm rising. "Veronica Hughes worked at the same law firm as her husband. She was the first target because she was working with Snyderman to bury Rosas."

"Why would Tupaz save Hughes at the scene of the accident?" Frisbee asked.

"She needed to find out where Snyderman stored the evidence he had against Rosas," Carlisle explained. "She killed the Jarquins because they were informants."

"Sharpe and Garcia sold drugs for Rosas," Ruiz chimed in. "After the drunken idiot blew up half of Pittsburgh, Rosas had to have them put down before they talked."

"Tupaz's involvement would also explain other questions," Carlisle continued. "We know Snyderman's laptop was taken from his car after Ortiz executed him. The computer is purported to have contained evidence against Rosas. Ortiz showed up in Highland Park at room temperature because the laptop also contained evidence against Tupaz, and Ortiz read it."

"Okay," Frisbee reluctantly agreed, "What about the attack last night? Why would she set that up?"

Carlisle stood, leaning partially over the table to guarantee Frisbee's attention. "Hughes had become suspicious and needed to be eliminated. If the attack is made to appear as if Tupaz were the survivor, she looks innocent, and she walks."

Carlisle sat down and let out her breath.

"I'm sold!" Frisbee said. "Hughes and Tupaz are still in residence at the hotel. I believe we have enough evidence to obtain a warrant to search her house. You can present it to her when you pick her up, Mel."

Hughes had an impressive network of powerful friends, as Frisbee learned firsthand when he approached Judge O'Connor to obtain a search warrant for Tupaz's house.

The judge reluctantly agreed to the warrant after thoroughly reviewing Frisbee's arguments and warning the detective to treat Tina with kid gloves.

Feeling Carlisle had the best rapport with the diminutive nurse, he assigned her to accompany the search team to Tina's home. He asked Ruiz to accompany Tina to headquarters, hoping the narcotics officer would avoid any of the problems the uniformed officers encountered.

Sadly mistaken, he soon learned the difference powerful connections can make.

The first roadblock came in the form of a refusal concerning Tupaz. Hughes would not permit Ruiz to accompany Tina to headquarters and question her without formally charging her with a crime.

Ruiz attempted to throw her considerable police experience at the issue.

Bill called the governor.

Following over an hour of arduous negotiations, they finally agreed on a compromise. Using a privately-owned vehicle, Hughes would deliver Tupaz to headquarters, where she agreed to be interviewed in an open conference room.

"I hate attorneys," Ruiz muttered under her breath as she exited the hotel.

Hughes decided the situation had progressed to the point where Tina needed to be represented by a criminal attorney, not a well-meaning investment lawyer.

He made a call, arranging for a legal representative to meet him at the hotel before proceeding to police headquarters.

Impatient, Ruiz returned to police headquarters to wait for Tupaz.

At the same time, Carlisle returned empty-handed from the search of Tupaz's house.

Tina arrived at headquarters more than an hour late, accompanied by Hughes and her new attorney, Monica Chang.

Carlisle moaned in shock.

"We are here under protest, detective," Chang maliciously intoned before completely entering the room.

She stared directly at Frisbee as she continued. "Nurse Tupaz has agreed to answer only specific questions. All questions will be filtered through her attorneys, as will her answers. If we feel Nurse Tupaz's constitutional rights are being violated at any time, we will promptly end this interview. Do I make myself clear?"

"Detective Sergeant Frisbee is not in charge of this interview, Ms. Chang, I am," said Ruiz, giving the attorney the icy stare she used to intimidate suspects.

It had no effect.

Ruiz sighed, waiting until Tina comfortably seated herself between her attorneys before continuing. "There are quite a few discrepancies between statements given by Ms. Tupaz and crime scene evidence."

"What statements are you referring to, lieutenant?" Chang asked. "I have not been allowed to review the results of previous interviews."

"Your client has not been charged with a crime, Ms. Chang; there have been no formal statements," Carlisle said. "We simply wish to ask a few questions."

Chang leaned closer to Tina, ostensibly to speak to her privately, but whispering loud enough for everyone to hear. "I strongly suggest we make them file charges with what they have, or release you. They have no solid suspects, so they plan on using you as a scapegoat. Pin the crimes on the Asian woman and look good for the press. They would be heroes for bringing in the Road Rage Killer, and to hell with the real murderers."

Chang's tactics were discussed earlier, along with the legal loophole permitting the police to hold Tina for twenty-four hours without a bond hearing.

Tina wasn't happy with Chang looking for chinks in the detective's armor and worried about the possible consequences of Ruiz calling her attorney's bluff, but she respected Chang's talent enough to play along.

Tina sat sphinxlike in her chair, allowing Chang free reign.

Chang stood, clenched fists resting on the table, her contempt almost palpable. "Detective Carlisle, following a vicious assault on my client, you pretended to show concern for the welfare of my client. You even touched her suggestively while attempting to coerce her into a false confession. I demand you recuse yourself from these proceedings."

Carlisle, shocked by Chang's vehement verbal attack, found herself speechless.

Frisbee, new respect forming for Chang's abilities, charged into the breech. "Forget it, Monica. We became aware of certain facts this morning, creating a need for additional information from Ms. Tupaz. Detective Carlisle stays."

Chang sighed, returning to her seat. "Fair enough, lawman. Just remember, Nurse Tupaz will only be answering questions through me. Any violations of this rule, we walk."

Ruiz took a cleansing breath. "My first question, Ms. Tupaz, has to do with your relationship with Alfonso Rosas. How well do you know him?"

Chang stood before Ruiz completed the question. "Really, Lieutenant Ruiz?

"During your last interview with my client, it was made clear she had never met Rosas. If this is how you plan to conduct today's session, we can skip ahead to the harassment charge and go home."

"I'm just reviewing some facts, Ms. Chang," Ruiz said. "Mister Rosas is wanted for questioning in connection to several crimes in the US, but we can't extradite him to stand trial.

We know he uses intelligent, competent people, not on the police radar, to run his various enterprises. Tupaz fits that description."

"We did not come here for lectures," Chang said, beginning to place files in her briefcase. "We can find our way out."

Ignoring Chang, Ruiz continued, "Can you tell me where you were the night of the original accident, Ms. Tupaz? Just to be clear, I'm referring to the accident that took the lives of the Hughes family."

"We spoke to your brother, Ms. Tupaz," Ruiz added. "He told us you left his house almost three hours earlier than you claimed."

Chang quickly wedged herself between Tina and the detectives. "What's this about, Tina? Is it true?"

"Yes," Tina mumbled. "I'd been having an affair with a doctor. He's married. I went to his house to break it off, but his wife was home. I parked down the street and waited until she left. He yelled at me when I knocked on his door. I was so upset I drove in circles before entering the freeway."

"Will he corroborate your story?" Bill asked, quietly.

"I don't know. He's a real jerk," replied Tina, her face red with embarrassment.

Chang patted Tina's hand, smiling. "They all are, sweetheart. Some are just worse than others. It's a good thing you found out when you did. Let me know who he is. I'll make certain he understands it's in his best interest to corroborate your story."

Turning to face the detectives, Chang said. "My client has personal reasons for the discrepancy in time between her departure from her brother's home, and her arrival at the accident, where she heroically saved the life of William Hughes. Her explanation, along with collaboration, will be provided. Please, continue."

Ruiz and Carlisle took turns interrogating Tina, concentrating on the estimated times of the killings and her whereabouts.

Despite the fact she had no concrete alibis for any of the killings, Chang ran a personal blockade against the detectives at every turn.

"Why were you at the Hughes residence the night Captain Decker was killed, Ms. Tupaz?" Carlisle asked.

Chang rolled her eyes in exasperation, "My client has answered this question several times, detective. Hughes called her and asked her for help. You have the phone transcripts."

"We have records stating Hughes placed several calls to Tupaz. We don't know what the actual conversations were, or why Tina left her friends to drive across town," Carlisle continued.

"Bill asked me to help him," Tina said. "He's told you that himself. At first, I refused to drive to his house because his contract with Best Nursing had expired, but I changed my mind. I left my friends after Jordon Best threw a tantrum about my relationship with Bill. I didn't want to be around him anymore."

Chang stood, gathering her papers. "We've had quite enough. Rehashing old testimony for two hours is not my idea of productive police work. It is well past a decent dinnertime. We're leaving." Taking Tina by the arm, Chang escorted her out of the conference room, Bill following closely behind.

Outside headquarters, Tina consulted briefly with her attorneys, making appointments for the following day.

After a few heartfelt thanks from Tina, they each headed off to their respective homes.

Inside headquarters, Carlisle had a fit, pacing and yelling, "Chang is a real ball-buster! We never had a chance!"

"I disagree, Caroline," Frisbee said. "I believe we learned a great deal."

Ruiz stared at Frisbee in disbelief. "We've just completed hours of interrogation, Sterling. It might help if you were a little more specific about what we learned."

"Tupaz mentioned she had a fight with Jordan Best concerning her involvement with Hughes," Frisbee answered. "The fight took place shortly before Decker was murdered."

"We heard her statement, Sterling. What difference does it make?" Carlisle asked.

Ruiz sighed in exasperation. "Do we know if it was a big fight?"

Carlisle rifled through her files. "According to witnesses, the argument was bad enough for Tupaz to strike Best before bolting outside."

"Do we know how long it took Tupaz to walk home from the bar?" Ruiz asked.

"Approximately twenty minutes," Carlisle answered from memory.

"Did she get in her car and drive directly to Upper St. Claire?" asked Frisbee, patiently.

"No," Ruiz answered. "She went inside her house, took a shower, and changed clothes."

Frisbee paused a moment in thought. "Any idea how long it was before she headed for Hughes' house?"

Carlisle and Ruiz traded looks and shrugs.

"At least an hour, maybe an hour and a half," Carlisle said.

"Where did Best park his car that night?" asked Frisbee.

"That's easy," Carlisle said. "Best always parks in the lot behind the bar. He's a close friend of the owner."

"Ah believe we need to talk to Mister Best. He may have information about Decker's murder that will shed some light on our investigation. He may also know something about the recent home invasion at a certain property in Upper St. Claire."

Frisbee's partners looked skeptical, causing him to add, "I think we have another suspect."

Chapter Forty-One: Hello Again

On her way home, Tina stopped at her favorite dumpling house for takeout.

She unexpectedly ran into a small group of nurses from the hospital, including Sue Cruller and Barb Wilson, the two nurses who had *almost* stood up to Decker.

Tina happily accepted their invitation to join them for dinner and a night out.

Several hours later, with the help of a designated driver, Tina and her car made it home safely, a packed SUV of co-workers right behind. After a half-dozen fierce hugs and a cacophony of shouted goodnights, they left her on the front porch, feeling slightly embarrassed, and very happy.

Fumbling with her keys at the front door, Tina gazed at her watch. Although her eyes were a little blurry, she read the time on her watch at a few minutes past 3:00 a.m.

With an inebriated sigh of relief, she announced to the world, "This day has been rough. I am so glad it is over."

A bout of dizziness made Tina lean her head against the door frame to keep from falling.

Tina felt her horrible day still had more to bring, but she was too inebriated to move quickly.

Before she could muster the courage to leave, her door swung open.

An unseen hand violently yanked her into the darkened house, causing her back to slam against the living room wall.

Gasping for air, Tina dropped her keys and began sliding down the wall.

A shoulder pressed against her chest, breaking her fall.

Then, a strong hand covered her mouth.

"Don't make a sound. You so much as squeak, I'll kill you!" a raspy voice whispered into Tina's ear. "I'm going to let go of you so I can close the door. If you scream or try to run, I'll hurt you in ways that will make you wish you were dead! Do you understand?"

Tina nodded, her eyes wide with fear.

The assailant closed and locked the front door.

Streetlights shining through the front windows provided Tina with a view of a large man dressed completely in black.

His head was covered with a black hoodie, and a ski mask covered his face.

Tina felt she had encountered death. Again.

The intruder plopped onto a nearby chair, leaned back, turned his face to the ceiling, and covered it with his hands.

Seeing an opportunity to escape, Tina inched her way toward the front door.

"Don't take another step, Tina," the prowler whispered. "I don't want to hurt you!"

Ignoring the warning, Tina turned to run for the door.

The intruder shot out of the chair like a bolt fired from a crossbow.

In two long strides, he crossed the room.

When he collided with Tina, the impact made her feel like she had been hit by a truck, lifting her entire body off the floor.

Their momentum carried them to the outside wall, the impact knocking the air out of Tina's lungs when she slammed against the wall, again.

Her head bounced off the plaster. She hit the wall so hard her chin split open, leaving a fine spray of blood.

Tina and her assailant ricocheted off the wall and tumbled heavily to the floor.

The intruder jumped to his feet, dancing like a defensive lineman after a quarterback sack.

"You see what you made me do?" he yelled, prancing around Tina's living room, smashing breakable objects on the floor. "You moved! I told you not to move! Now, I have to punish you!"

The masked man drew back his leg and kicked Tina viciously in the ribs.

She folded her body into the fetal position, covering her face.

He stomped on her hip.

Instinctively, Tina moved her hands from her face to cradle the new injury.

The assailant's next kick was aimed directly at her head.

She blearily witnessed her assailant looking down at her damaged body as she slipped into darkness.

Chapter Forty-Two: Where Is Tupaz?

Early the following morning, when Frisbee arrived at his office, Carlisle and Ruiz were seated in front of his desk, staring in disbelief at his high-backed office chair, turned to face the wall, making the chair's occupant invisible.

Watching from the doorway, Frisbee observed the chair as it spun slowly around, stopping only when the angelic features of Monica Chang came into full view, her elbows resting on the desk and her fingers tented as if in prayer.

"Where have you hidden my client, Sterling?" Chang asked in a cat-like purr, making Frisbee think of a feline pouncing on its prey.

"I honestly don't know what you're talking about, Ms. Chang," Frisbee replied, remaining in the doorway, prepared for a quick getaway.

Chang leaned forward, showing her perfectly formed, feline-like neck. "Tell me, Sterling, what are the consequences to the police when they hold an innocent citizen incommunicado for twenty-four hours?"

"I don't know what you're talking about, Monica. What innocent citizen am I supposed to have placed incommunicado?"

Chang slammed her hands on the desk. "Frisbee, where have you hidden Christina Tupaz?" she screamed, causing everyone in the room to duck.

Frisbee looked to Ruiz and Carlisle for clues.

"She came into the office about ten minutes ago, sat in your chair, and turned it around to face the wall, without saying a word," Carlisle whispered.

Frisbee nodded slightly.

"We don't have Tupaz. When was the last time you spoke to her?" asked Frisbee.

"I spoke to her after your interview. Tupaz agreed to meet with Hughes and me, but he received a text from her stating she was ill."

Frisbee took a deep breath, "Then, she is simply ill. What makes you think we have her?"

"Hughes tried to contact her. When she didn't reply, he went to her house. Her car was parked across the street; he found that unusual. When he peeked in the window to see if she was okay, the place looked torn up. I assumed you had gone back to arrest her and trashed her house in the process."

"We haven't seen her," said Frisbee.

He snatched his cell phone out of his jacket, quickly arranging for patrol cars to be sent to Tina's Shadyside address.

"Anything y'all want to report before I call the chief?" Frisbee asked his partners, his phone in hand.

Carlisle shook her head.

Ruiz looked at Chang and shrugged.

Frisbee left a voicemail informing Chief Smith he would be in Shadyside. Then, he hurried out of the office, his partners hot on his heels.

Chang stayed behind, seated at Frisbee's desk.

She looked at the dust and clutter of the small room, mentally congratulating herself on her chosen profession and on her decision to wear one of her least expensive outfits before invading Frisbee's office.

She gingerly wiped the dust off the sleeve of her Moda Operandi silk suit. It still managed to turn heads and cost her less than $1,500.00.

She sighed in resignation, deciding it needed to be donated to charity after having been exposed to this room.

Chang pulled a pair of custom-made leather gloves out of her Michael Kors purse, seductively pulled the gloves over her hands, and began to peruse the folders on Frisbee's desk.

Finding the Tupaz file, she scanned the folder, taking photos of several pages with her phone.

Chang closed the folders, returning them exactly as she found them.

She tented her fingers on the desk, lost in thought.

After a few minutes, she peeled off her gloves, returning them to her purse. She swiveled the chair back and forth like a child, a slight smile playing across her face.

Still smiling, she tapped a number into her cell phone.

A voice came on the line after two rings.

"Put him on," Chang said, without preamble.

She waited patiently for several minutes, swiveling the chair and humming a nameless tune, her smile broader than before. A heavily accented "Hello?" came from the other end of the line.

"The police are getting close. We need to take appropriate action. You know my fees."

Ending the call, Chang rose and gracefully exited the office. An evil smirk spread across her face.

Frisbee and Carlisle raced to their unmarked police vehicle.

Unused to being chauffeured, Frisbee paused to glance at Carlisle weaving in and out of traffic as she raced across Pittsburgh with her siren blaring and her lights flashing.

Frisbee's cell phone sounded, breaking his reverie.

"Frisbee. What is going on?" Chief Smith asked as soon as Frisbee answered the call.

"I'm not sure, chief," said Frisbee. "As I said in my message, we've had no contact with Tupaz since her interview. Neither has Chang. I have a feeling she's skipped on us. I wanted to talk to her buddy, Jordan Best, but the uniforms I sent to his workplace say he's a no-show."

Frisbee clutched the dashboard as Carlisle turned onto Tupaz's block, disconnecting the call. *And she had the nerve to criticize* my *driving*, he thought.

Patrol cars blocked both ends of the street, forcing Carlisle to slide in sideways.

Ruiz, following close behind, added her SUV to the blockade.

The team jumped out of their cars and strode purposefully toward Tina's house.

"Has anyone been inside?" Carlisle asked the patrolman stationed on the front steps.

Without waiting for a response, Carlisle jumped the railing and looked inside the living room windows.

"Be careful, Caroline," Ruiz muttered.

Frisbee stepped over an upended lounge chair to peer into the window next to Carlisle. "You're right, Mel. We do this by the book. The living room looks trashed, but I don't see anyone in immediate peril. We call the bomb squad. Once they've cleared the house, we can go in."

"The bomb squad is in transit," said Ruiz, looking up at Carlisle and smiling. "I called on the way here. I am the queen of multi-tasking!"

Carlisle rolled her eyes.

"Okay. We should probably move away from the house until the cavalry arrives," Frisbee said, smiling at his partners.

The patrolman guarding the house overheard the conversation. "I'll check on the bomb squad's ETA," he said as the detectives started to cross the road.

The patrolman had his cell in his hand, pushing the call button, when Carlisle turned, yelling, "No cell phones! The signal might set off a—"

Carlisle never ended her warning. A dull thump came from somewhere within the depths of the house, followed by a massive explosion sending shrapnel flying in all directions. A huge fireball mushroomed upwards through the roof.

The force of the blast threw Frisbee and Carlisle over the hood of a nearby car and onto the opposite sidewalk while hurling Ruiz through the air, her momentum broken by the trunk of an old oak tree.

Unconscious, Ruiz spewed blood from dozens of lacerations.

An EMS van rolled onto the street seconds later.

They quickly loaded Ruiz into the ambulance, rushing her to the nearest hospital, but not until Carlisle double-checked the vehicle, paying close attention to the crew.

It had been a bad morning for Frisbee's team.

With Ruiz on her way to surgery, they had misplaced their prime suspect, and the Road Rage detectives were out of ideas.

Just to make sure everyone knew they were still in Pittsburgh, it started to rain.

Ruiz needed several pieces of shrapnel removed from her right side.

Investigators praised Ruiz's ability to turn herself to stand at an angle to the blast, exposing a relatively small portion of her body to flying debris.

Her doctors believed she had escaped the worst but insisted she stay overnight for observation.

Relieved to hear their friend stood a good chance at complete recovery, Frisbee and Carlisle left her in the company of loved ones and stepped out of the hospital to be met by the sights and sounds of late-night Pittsburgh.

Despite heavy traffic, pedestrians ignored crosswalks to wander aimlessly across busy streets, and the noise level at local bars reached ear-shattering levels.

"At least it's stopped raining," mumbled Carlisle.

"We should go ruin somebody's day," Frisbee said, an evil grin on his face.

With Jordan's last known address listed as his childhood home in the Oakland area of Pittsburgh, Frisbee called Judge O'Connor.

He arranged for a generic search warrant to be obtained because the suspect left the area while under investigation. He arranged for a patrol car to pick up the warrant and deliver it to Best's house.

The homes in Best's neighborhood, overlooking majestic Schenley Park, had wide front lawns and paved driveways, highly unusual for city dwellings.

Carlisle parked on the street within view of Best's house, patiently waiting for the backup teams to arrive with the warrant.

As they watched the house, a fire engine red Mustang pulled into the driveway. Motion-activated spotlights brightly illuminated the driveway and yard.

Carlisle entered the vehicle's license number into her onboard computer, confirming Jordan Best as the legally registered owner of the Mustang.

The driver remained behind the wheel, engaged in an animated cell phone conversation.

"That's got to be Best," Carlisle said, fidgeting nervously with her steering wheel. "The car's still running. He's going to escape if I don't move up and block the driveway."

"We need to wait for the search warrant, Caroline," Frisbee hissed. "Ah don't want him walking on a technicality."

The spotlight's timer ran out, the darkness now total under Pittsburgh's overcast skies.

The Mustang sat in the house's gloomy shadow while the detectives watched, nervously awaiting the search warrant.

The Mustang's motor shut down, the driver's door flew open, and a darkened figure stepped out, reactivating the floodlights.

The driveway, the car, and a male over six feet tall wearing a black hooded sweatshirt were fully exposed.

"Jesus Christ!" exclaimed Carlisle. "That's our guy! Just as Hughes described him. Right down to the black hoodie."

Frisbee's cell phone picked that moment to ring.

Modern cell phones provide a wide variety of ringtones for operators to personalize their phones and add a unique identity to their contacts. Frisbee, in one of his rare witty moments, set a code two siren as his identifying ringtone for calls from the police department. One of the officers tasked with retrieving Frisbee's warrant had called as he turned onto Best's Street.

The ringtone carried through Frisbee's open window and across the night.

The hooded figure darted to the Mustang.

Carlisle sprang into action. Broadcasting "Officer needs assistance!" into her radio. She had her vehicle in gear before the suspect reached the Mustang.

Fast, nimble, and scared, the dark-clad figure dove behind the wheel, fired up the high-performance engine, and dropped the gearshift into reverse.

Carlisle brought the unmarked Chrysler into position, blocking the driveway.

His escape route blocked, the driver of the Mustang changed gears, dropping the gearshift lever into first gear.

With its tires kicking up grass and dirt, the Mustang headed across the neighbor's front lawn, its speed increasing with every foot.

The high-performance engine of the Mustang proved to be too much for the police car.

Carlisle gave pursuit, but she didn't have the engine power to prevent the Mustang from reaching the street and escaping.

Fortunately for Carlisle, fate had other plans.

The Mustang's driver failed to notice a bicycle lying half-hidden in the neighbor's grass, until he almost collided with it.

He yanked on the Mustang's steering wheel to move the car out of the way.

The Mustang's rack and pinion steering reacted, and the vehicle went into a slide, the driver heaving a sigh of relief as he skidded past bicycle tires, but he was not home free.

The sliding sports car's right-front tire clipped the bicycle's handlebars.

The tire disintegrated, spinning the bike frame into the Mustang's high-performance suspension, tearing it to shreds.

The car flipped onto its roof and slid rapidly across the lawn and onto the street, where it finally came to a stop in a shower of sparks.

Carlisle slammed on her brakes, sliding the unmarked cruiser at an angle to the street.

Frisbee jumped out, his sidearm drawn, screaming "Police! Freeze!" as he bolted toward the Mustang, with Carlisle close behind.

Frisbee slowed as he neared the wrecked vehicle, handgun extended in front of him, standing sideways to present the smallest target.

Using hand signals, he directed Carlisle to the passenger side of the Mustang.

The officers delivering the warrant arrived formed a defensive line behind the detectives.

As more officers answered Carlisle's request for backup, they fanned out along the street, making certain residents didn't wander into the police action.

Frisbee moved cautiously to the left rear fender of the Mustang, Carlisle mirroring his actions on the right.

She hugged the car's right rear fender, peering inside to check for passengers.

Finding no one, she signaled an all-clear to Frisbee and then darted ahead and away from the vehicle.

Frisbee darted forward and outward for a better view of the driver's seat, his backup team training their flashlights on the vehicle.

Inside the Mustang, a hooded figure hung upside down, supported by a seatbelt harness designed to mimic NASCAR safety devices.

The hood of the driver's black sweatshirt obscured his face.

Frisbee moved directly in front of the vehicle while Carlisle, still several yards away from the car, looked through the shattered passenger window.

"What's wrong with his hands?" Carlisle asked.

Frisbee froze. "What do you mean?"

"He's hanging upside down, but his hands aren't visible," Carlisle said, breaking into a run, yelling as she moved away from the car: "Sterling! Run! He has a bomb! Run! Run! Run!"

Ignoring Carlisle's warnings, Frisbee moved closer to the Mustang, trying to find a better view of the driver's face.

His backup team focused their flashlights on the figure inside the Mustang.

As the lights hit his face, the driver, wearing white face paint, heavy black eyeliner, and black lipstick, opened his eyes and smiled.

He slowly pulled his right arm out of the marsupial pouch of his sweatshirt.

Holding a cell phone with his finger over the send button, his smile turned to a wide grin reminiscent of the Joker from Batman.

Frisbee and his backup team bolted for cover.

The Mustang disappeared in a ball of flame.

The force of the explosion shattered windows in neighboring houses.

Simultaneously, a series of dull thumps sounded from the basement of the Best residence, followed by rapidly spreading fire.

Miraculously finding a Honda Accord in a nearby driveway, Frisbee dove behind it as the blast from the Mustang roared across the sleepy community.

The force of the explosion rolled the Honda, pinning the detective beneath it.

All the commotion had brought a lot of their neighbors outside. Many of them bemoaned the fact they would have to replace their windows, but they all agreed they were happy to be alive.

One of the bystanders had called 9-1-1, and Frisbee was rushed to the hospital.

Luckily, he wasn't badly injured, having only suffered a broken arm and collarbone.

Chapter Forty-Three: Trapped

Like traveling through a thick fog, Tina slowly regained consciousness, her memory returning in brief flashes.

She recalled being attacked and kicked in the head. She also knew she had suffered from a severe concussion, but the fogginess indicated something more.

Tina looked at the parts of her body she could see, and she saw needle marks in the crook of her arm. Realizing she had been administered drugs, her first reaction was to thank God she hadn't died.

However, as Tina's mind continued to clear, awareness of her situation made her wonder if clarity were such a good thing.

She was lying on a rancid-smelling, lumpy, old single mattress in a dark room with her arms taped to her sides, her legs taped together, and a metal shackle attached to her right ankle. Whoever had captured her was determined to give her no chance of escaping.

Moving caused her head and shoulders to throb, but Tina eventually powered through the pain and managed to sit up.

Her eyes adjusted to the gloom, finding enough ambient light to create long shadows.

Concentrating on figures she could readily identify in her little prison, Tina was able to locate an old furnace, a hot water tank, and a workbench.

I'm in a basement, she thought. *If I'm still in Pittsburgh, that narrows my location down to 250,000 possibilities. Not the greatest odds.*

"How could someone do this to me?" Tina screamed, furiously.

She thrashed about, trying to loosen the duct tape. Still affected by the drugs, she tired quickly, lay on the ragged mattress, closed her eyes, and fell into a restless sleep.

Tina awoke with a start at the sound of a slamming door.

The overhead lights were on, providing Tina with an unimpeded view of her prison.

Groggily, she inventoried her immediate surroundings, beginning with herself.

The tape had been removed from her arms and legs. The steel cuff bolted around her ankle connected her to a length of ¾ inch chain leading around an old, rusty, forced air furnace.

A fresh needle mark on her arm indicated Tina's captor had injected her with additional drugs. Tina assumed the narcotics were administered to make certain she didn't wake up while her bindings were changed.

"What kind of a monster kidnapped me?" Tina asked herself, quietly. "Why are you doing this to me?" she yelled.

She listened in fear for the sound of footsteps.

After several minutes passed, she let out a blood-curdling scream.

No one answered.

Ignoring the pain in her chest and shoulders, Tina forced herself up on her feet, stretching to her full five-foot height.

Wrapping the loose lengths of chain around her arm, she limped, following the chains as they stretched around the furnace, finding the far end attached to the main water line with a heavy padlock on it.

A rickety wooden staircase ran parallel to the outside wall, leading to the ground floor, a large plastic bag was attached to the bottom of the fourth step with duct tape.

As Tina moved closer, her mind registered the bag as an IED. Her eyes grew large in fear. She knew she had to find a way out, and quick. Given her circumstances, that was much easier said than done.

The lights went out, leaving Tina in darkness.

Discouraged, she stumbled her way back to her filthy mattress to think.

Tina sat cross-legged on the mattress until daylight filtered through the plywood shutters covering the windows.

When she determined she'd had enough light, she ignored her pain and lurched to her feet, determined to find a means of escape that didn't include the booby-trapped stairway.

Mentally cordoning the basement into measured squares, Tina moved about her prison, studying each nook and cranny.

Moving quickly from square to square, she checked each one off in her mind once she completed searching it thoroughly.

Making quick work of the open areas, she moved to the darkened, windowless side of the basement.

Without shoes, Tina walked slowly, wary of booby traps her kidnapper might have placed around the area. She couldn't be too careful.

Allowing time for her eyes to adjust to the gloom of the unlit side of her basement prison, she felt the floor change from concrete to dirt. "They only poured concrete where it was necessary to hold the furnace," she said to herself. "I hate cheap people."

Hoping the unfinished section of the basement would provide what she needed, Tina concentrated her search in the areas where she could feel the dirt under her shoeless feet.

After staring at the far wall of the basement for what seemed like an eternity, Tina finally spied a hammer in the far corner.

Forgetting her chains, she rushed toward the newfound treasure, stopping several feet short of her goal when she reached the end of her chain and fell, much like a dog at the end of its leash.

She lay down, stretching her hand out to the farthest point, but could not reach the elusive tool.

Lying down on the dirty floor, her gaze locked on the hammer; Tina noticed a medium-sized steel access door mounted on the wall.

It sparked an old memory. Before purchasing her home, Tina looked at a less expensive, much older house. It had a tunnel running from the basement to the city's old sewage system, accessed through a steel door mounted in the basement wall. That's why the previous homeowners were selling it so cheap. Of course, Tina would have never discovered the often-overlooked opening.

Tina had discovered her escape route.

Jumping to her feet in excitement, she nearly bumped her head on the low basement ceiling. Because she was somewhat short, Tina hadn't noticed the low ceiling height. She thought that would be to her advantage because an average-sized person would need to duck to avoid the low-ceiling joists.

Tina's excitement upon finding the access door grew when she remembered a homeowner's class she took shortly after she had moved into her current home. During the class, a plumber explained heavy corrosion at the point where two materials, such as copper and brass, are connected, usually signified a weakened fitting.

A little while earlier, Tina had noticed badly corroded fittings where her chain connected to the waterline. Heedless of her bare feet, she rushed across the basement as fast as she could manage.

Using her fingertips to pinpoint the weakest spot, Tina looped an end of her chain around the worn plumbing. She walked purposefully to the nearest support column, wrapping the chain once around the post.

Sitting on the floor, Tina braced her feet against the furnace.

Using the column as a fulcrum, she pulled until the muscles in her back strained to the bursting point, a primordial scream rising from her chest.

The corroded pipes had moved several inches, but the fitting did not fail.

Tina collapsed to the floor in exhaustion and pain.

Removing the pressure from the chains caused the corroded fitting to snap back into place and fail with a loud crack.

The heavy padlock flew across the basement, smashing into the support post inches above Tina's head.

Water spewed from the broken fitting like a rushing stream. It ran across the basement, over the edge of the concrete, and onto the dirt floor.

The lights suddenly ignited.

The door at the top of the stairs flew open with enough force to be heard above the rushing water.

Tina scurried behind the furnace, wrapping the excess chain around her waist.

From her hiding place, she heard a loud screeching noise as someone turned a seldom-used valve.

The flow of water slowly stopped, now in its place a deafening silence.

Holding her breath, her back pressed against the furnace, Tina heard a soft sigh, followed by a familiar voice.

"You are a resourceful girl, Tina," Joan Best sneered, "but the basement is soundproofed. You could have screamed for days on end, and no one would have heard you, including me. But when you disrupted the water supply, *you screwed everything up!*"

"I have a gun, Tina," Joan continued, "I don't want to take a chance of getting too close to you, so I'm going to leave you down here, go back upstairs, and reset the trap on the steps."

Hearing a shuffling noise coming from the other side of the furnace, Tina realized someone, using Joan's monologue as a diversion, attempted to sneak around the ancient appliance.

Tina steeled herself for a showdown.

With the bulk of the chain wrapped around her waist, Tina set her feet, both hands holding tight to the remaining five feet of chain, the heavy padlock hanging from its end.

Locking her elbows like a tennis star, Tina spun her entire body, aiming in the direction of the shuffling footsteps, targeting the end of the chain just below the ceiling joists.

Using her pent-up anger for motivation, Tina swung the chain, catching Jordan, bent slightly at the waist, as he rushed around the side of the furnace, a nine-inch butcher knife in his hand.

Six inches of chain, with a heavy padlock at its end, smashed into Jordan's face, ripping skin and splattering blood across the room.

Links of the chain smashed his nose, twisting it to the side and tearing one of the nostrils. The edge of the padlock struck his head, ripping his scalp.

Dropping the butcher knife to cover his damaged face with his hands, Jordan bolted upright. He slammed his head into the low basement ceiling with a resounding thump, momentarily lost consciousness, and crumpled to the floor.

Tina calmly retrieved the knife, experimentally turning it in her hand.

Jordan pulled himself to his hands and knees, the blood from his damaged forehead streaming into his eyes.

"You bitch!" Jordan screamed in a fit of rage. "I'm going to kill you!"

Pushing off from a four-point stance like an enraged football player, Jordan rushed forward, instinctively reaching for Tina's throat. Blinded by a black mist of hatred, Jordan didn't see the knife clutched in Tina's hand.

They tumbled to the floor, arms and legs tangled as they struggled.

The knife plunged under Best's ribs and into his heart, killing him instantly.

Gasping for breath, Tina squirmed out from under the lifeless body of her old friend.

She scooted across the floor to sit with her back against the ancient furnace, eyes tightly shut against the tears running down her cheeks.

Hearing someone clear their throat, Tina opened her eyes to find Joan Best standing ten feet away, a large revolver in her hand.

They stared at each other, silently taking measure.

"Before you kill me, may I ask why?" queried Tina, surprisingly calm.

Joan looked at her nephew's lifeless body, and anger spread out all over her face. "Did you know he never liked you calling him Jordy? He thought it was childish, but he allowed it because he was so much in love with you! Jordan was only fifteen years old when his parents died, and I took him in. He was the only family I had left, and you just took him from me!"

Tina stood, her heart full of pain, "How could he do this to someone he loved?"

"*You betrayed him!*" Joan screamed, waving her pistol.

Tina noticed Joan had acquired a slight accent and became extraordinarily mean in just the few moments that had passed since her nephew's demise.

"What are you talking about? I would never do anything to hurt Jordan," Tina quietly answered.

"*Liar!*" Joan screeched. "Look at his lifeless body on the floor; you did that! Before, you were having an affair with a married man! Do you have any idea how much that disappointed him?"

"He never said anything to me," whispered Tina.

"Well, he should have!" Joan spat, her face turning red with anger. "It would have saved all of us the mess of going after you. But all the others, they had to go."

Tina's eyes opened wide in realization. She gasped. "The police think I'm involved in the Road Rage Killings, but it was you!"

Joan lowered the heavy pistol. "Jordan began the killings after the Hughes accident."

"Jordy killed the Burns family?" Tina asked.

"*Stop calling him that!*" Joan shouted in an enraged voice.

"What possessed Jordan to kill all those people so viciously?" Tina asked, quietly.

"After the accident, Jordan changed." Joan began.

"He became withdrawn and mean. He even researched the areas where the Hughes family died and learned some of its secrets."

"Did you know the original construction on I-279 was halted for a brief time in 1972, while government flunkies from the Smithsonian Institute relocated a forgotten cemetery full of Western European immigrants?

"They were later tasked with finding an unmarked crypt located in an unconsecrated area of the cemetery, but they failed. The crypt was the final resting place of a servant who was falsely accused by members of the community of bringing a catastrophic disease to the town.

"The townspeople buried her alive in the crypt with the hope that their God would forgive them and lift the curse of the disease. Instead, they created a *sorgina*. A *sorgina* is not specifically evil, but this woman's resting place was disturbed on at least two occasions, making her very angry. She retaliated, eventually becoming the one responsible for the many accidents on the freeway. You might have even seen her walking across the road that night of the first accidents."

Still in shock for having killed her former best friend, Tina whispered, "What about Jordan? Did you tell him to kill all those people?"

"Jordan presented no problem. His unbridled love for you made him especially vulnerable, and it was easy to bend him to my will. It did not take much to convince him Burns was responsible for your pain and suffering. Jordan killed to protect you from harm, Tina. That's why he killed Decker. He went after Hughes the night the two of you were together. But he wasn't able to kill him because you just had to interfere!"

Joan paused for a moment to catch her breath. "The Rosas family were a little harder to convince, but I sweetened the deal by having Jordan steal medical supplies from the hospital for them. You won't believe the kinds of things they use to torture their victims."

"We were scheduled to leave the country today," Joan continued softly. "The boys rigged Jordan's Mustang and house with explosives to destroy evidence and create a diversion."

Joan looked down at the bloody mess that had once been her nephew, slowly shaking her head. "Jordan wanted to take you with us. Jordan and Franky had a big fight about you. Jordan was livid about Franky stashing explosives in your basement. Franky couldn't believe Jordan had kidnapped you. Men are such fools." Joan scoffed.

"Franky took off in the Mustang, but the argument continued over the phone. Before he hung up, he said he wanted to check on a few things at Jordan's house. I believe Franky is gone."

Joan strolled over to the rickety wooden staircase. "His argument with Jordan was cut short, and we assumed the worst, because neither of them heard anything from Franky since then. Jordan brought you here to convince you to run away with him, but that ship has definitely sailed!"

Her accent had grown increasingly thicker, and her eyes were now completely black. Joan extended the pistol, aiming it at Tina's head.

Much to Tina's surprise, she lowered the gun and began to walk slowly up the stairs, carefully avoiding the explosive on the last step. "I can't harm you, Tina. You are the *mangkukulam*, the one who is supposed to destroy me. I am the *sorgina*, but I just can't bring myself to shoot you. My name is Nekane."

Tina's eyes widened in alarm. She couldn't believe what she was hearing. Sure, as a child she'd heard mythical tales about *sorginas* and *mangkukulams*, but she never took them to heart. After all, as her parents told her, there were no such things as witches. However, there was proof right there she was dealing with a wicked *sorgina*.

"No matter; I'll leave you and Jordan alone now," Joan called from the top of the stairs, deeply breathing, her anger still evident. "You possessed my nephew's soul like a witch, so it's only appropriate you burn like one!"

Tina heard the door slam shut. The basement lights still lit, but she didn't think that would do her any good now.

She wrapped her chains tightly around her waist and hurried to the far corner of the basement. In her moment of distress, she cried out again. "How am I going to get out of this one?"

Chapter Forty-Four: Go Time!

A distraught Carlisle wandered the hospital halls. She was too upset to wait for the final word on her partner.

A veteran of the U.S. Army, she believed she had witnessed the worst atrocities any human being could perform on another during her four-year tour of what is commonly known as the sandbox. She had been with the Pittsburgh Police Department for less than two months. She had been blown up twice. Her newfound friends had each been seriously injured.

Carlisle wanted to shoot someone. Instead, she continued to stalk the hospital's halls, growling at anyone foolish enough to confront her.

Pausing to stare out a window, Carlisle caught the reflection of someone approaching her from behind.

In one fluid motion, she spun her body around, kicking the legs out from underneath the interloper.

She had the man in a stranglehold before she realized she had just attacked Chief Smith.

"Sorry about that, chief," Carlisle said, attempting to untangle herself with a modicum of dignity. "It's been a rough couple of days; I guess I'm a little jumpy," she added with a smile, offering Smith her hand.

"Thank you, Carlisle, but I will stand on my own. I believe I would only succeed in bringing us both back to the floor." Smith chuckled.

"Did you just get here, chief?" Carlisle asked. "Or have you been talking to the doctors?"

"I have been too busy cleaning up your mess to have time to talk to doctors, Caroline," Smith said with a sad smile. "That Road Rage boy of yours created quite a bit of trouble, but I'm sure things will start to calm down now he's been stopped."

"That wasn't him in the Mustang, chief. It must have been one of his lackeys."

Smith's smile disappeared. "Are you certain? We can get a DNA test once the scene is cleared. Hua is scraping up remains, but the suspect was so spread out by the blast she needs to use a stick and a spoon."

"I'm positive, chief," Carlisle said, chuckling at Smith's macabre joke. "His hood shifted when he pulled the phone from his sweatshirt, exposing most of his head. He was wearing white makeup, black eye shadow, and black fingernail polish. Best didn't dress like that."

Carlisle paused before asking quietly, "What about the rest of the team?"

"Your warning came in time, Caroline. The uniformed officers working with Frisbee were injured, but are recovering. The rest of the team credits your quick reaction and highly audible warning with saving their butts."

Smith gingerly patted Carlisle on the shoulder. "Good work, Caroline!"

"Thank you, sir," Carlisle said.

"Best's house burned to the ground, just like Tupaz's They must have used the same kind of explosives in both houses. It will be hours before the fire department clears it, but I have cadaver dogs on standby."

"I doubt the dogs will find anything, chief, but I have a lead I want to run to the ground."

"I'm sorry, Carlisle; your lead detective is unavailable, and you don't have the experience to run the investigation on your own."

"But I do," Ruiz said, leaning against an open doorway. "All the heavy lifting has already been done, chief, and if anything comes up, Caroline can take care of the ass-kicking. I saw how she took you down." Ruiz chuckled.

"I certainly don't question your qualifications, Lieutenant Ruiz," Smith replied, "but I can't let you on the job without a written release from your doctor. It's a non-negotiable departmental policy, enforced by insurance, and union contracts."

Ruiz smiled and handed Smith a signed release form.

"Keep me posted," Smith said, tucking the form in his pocket and walking away.

"I've been on every floor in this hospital, going over all the evidence in my head. I think we've been barking up the wrong tree," Carlisle said as soon as Chief Smith turned the hallway corner.

"What do you mean, Caroline?"

"We were on our way to search Best's house when 'the fertilizer hit the ventilator,' as Sterling would say. The clown driving Best's Mustang was probably his partner, Francis Sinatra. We won't know for certain until the DNA results come back, but Franky was known as a Goth, and he wore the white makeup when he wasn't working."

"My research into the EMS crew tells me Sinatra rarely took initiative. That could only point to Best being deeply involved in the killings, but how?" Carlisle asked, rhetorically, without waiting for an answer. "As I see it, there are three possibilities: one, he has been helping Tupaz all along; two, he is helping someone else; or three, he's as crazy as a runover cat."

"Just for the hell of it, let's say Best is borderline until the Hughes incident. The severity of the accident pushes him closer to the edge. He learns the Burns boys caused the accident but are going to walk. He plummets down the dark side, planning to punish the perpetrators. Before you ask, he has access to the drugs and nitrile gloves."

"Crazy as a runover cat?" laughed Ruiz. "You sound more like Sterling every day. I have a question about your theory. Where does the murder of the Jarquins fit in?"

"I think Franky worked for Alphonso Rosas," answered Carlisle. "He followed Jordan to the Burns residence to kill Guillermo. He stumbled upon the dart gun, a curare, and a drunken Raul when searching Guillermo's living quarters. He used the curare to murder the Jarquins and send a message to Rosas's enemies."

"What about the other murders?" Ruiz asked, her curiosity piqued.

"I'm glad you asked that, Mel," answered Carlisle. "I have theories on the other killings, too."

She began to count out details on her fingers. "One, all the Road Rage Killings were revenge murders for accidents involving people associated with horrible traffic accidents. Best's EMS team was called and showed up for every accident. The crazy SOB wanted to make certain the perpetrators paid.

"Two, Ortiz is brought in to help find the evidence Snyderman has on Rosas. Ortiz knocks Hughes out before searching his house. He wants Hughes alive for questioning if he can't find what he's looking for. Decker shows up. Ortiz kills him and runs."

Carlisle pauses to regroup.

Ruiz begins to ask a question, but Carlisle holds out her hand. "Hold that thought, Mel! There's more!" Carlisle exclaimed. "Since Ortiz didn't take care of Hughes, Franky steals a shotgun, planning to do the job himself. He didn't count on Tina or the police being there. He barely manages to escape."

"I believe we are wrong about Ortiz, too," added Ruiz.

"I agree, Mel," Carlisle said, a gleam in her eyes. "Sinatra's connection to Rosas runs through Joan Best. She is young enough to interest Rosas, and certainly pretty enough to turn Ortiz's head."

"That brings us back to Jordan Best. Joan Best is his only living relative. Since we know he wasn't driving the Mustang, he is probably with his Aunt Joan. Tupaz disappeared shortly after publicly ending her relationship with Jordan Best. Jordan wouldn't risk keeping Tupaz at his house, so I believe they're all at Aunt Joan's!"

Ruiz smiled, "Thanks, Caroline. You get the warrant; I'll get back up."

Joan strolled from the basement door to her office. She carefully erased several files from her laptop before slipping it into a custom-made leather briefcase.

Locking the front door behind her, Joan walked leisurely to her Jeep, a Gucci bag hanging from her shoulder.

She had her briefcase swinging by her side and was pulling a suitcase behind her. Daydreaming about Latin America, where a new life awaited her, she didn't spare a thought for her recently late nephew, or her former employee. All she cared about was leaving the country before she got caught.

Tina flew into escape mode the moment Joan closed the basement door. She rushed across the dirt floor to the access door, tossed aside the bricks piled in front of it, and pulled on the small handle. The door opened a fraction of an inch before sticking, the handle breaking off in her hand.

Picking up the hammer and using it like a small shovel, Tina frantically dug dirt away from the bottom of the door.

When she felt she moved enough dirt out of the way, she wedged a portion of chain around the top corner of the door and pulled.

The door opened almost a third of the way before sticking again.

The door itself measured only thirty inches wide, but Tina didn't need the entire opening. She managed to get the door halfway open, with plenty enough room to squeeze through. Wriggling inside the crawl space, she encountered the complete darkness of a musty, hundred and twenty-five-year-old tunnel.

Tina began walking away from her prison, immediately encountering a thin chain hanging from the ceiling.

"My first real break in days," muttered Tina.

She followed the chain upwards through a multitude of cobwebs to find what she had hoped for, a ceramic light fixture, complete with a bare lightbulb.

Tina pulled the chain. The fixture clicked, but the darkness remained.

Undeterred, Tina spun around. She returned to her basement prison to retrieve light bulbs. She determined three bulbs would be enough to provide insurance against breakage.

Removing her shirt, she made a pouch to carry the bulbs.

Running to the farthest fixture, she unscrewed the bulb with her shirt sleeve and carefully placed it in her makeshift bag.

Carlisle, search warrant in hand, rode shotgun in Ruiz's SUV.

Lights flashing and sirens blaring, they roared from HQ to Best's South Side residence, arriving as Joan tossed her suitcase into an immaculate white Jeep Wrangler.

Joan hardly took notice when Ruiz screeched to a stop behind her, but a slight sign of irritation showed on her face when patrol cars arrived to box her in.

Carlisle jumped out of the SUV, her sidearm drawn.

Ruiz raised her handgun and rested it in her open window. "Please don't move, Ms. Best," she said.

"I have been looking forward to meeting you, Lieutenant Ruiz," Joan said in perfect Spanish, a broad smile crossing her face.

A cell phone appeared in her hand.

Ruiz and Carlisle began moving at the same time, reaching for the device, and screaming for everyone to move away from the house.

Time seemed to slow down for the detectives.

Ruiz, closest to Joan Best but moving slowly because of her injuries, couldn't seem to reach the suspect in time.

Carlisle moved faster but couldn't get around the SUV to reach Ms. Best and stop her.

Joan entered the final digit of the device code just as Ruiz grabbed the sleeve of her Valentino jacket. A series of small blasts came from the house, followed by searing flames.

Ruiz slammed Joan Best to the ground.

Injured and angry, Ruiz took one look at the burning hatred in Joan Best's eyes, pulled back her arm, formed a fist, and punched her in the jaw, knocking the suspect out cold.

"You have the right to remain silent, bitch," Ruiz said, rolling Joan over and handcuffing her.

"Take her downtown and put her in a cell, please. Detective Carlisle and I have a few loose ends to tie up," she commanded a nearby uniformed officer.

She joined Carlisle, standing on the sidewalk, quietly watching the fire.

"Nice takedown, Mel," Carlisle said, moving aside for rushing firefighters.

Chapter Forty-Five: Tina's Escape

Explosions ripped the building as Tina unscrewed the second bulb, knocking her to the basement floor. Flames quickly ran along the low ceiling.

Tina suddenly understood Joan's earlier reference about burning like a witch but found herself a little too busy to enjoy the pun.

Heavy black smoke swirled through the basement, and fire consumed the joists above her head, crackling and snapping as it ate away at the arid 120-year-old lumber.

Tina snatched a third bulb from its fixture.

Clutching the makeshift package of bulbs to her chest, she began to duck walk back to the crawlspace door, covering only a short distance before bumping into the body of her old friend.

Sadness engulfed her, threatening to freeze her in her tracks.

Tina looked lovingly at her Jordan, deciding to escape now and grieve later.

She rifled through his pockets, retrieving a Notepad, a set of keys, and a small flashlight. Even in death, Jordan continued to save her.

Adding her newly acquired items to her bag of bulbs, she crawled the remaining distance to the tunnel.

Using the flashlight, she quickly found the light fixture, changed the bulb, and yanked the chain.

Nothing happened.

Screaming in frustration, Tina swung at the light, missing the bulb, but catching the old ceramic fixture with a glancing blow. The bulb emitted a slight glow.

Tina took the fixture in both hands and shook it, shedding decades of dust and corrosion from the wiring. The bulb came to life, illuminating the tunnel and another roadblock.

Less than ten feet ahead, a solid wall blocked Tina's path to freedom. The city had bricked off the shaft.

Tina stared at the wall in shock.

Smoke was beginning to seep into the small tunnel.

Refusing to stand in place and die, Tina dove through the access door, blindly reaching out for the hammer she left behind. She grabbed it on her second try, her lungs screaming for relief.

Armed with fierce determination, and a big hammer, Tina began to pulverize the obstruction to her freedom.

Swinging the hammer repeatedly at the old, brittle bricks, she soon had an opening.

Fresh air rolled in. Sticking her face in the opening, she took a breath of clean air before continuing her assault on the obstruction.

As soon as she removed enough bricks for her to escape, she wriggled through.

Standing in an unused portion of Pittsburgh's original sewer system, Tina once again found herself shrouded in darkness.

She attempted to use the small flashlight she had found on Jordan's body, but the battery was too low for her to see anything clearly. Fortunately, the darkness lasted only a moment before Tina caught a glimpse of a thin light shining in the distance. The light, soon joined by several others, seemed to be coming closer.

Tina turned toward the distant ray of hope, wrapped her chains tightly around her waist, and began to walk.

Chapter Forty-Six: The End?

The principal investigators were crammed into Chief Smith's office to celebrate the end of what the press had named the Road Rage Case.

Smith, sitting comfortably behind his desk, grinned as he addressed his favorite detective. "I think I have a new team of top detectives, Frisbee. Once they got you out of the way, everything just seemed to fall into place."

"Very funny, chief," Frisbee said. "Caroline, how did you know where to find Tupaz?"

Carlisle chuckled. "We were certain she was with Jordan Best. Since we knew they weren't at *his* house, we moved in on the aunt."

"Caroline's instinct told her Joan Best was our Rosas connection, and Tina was only a pawn," Ruiz continued.

"When we arrived at Joan's residence, we caught her in the process of running away, and we nailed her," Carlisle said. "But we were too late to prevent her from torching the house. We were watching Joan's house burn when firefighters rushed past us, in the opposite direction of the fire.

"I followed them to an open section of sewer line where workers had smelled smoke. One of the workers noticed a dim light coming from an abandoned section of the tunnel. He followed the light and found Tina.

"She escaped from certain death and walked out of that access tunnel in her bare feet, wearing nothing but a skimpy bra and torn underwear. She was covered in blood and dragging a chain. She staggered up to a very startled sewer worker and told him she wanted to report a murder."

"Is she going to be okay?" Ruiz asked, looking at Doctor Hua.

"Yes," Hua said. "She'll be fine. She's a tough one."

"What about your other case, Mel?" Frisbee asked.

"If you mean Rosas, I believe we put a dent in his operation, but he still isn't down. Joan Best managed to destroy the evidence on her laptop, but Tina carried Jordan Best's Notepad out of the tunnel. Our experts are searching the Notepad for evidence against Rosas. Unfortunately, most of Jordan's files were about Tina or the murders," Mel said.

Ruiz paused. "Jordan kept meticulous records. They collaborate Tupaz's testimony."

"Franky killed Rosas's men?" Frisbee asked.

"We believe Franky worked for Rosas. He searched the carriage house while Best butchered Burns' family."

Ruiz shook her head. "He found the dart gun and the curare, shooting Raul as he slept, and Guillermo after he exited the Maybach. He tossed Raul in the dumpster as a diversion and hid Guillermo's body in the winery."

Ruiz took a cleansing breath. "He shot Princess with the same dart he used on Guillermo. It had enough residual poison to knock her out, but not enough to kill her."

"Rosas hired Ortiz to eliminate Snyderman and retrieve any evidence he had. Ortiz got curious and accessed the files, essentially signing his death warrant," Ruiz added in conclusion.

"Why would Jordan Best murder his victims so violently?" Hua wondered.

"Joan kept ranting and raving about something called a *sorgina*," said Frisbee. "She said she had caused all those accidents and killed those people because she was getting revenge on the descendants of those who buried her alive during the 1500s and disturbed her resting place in 1972, when I-279 was being revamped. Of course, no one seemed to buy it; that woman was looney tunes!"

Hua opened her mouth to speak, but Carlilse interrupted. "Before you ask, Best believed the *sorgina* possessed her and sent her after survivors because she couldn't stand the thought of anyone escaping her handiwork. Joan and the *sorgina* were going to enjoy a more symbiotic relationship, living to fulfill each other's needs," Carlise intoned. "At least, that is what the colonel said when I dropped Thadeus off at the bus station."

"You spoke with the colonel?" Hua asked, incredulously.

"What, wait, huh?" said Frisbee.

Smith's cell phone rang.

He stepped out of the office to take the call.

"How did Joan get involved with Rosas to begin with?" Hua asked, changing the subject.

Ruiz grinned. "She seduced him when she was on one of those missionary hospital trips your medical school people like to take."

"Really?" Hua asked, wide-eyed.

"Who knows, Charlotte?" Frisbee chuckled, "Anything is possible."

"She and Rosas are lovers," Ruiz said. "There are some pretty hot and heavy emails on her computer."

"We found the directions to the explosive devices on Jordan's computer. He downloaded them from the internet. We also found the recipe for the drug cocktail they gave Tupaz," added Carlisle.

Smith re-entered the room, shaking his head. "Joan Best's attorney convinced a judge to release Best on her own recognizance. About an hour after she was released, Best disappeared."

Everyone turned to look questioningly at the chief.

"Her attorney is Monica Chang," Smith said with a shrug.

"I don't think we have heard the last of either Best or Chang," Carlisle added, her tone of voice ominous.

Suddenly, the room seemed to grow colder, and Carlisle swore she heard the sound of distant laughter.